continued . . .

"An excellent blend of mystery, paranormal, and light humor, creating a cozy that is a must-read for anyone with an interest in literature with paranormal elements."
—The Romance Readers Connection

"It's a fun story, with romance possibilities with a couple hunky men, terrific vintage clothing, and the enchanting Oscar. But, there is so much more to this book. It has serious depth." —*The Herald News* (MA)

Praise for the Art Lover's Mysteries by Juliet Blackwell writing as Hailey Lind

Brush with Death

"Lind deftly combines a smart and witty sleuth with entertaining characters who are all engaged in a fascinating new adventure." —*Romantic Times*

Shooting Gallery

"If you enjoy Janet Evanovich's Stephanie Plum books, Jonathan Gash's Lovejoy series, or Ian Pears' art history mysteries . . . then you will enjoy *Shooting Gallery*."
—Gumshoe

"An artfully crafted new mystery series!"
—Tim Myers, Agatha Award–nominated author of *A Mold for Murder*

"The art world is murder in this witty and entertaining mystery!" —Cleo Coyle, national bestselling author of the Coffeehouse Mysteries

Feint of Art

"Annie Kincaid is a wonderful cozy heroine. . . . It's a rollicking good read." —*Mystery News*

DEAD BOLT

A HAUNTED HOME RENOVATION MYSTERY

Juliet Blackwell

AN OBSIDIAN MYSTERY

OBSIDIAN
Published by New American Library, a division of
Penguin Group (USA) Inc., 375 Hudson Street,
New York, New York 10014, USA
Penguin Group (Canada), 90 Eglinton Avenue East, Suite 700, Toronto,
Ontario M4P 2Y3, Canada (a division of Pearson Penguin Canada Inc.)
Penguin Books Ltd., 80 Strand, London WC2R 0RL, England
Penguin Ireland, 25 St. Stephen's Green, Dublin 2,
Ireland (a division of Penguin Books Ltd.)
Penguin Group (Australia), 250 Camberwell Road, Camberwell, Victoria 3124,
Australia (a division of Pearson Australia Group Pty. Ltd.)
Penguin Books India Pvt. Ltd., 11 Community Centre, Panchsheel Park,
New Delhi - 110 017, India
Penguin Group (NZ), 67 Apollo Drive, Rosedale, Auckland 0632,
New Zealand (a division of Pearson New Zealand Ltd.)
Penguin Books (South Africa) (Pty.) Ltd., 24 Sturdee Avenue,
Rosebank, Johannesburg 2196, South Africa

Penguin Books Ltd., Registered Offices:
80 Strand, London WC2R 0RL, England

First published by Obsidian, an imprint of New American Library,
a division of Penguin Group (USA) Inc.

First Printing, December 2011
10 9 8 7 6 5 4 3 2 1

To Shay and Suzanne:
You take "neighborly" to a whole different level.
Thank you for being family.

Acknowledgments

Writing a book takes the support, patience, and knowledge of a huge number of people. I can't thank you all by name, but I carry you in my heart.

Special thanks are due, as always, to my editor, Kerry Donovan, and to Kristin Lindstrom of Lindstrom Literary Management. And to my incredible network of friends and family, for inspiring my writing, for holding my hand when things get tough, and for always being there. I hope by now you know who you are, and how much I appreciate you! A special shout-out to my long-lost friend Antonio Jimenez—I missed you so much, for too many years. Can't wait to eat lobster on the beach again, and soon.

To all the Pensfatales, without whom I couldn't function, and in particular Gigi Pandian, for her courage and humor. I can't wait for Scotland, when you'll be well beyond today's challenges. To Adrienne and Tom Miller, for showing me their cool ghost-busting equipment and checking my old house for ghosts. To Rachael Herron, for cemetery walks and endless plot lunches that de-volve into gossip, each and every time. And to Sophie Littlefield . . . there really are no words. Without you I'm sure I would be huddled in a dusty corner somewhere, unable to write. L. G. C. Smith, Lisa Hughey, and Martha Flynn—you guys make this crazy business *fun*, and never fail to inspire me.

To Victoria Laurie, for her wonderful ghost tales, con-ference hijinks, and encouragement. To Nicole Peeler—looking forward to getting into lots of trouble in the future, professionally, personally . . . in all sorts of ways, from rural Pennsylvania to Scotland! And to Lesa Hol-stine, librarian and book reviewer extraordinaire!

To JC Johnson, who really knows the meaning of providing "helpful critiques"—thank you so much for your time and suggestions, and for your steadfast love of reading and your passion for the written word. To Carolyn Lawes, for all the ideas, jokes, and very tactful suggestions, even when I'm catatonic from deadline pressures.

And finally . . . to Sam-the-brown-dog, we miss you so much, especially "single bark." Thanks for sticking around in ghost form.

Chapter One

My father always used to say: There's nothing quite like a protracted remodel to test a person's sanity.

Still, one thing was very clear to me: The handprints on the ceiling were real, not a product of my imagination.

Damn it. My mind cast about for a way to explain them to my clients. They weren't flat, as if someone had used their hands to steady themselves while teetering atop scaffolding or a tall ladder. Rather, it looked like someone had dragged five fingers along the surface of the ceiling's wet plaster or paint, resulting in a subtle chicken-scratch pattern fanning out in concentric circles around the hole for the light fixture.

The ceiling had been perfectly blank yesterday.

As with so much of what was happening on this job site, it was . . . disturbing.

My clients, Katenka and Jim Daley, stood with me amidst the construction debris and dust. The workers had finished for the day, and the house was quiet save for the loud cooing of eleven-month-old Quinn, who squirmed like a baby kangaroo in a padded pouch slung across his father's stomach.

We gazed up at the twelve-foot-high coffered ceiling of what would be an elegant dining room as soon as the walls and ceiling were patched and painted, the antique light fixtures rewired and remounted, and the inlaid wood floors sanded and stained. The Daleys' home, an 1890s Queen Anne Victorian in San Francisco's Cow Hollow neighborhood, was structurally sound—a pleasant surprise, rare for structures from that era—but decades of operating as the Cheshire Inn, a boardinghouse for drifters, down-at-the-heels bachelors, and homeless cats had left their mark. The home's bones were exquisite, but the rest required plenty of renovation, repair, and ornamentation. Queen Anne Victorians were celebrated for their elaborate decorative designs and lavish "gingerbread" details.

This is where I come in. Mel Turner, General Contractor, Jill of All Trades.

But at the moment, I feared my crew and I weren't the only entities at work within the ornate halls and chambers of the historic house. I had been trying—and failing—to ignore or explain away the series of strange events that had plagued the project from its inception: lumber and sheetrock disappearing from one spot and then showing up in another; work gloves and safety goggles *right there* one moment and gone the next; rusty old dead bolts locking and unlocking though the keys had long since been lost; footsteps resonating overhead when no one was upstairs. A handful of workers had already walked off the job, unwilling to deal with the unexplained occurrences.

"Are those . . . *handprints*? On the ceiling?" Katenka's heavy Russian accent made it sound as though she were swallowing her vowels. Dark, wavy hair hung halfway down her back; her big brown eyes were limpid; her posture languid. She had just celebrated her thirtieth birthday but appeared much younger. This was due to her petite stature as well as her penchant for gauzy babydoll dresses, a wardrobe choice completely unsuited to a foggy San Francisco December.

Since I was known for my own offbeat fashion choices, I wasn't about to cast stones . . . still, whenever I was in the same room as Katenka, I had to stifle the entirely uncharacteristic urge to bundle her up in a big fluffy sweater.

If Katenka inspired such protectiveness in someone as cynical as *me*, I could only imagine what havoc she wreaked upon the average heterosexual man.

"Yep, they look like handprints to me," I answered with a nod.

"Maybe from the painters?" Jim offered.

"Sure, that must be it," I lied, hoping he didn't notice there wasn't a paintbrush in sight. This project was nowhere near ready for the final decorative stages; we hadn't even started with plaster repair, patching, and mud. "We'll take care of it. Don't worry. You won't even notice them once we're done."

"Great." Jim was a typical thirtysomething Bay Area high-tech professional: He wore stylish eyewear, his hair was artfully cut and tousled, and he spent what few leisure hours he had training for triathlons or bicycling up Mount Tamalpais. At least he had until his son was born. Now he threw his energy into parenthood, which was a good thing: Jim seemed better cut out for it than

Katenka, who struck me as bemused, even outright dis-
comfited, by her wriggling, demanding bundle of joy.

At the moment little Quinn was enthusiastically gum-
ming his father's thumb, a long trail of drool marring the
front of Jim's shirt as though left by a giant snail.

"He's cutting a tooth," Jim said with an indulgent
chuckle.

I returned his smile, enjoying the sight of a dad with
his beloved boy. Jim was easy to work with . . . with one
exception: He had been adamant about living in the
basement apartment while we worked on the house. My
own father, the original Turner of Turner Construction,
had cautioned me against allowing clients to remain onsite during renovations. Apart from the obvious problems with the dust, the noise, and the early-to-rise hours
of the construction trade, there were aspects of the job
that clients really didn't need to know about. Incessant
raunchy jokes and blaring rock music were only the beginning. There were also the occasional, but inevitable,
minidisasters: broken windows or fried wiring, any number of "oopsies" that we would make good in time, but
that I'd rather the clients didn't witness.

Maybe because I was a woman—not a gruff former
marine like Dad—or simply because I lacked sufficient
backbone, I had a hard time enforcing this policy.
Katenka and Jim insisted on living downstairs, and they
were paying the bills. In the high-end construction business, the one with the checkbook rules.

As a principal in a successful Internet start-up, Jim
had pockets deep enough to return this Queen Anne to
its former glory. In fact, he possessed an almost messi-
anic drive for historical restoration, and spared little ex-
pense.

These are highly attractive traits in a client.

"Is very *dusty*. Dust everywhere," Katenka commented as she glanced around the dining room, delicate nostrils flaring.

"Hard to avoid on a construction site, I'm afraid."

"Oh, by the way, Mel," Jim said. "I've taken the liberty of calling in a green construction consultant."

"Is that right?" I said, trying to keep a neutral expression on my face. I'm territorial about my construction sites. When a general contractor is on The Job, they own The Job. I might cave in to clients, but there was a reason my workers called me "the General" behind my back.

Apparently my attempt to cover up my feelings was not successful. No surprise there. Diplomacy has never been my strong suit.

"I know you're pretty green already, but it makes me feel better to have an expert on the job," said Jim, his tone conciliatory. "I'm sure you two will get along great. As a matter of fact, he mentioned you know each other—his name's Graham Donovan."

"Yes, I do know Graham," I said, my emotions reeling. The sexy contractor and I had history. The kind of history I didn't want to dwell on while in the company of clients.

"And check this out," Jim said, using his free hand to pick up a package from a plywood plank laid across two sawhorses. "I had this plaque made. I was thinking you could put it up when we're all done."

The gleaming brass plaque read:

CHESHIRE HOUSE, CIRCA 1890
RESTORATION BY DALEY FAMILY
AND TURNER CONSTRUCTION, 2011–2012

"That's beautiful, Jim," I said. Okay, Jim Daley had more going for him than just deep pockets: He *loved* this house. As one who is enamored of historic homes, I felt a certain kinship.

Quinn's adorable coos escalated into a fretful whimper. His chubby legs danced and his tiny arms flapped.

"Chow time! I'd better go feed the baby," Jim said. "Coming, honey?"

"You go. I come after. In a minute." Katenka's mouth tightened and one side pulled down in a barely-there grimace. I'd noticed that expression before. It was usually directed at unpleasant tasks . . . or just about anything involving her son.

Still, in her big hazel eyes I read a mixture of eager concern and trepidation. I found it hard to warm to Katenka, but a part of my heart went out to her. The unceasing demands of an infant would be tough for anyone, especially someone living in a foreign country without her family.

"Take your time," Jim said, kissing the top of her head. "Let's order Thai tonight. What do you think?"

She shrugged.

"Indian?" The baby's distress spiraled up, his whimpering ceding to crying.

"Is greasy."

"Pizza?" Quinn started to wail.

"We decide *later*," Katenka said.

"Okay, sure. Let me know when you're getting hungry, honey. See you tomorrow, Mel." Jim headed down the servant's hall to the rear staircase that descended to the basement-level apartment.

"Crazy," Katenka said, rolling her eyes. "He drive me crazy."

"The baby, or Jim?"

"*Both*. Mel, I must ask you some advice."

"I'm not much good at advice, Katenka. . . ." At least with regards to one's personal life. Got a leaky faucet? I'm your gal. Trying to expedite a construction permit down at city hall? I can give you a name. But problems with your marriage? You'd be better off soliciting advice from Larry King.

"I think we have uninvited guests in this house," said Katenka.

"I'm sorry?"

"Spirits. Ghosts. The souls of the dead still with us."

"I . . . uh, why would you think that?" Giving marital advice was sounding easier all the time.

"At night, I hear knocking. And footsteps."

"There could be any number of expla—"

Katenka's imploring gaze silenced me. She played with the filigreed crucifix that hung from a fine silver chain around her swanlike neck. "*Please*, Mel. I did research. It is said the spirits of the departed do not like to have their surroundings disturbed. And the renovation work, it disturbs surroundings, no?"

"Well, sure. That's sort of the point. . . ."

Unfortunately, I couldn't dismiss Katenka's fears out of hand, given the odd events on this job site. Besides, this wasn't my first run-in with the unexplainable. Several months ago I'd met up with the confused spirit of a murdered acquaintance, and once I recovered from the initial shock, I'd found the experience both annoying and fascinating. Since then I'd read up on the subject but hadn't sensed anything more ghostly than the vague sensations of welcome—or the lack thereof—I had always felt in historic homes. I had come to think of that paranormal experience as a onetime deal. Like the measles. Once you had it, you were immune.

Seems I was getting a booster shot.

"And when I go . . . when I go into Quinn's room," Katenka continued, "sometimes there feels like a black . . . What is the word? A black shadow? Following me."

"A black shadow? In the baby's room?"

"I feel it over my shoulder. As though it is trying to get in the room with me and the baby."

I swallowed, hard. The ghost I'd gotten to know had been irritating, but at least he never lurked over my shoulder in the form of a black shadow.

"I put up amulets," said Katenka. Her voice started to shake, and tears welled in her huge eyes. "I sweep and sprinkle the Holy Water. I tell the ghosts to leave. I was very forceful, but it makes things worse. Now they are worse."

That explained the smudge bundles I had noticed earlier amidst bits of wood and wallboard. The scent of burnt sage reminded me of walking down Telegraph Avenue in nearby Berkeley, and was said to cleanse places of bad vibrations. It also reminded me of Thanksgiving turkey, but maybe I was a little food-fixated.

"It's unsettling to live in a home while construction is going on around you," I said. Though I believed her, I didn't want to jump to conclusions. "The knocking could be a twig against a windowpane, or the sound of old pipes. And the creaking in the walls—"

My attempt to explain away the unexplainable was interrupted by the high-pitched whine of an electric drill that started spinning atop the temporary plywood worktable.

Katenka and I stared at the out-of-control contraption.

"Probably an electrical short," I said as I hurried to hit the OFF switch and unplug it from the wall. "Happens all the time in these old houses."

"Is no short," Katenka said, her tone fatalistic. "Is ghost. Maybe more than one. Even I think there is a cat ghost here. Is in the walls."

"A cat ghost?"

"I think maybe. I hear it, smell it sometimes."

"It could be an actual cat. I'll check the foundation for access—"

"Have you found history of the house?" Katenka interrupted. "Maybe history could tell us about these ghosts."

I shook my head. A crucial element in restoring a historic structure was conducting thorough research into its past. But a trip to the California Historical Society hadn't turned up anything on the Daleys' Queen Anne Victorian. Not even the name of the family that had built it. It wasn't that the history of the place was sketchy; it was nonexistent. And that was odd. San Francisco isn't that old, or that large. Usually it was easy to find the paper trails left by its well-to-do citizens, whether articles in the newspaper's society section, or tax records, or architectural blueprints.

But not this time.

"You know the lady who used to live here?" Katenka asked. "The cat lady?"

"I've heard of her, but we haven't met."

"I went to see her yesterday. She admit to me she leave this house because of the ghosts. She say they try to kill her."

Our eyes met in silence.

"That's a bad thing, no?" Katenka demanded.

Why yes, I thought. In general, death threats were a bad thing. Death threats from the beyond? Worse.

Katenka's gaze shifted to a spot behind me, and her eyes widened. Her face went pale, her body rigid. I swung around to see what she was staring at.

But I saw nothing except the kitchen door. Standing open.

Wait—hadn't it been closed?

And then I saw it: a footprint in the dust on the floor.

I turned back to Katenka just as she wobbled, then crumpled, overcome with fright. I caught her before she fell to the floor.

Another footprint appeared. Then another. Coming toward us.

Chapter Two

I stifled the urge to abandon my client and hightail it out of there. Self-preservation is a powerful, if at times undignified, instinct.

My heart beating a crazy tattoo against my ribs, I took a deep breath and gave myself a stern talking-to: *Keep calm, Mel. Last time, the ghost didn't hurt anyone. If anything, he helped. Why would this time be any different? It's just trying to make contact. Maybe it senses that you feel more, see more, than the average visitor.*

The footprints came together and stopped, as though someone were standing right in front of us.

"What is it?" Fear made my voice shrill. I tried to steady myself. "What do you want?"

Silence. I hadn't really expected an answer, but it was worth a shot.

Checking compulsively over my shoulder, I dragged Katenka to a horsehair settee that had been left by the former tenants, and eased her onto the dusty cushions as gently as I could. She moaned, stretching her arms over her head, her lips forming a Mona Lisa smile. The gesture and the smile were so sensuous—and so unlike her—that I was doubly shaken.

I straightened and surveyed the dining room, paying attention to my peripheral vision. The last ghost I had seen disappeared when I looked straight at him, only appearing in my side vision, or in the reflection of a mirror. Ever since odd events had started plaguing this job site, I had been driving myself crazy searching the premises out of the corners of my eyes.

I saw nothing. Nothing but the tracks in the dust. They weren't boot prints, but footprints—bare footprints. They were large, as if made by a grown man; here and there were droplets as though the . . . *entity* . . . had just stepped out of a bath.

But there weren't any new ones once they came together.

Last time this had happened to me, I was the only one who could see the ghost. He hadn't left any physical signs, hadn't even opened doors, just appeared at random. Despite my research, I wasn't that familiar with different sorts of ethereal apparitions. For all I knew they grew in power over time, like the vampires of lore. And maybe they loved to soak in the tub.

Seems I would be going up against some spirits. Again.

But I would *not* do it alone. I had learned that much, at least. This time, I was calling in backup from the start. Since I knew I wasn't hallucinating, I refused to be shy about asking for help. Awkward, maybe—reluctant, definitely—but not shy.

I stood over Katenka, pondering what my next move should be. Call Jim? Hire a psychic? What I really wanted was to rent a U-Haul and get this young family *out* of here before dusk.

The back of my neck tingled.

In my peripheral vision, I saw a black, amorphous shape. And felt a wave of dread, and rage, wash over me.

As soon as I looked straight at it, it disappeared.

It left me feeling off-kilter, uncentered, as though looking into the distortions of a funhouse mirror. It was hard to know what was real, and what was not. This was nothing like the last ghost I had seen.

I reached down and shook Katenka, calling her name.

"Mm . . . wha . . ." She opened her eyes and, after a long moment, focused on me. Fear returned to her face as she scanned the room. Seeing nothing, she relaxed into the cushions and fixed me with an accusatory glare. "You saw it, no?"

I nodded.

"I think you must stop this project."

"But . . . we're nowhere near finished."

"Is fine. I live in worse in Russia, believe me. I have placed the amulets and magic water in our bedroom and the baby's; nothing has happened in there. In there we are safe. I will talk to Jim to stop renovation. Then ghosts will be quiet."

"Wouldn't it make more sense if you and Jim moved out for the interim?"

She held up a delicate palm, closed her eyes, and took a shaky breath. "No, this is not possible. I have told you before, Jim will not even discuss it—he says we must live in our home to create . . . tradition and stability for the baby. Jim says this is our home and we stay here, forever."

"Forever" seemed like a chilling word to bandy about

at the moment. If the ghosts were indeed malevolent and threatening, I sure wouldn't want to spend the night under the same roof with them. Especially not with a child.

"But if there's something here, something unsettled, or dangerous—"

"If you stop construction, perhaps the spirits go back to sleep. Or if they do not—perhaps we must sell, find someplace else for our forever home for baby. I will talk to Jim."

"Sell? Now?"

"Perhaps is best."

"Katenka, please, we might be able to figure something out—"

I should have saved my breath.

She was already heading downstairs to talk to her husband, the man who couldn't refuse her anything.

I drooped onto the lumpy settee. A moment ago I had been contemplating running away from the house myself. But apart from the obvious financial ramifications of shutting down the job—Turner Construction employed a crew of seven full-time workers, as well as numerous subcontractors—a Queen Anne like Cheshire House was one of a kind.

I had been itching to return this place to its former glory from the first moment I laid eyes on it. As had Jim Daley. He told me he had searched for a Queen Anne of this magnitude and historic import for more than a year, only to find it right down the street from where he used to live, in a duplex on Union Street.

Unlike many grand homes, Cheshire House survived the 1906 earthquake and fire that devastated San Francisco. Built of solid redwood brought by ship from the lush old-growth forests that used to thrive along California's rugged north coast, a home of this stature show-cased the skill and dedication of turn-of-the-century workers: Italian mold makers, Polish stonecutters, Irish carpenters, Mexican builders, Chinese laborers. It had the beautiful arches and tall ceilings common to Victorians, but its copious gingerbread moldings made it a rare treasure. San Francisco boasts some fabulous Italianate and Stick Victorian homes, but the Queen Annes reign as the city's true royalty.

Whoever the original owners were, they had spent a fortune building the home. And it had been the recipient of the love and care of scores of talented workers whose energy had seeped into its very walls.

I love old houses. Passionately. I'm driven to preserve them for the future, for the environment, for our children. I understand them.

But Katenka didn't want to live with ghosts, and I couldn't blame her. Not to mention the alleged death threats from beyond the grave.

Time for some serious ghost busting.

Since I'd been through this once before, at least I now knew who to call. I rang Realtor Brittany Humm, of Humm's Haunted Houses, and asked her to meet me tomorrow for lunch and ghost-talk.

"Lovely!" she gushed. "I was hoping you'd be contacted again! I'm so excited!"

"Yeah. . . . Me, too," I lied.

Rather than intrude on Jim and Katenka's private discussion, I decided to let it go until morning. Jim loved this house so much I doubted he'd be willing to sell, even for the wife he adored. So the real question was whether or not I could get them to vacate while I rid the place of ghosts . . . presuming I figured out how to do that. Which was a rather large presumption.

After gathering my paperwork and tucking it into my satchel, I turned off the lights and locked the front door behind me.

As I descended the stone steps to the street, I spotted an apparition only slightly less frightening than ghostly footprints and black shadowy figures: Emile Blunt.

Super. The perfect ending to a perfect day.

Emile owned the upholstery shop across the street and though he wasn't quite as old as the building that housed his business, he was at least as broken down and crotchety. Like a tough old rooster, he led with his chest when he was bothered, and he was bothered a lot. The Daleys' construction project had irritated him from the start, and he wanted everyone to understand the extent of his frustration.

I used to nod and try to be pleasant, but lately I just avoided him. I moved quickly toward my car, hoping to outrun yet another of his tirades.

I almost made it—I was reaching for the door handle when I heard Emile's gruff voice behind me.

"Miss Turner."

Giving in to the inevitable, I turned around and forced a polite smile.

"Mr. Blunt, how are you today?"

"Not well. Not well at all. How long am I going to have to put up with this?"

"I'm sorry about the inconvenience, but—"

"I'm filing a complaint with the city."

I gritted my teeth. "You can if you wish, of course, but it won't do you any good. We have all the necessary work permits, and we're following the time guidelines, doing more than we're required to by law, even. I'm sorry you're unhappy, but construction projects always involve some noise and mess. We're doing everything we can to hurry things along and cause a minimum of—"

"Screw your minimum."

"Okaaaay," I said, wondering where to take it from there. If my practiced "please be patient and reasonable" speech wasn't cutting it, I didn't have a lot of other tricks up my sleeve.

Neighborhood relations are an ongoing concern for those of us doing residential renovation, but sooner or later just about every homeowner in San Francisco will undertake some sort of home improvement—a new roof, backyard landscaping, plumbing repairs, foundation work—and will need to call upon the patience of their neighbors. Most folks seem to realize this and suffer in silence, knowing their turn will come.

Emile Blunt was not one of these. One look at his front room was all it took to realize he hadn't so much as changed his curtains in the decades he had owned his shop.

He seemed to regroup, relaxing his aggressive stance and even attempting a gap-toothed smile. "If you would come inside for a minute, we could talk. Please."

I hesitated. I was tired and grumpy and preoccupied with ghosts. But Emile was old and grumpy and worried about lord-knows-what. Plus, he was a neighbor, and my elder, and he'd said please. I'm a sucker for "please."

Besides, it was almost Christmas, so I was trying extra hard to be nice. With a sigh, I followed him into his upholstery shop.

A rusty bell let out a lonely little tinkle as we passed through the door.

I always introduce myself to the neighbors at the start of any project, so I had been inside the upholstery shop once before. It was even worse than I remembered. Glancing around, I tried to avoid breathing.

The room stank of must, mildew, and something far worse. Thick bolts of dusty fabric stood in every corner; hundreds of sample books and loose fabric swatches littered the tables and hung from nails along the back wall. The main source of light was the tepid incandescence of a bare bulb hanging from a carved and gilded ceiling medallion that had once featured a grand chandelier. Thick cobwebs claimed every corner, the patterned wallpaper was water-stained and peeling away from the dirty plaster walls, and scarred wainscoting ringed the room, occasional panels cracked or missing altogether. Every horizontal surface was covered in fuzz, feathers, and filth.

"Nice place," I said.

Emile snorted.

A red fox sitting atop a worktable scowled at me, and I jumped before realizing it was stuffed and mounted. Upholstery was Emile's bread and butter, but he was also an amateur taxidermist. A stuffed tortoiseshell cat sat upon the mantel of a long-unused fireplace, next to several ceramic feline figurines. It was one of a variety of small animals that stared down from their perches with glassy, unseeing eyes. Around the cat's neck was a glittery rhinestone collar sporting a large metal charm. The decorative detail made its stuffed presence even sadder.

I couldn't understand how Emile managed to find customers who didn't mind having their antique Stickley sofas reupholstered alongside a stuffed California turkey vulture, but Emile was surprisingly slick. Plus his

rates were really, really cheap for Union Street, a neighborhood known more for chic restaurants and wine bars
than old-school shops like this. Emile must own the
building, I thought; otherwise he would never be able to
afford to stay in business.

"I see you like cats."

"What's wrong with that? Can't have a live one, on
account o' all the hair." He gestured at the stuffed tortoiseshell feline, his gaze lingering, lovingly, for a moment. "Did a great job on that one, though, didn't I?
Real lifelike."

I'm a strong believer in pursuing one's passions, but
taxidermy . . . ? Outside of the Museum of Natural History, it just seemed creepy.

"I understand the former owner of the Cheshire Inn
liked cats," I said.

"That crazy cat woman?"

"I take it you didn't get along?"

"You know she buried a bunch of her cats in the
yard? I offered to take care of 'em for her, but she
wouldn't have it. Anyway, I didn't ask you here to talk
about her. I want you to help me. I wanna make an offer
on the house."

"What house?"

"The Cheshire Inn," he said, giving me a "what an
idiot" look.

My cell phone rang. As much as I wanted to extricate
myself from this conversation, I let it go to voice mail.
Better to finish with the eccentric Mr. Blunt before taking calls.

"It's not my house," I said.

"I *realize* that," he said, his voice betraying what he

thought of my intelligence quotient. "I want you to facilitate things for me with the husband. He's being difficult."

"I'm sorry, Emile. I'm having a hard time wrapping my mind around this. You've hated this project since it began, and now you want me to help you buy a house that's not for sale. If you wanted it, why didn't you bid on it when it was on the market a couple of months ago?"

"I wasn't in the position to buy it then. But I understand the current owners might be unhappy. That little Ukrainian gal talks to me sometimes. She wants me to upholster an old settee."

"She's Russian, not Ukrainian." I stopped myself before adding that she was a grown woman, not a little girl. Weariness washed over me. It had been a long day, and I had just seen a ghost . . . or something. Why was I bothering with Emile Blunt?

"Listen, if you're seriously interested in the house, you should speak directly to the Daleys," I said, glancing at my watch. "I really do need to get going. I'm already into rush hour traffic."

Without waiting for an answer I fled the shop, relief wafting over me as I stepped out into the fresh evening air.

Unfortunately, Emile Blunt was hard on my heels.

"We're not finished!"

"I believe we are," I said, hurrying to my car. "If you want to buy the house, you'll have to speak with the owners, who happen to be home at the moment. I have to go."

"Listen to me, lady: If you refuse to help me, you'll be sorry."

I opened the car door but paused to look at him.

"Are you . . . *threatening* me?" I wasn't sure I could

believe my ears. When he didn't answer, I climbed into my boxy Scion, locked all the doors, and started the engine.

Blunt planted himself, sumo wrestler–like, in front of my car.

I glanced behind me. A brown delivery truck was parked there, preventing me from backing up.

I seethed. What in the world had gotten into this guy?

On the sidewalk a bearded homeless man watched the action, a broad smile on his face. He gave me the thumbs-up. At least the Roman crowds were with me.

My phone rang again.

"What?" I answered, adrenaline pumping through me.

"Um, sor-ry. Maybe I'll talk to you later," came the voice of my sixteen-year-old stepson, Caleb.

"No, *I'm* the one who's sorry, kiddo. A grumpy old man is standing in front of my car because I told him I wouldn't sell him a house I don't own. Go figure. Plus my clients might be firing me." I skipped the part about seeing ghosts. "And how's *your* day been?"

"I'm just so sick of it all. I wish I were, like, dead."

Nothing like the histrionics of a teenager to put things in perspective.

"What's going on?"

"Dad, like, left on a research trip. Valerie's here. I so totally don't want to be here with *her*. Could I crash with you for a couple of days, a week max? Mom'll be home next Monday, and I can go to her house."

"It's okay with me if it's okay with your folks. Want to check with them first?"

"Valerie kinda, like, kicked me out? So I'm pretty sure it's all good with her."

"And where's your mom?"

"She's in LA for a couple of days. I already talked to her and she said it was fine if it was okay with you."

Luckily, I got along great with Caleb's mother, Angelica. Caleb disliked his father's newest wife, Valerie, so intensely that it wasn't unusual for him to wind up at my house rather than stay at his dad's when Angelica was out of town, as she frequently was with her high-powered job.

A little over two years ago I had walked away from my ex-husband Daniel with nothing but a sigh of relief—and an abiding regret at having wasted so many years on the relationship. But his son was another matter. Caleb had been only five years old when Daniel and I married; he wore a pirate costume and stayed in character for the better part of a year. It was love at first pretend sword fight. During the eight years I was married to his father, I helped teach Caleb to swim and to read. I packed smoked salmon sandwiches because he was the only kid in America who hated PB&J, laughed at countless knock-knock jokes, kissed dozens of boo-boos, and attended never-ending PTA meetings. So even though I no longer wanted Caleb's dad, I figured I had earned my status as Caleb's backup mom.

Emile Blunt still stood in front of the car, arms crossed over his chest, channeling a particularly stubborn rooster. As a city girl, I have no idea whether roosters are particularly stubborn, but it wouldn't surprise me.

"I'm ten minutes away," I told Caleb. "I'll swing by and pick you up. Get your stuff together and be ready to go when I get there, okay?"

"'Kay. Can you get here any faster?"

"I'll do my best, but at the moment I've got a man standing in front of my car."

"Is he trying to wash your windshield? Just give him a buck and he'll move. Or rev your engine. Maybe he'll leave."

I gunned it. Emile crouched, hands out, as though prepared to wrestle the Scion.

"Get this—now he's gone into some sort of karate stance!"

"Dude!" Caleb started laughing. I joined him.

"Okay," I said, still chuckling. "I'm going to hang up and either run this guy over or talk him into leaving. If I don't show up soon, come post my bail, will ya?"

I respect my elders. Really I do. That's what my parents taught me, and most seniors deserve it. But ever since my divorce I was less inclined to deal with recalcitrant men of any ilk. Plus, I had lots of experience with aging curmudgeons—my father was one of the highest order. Caleb was the only male I had patience for right now.

I leaned out the window.

"Listen, old man," I called. "Move it or I'll run you over. I'm not kidding."

Chapter Three

Emile Blunt glared and seemed to be swearing at me under his breath. Other than my managing a construction site near his shop, I couldn't imagine what could have inspired such animosity toward me. It was a little tough not to take it personally.

I took my foot off the brake. The vehicle started to creep ahead, though my boot still hovered over the pedal.

Blunt finally stepped aside, glowering.

I forced myself not to floor it.

As I prepared to turn the corner, the hairs on my neck stood up. I checked my peripheral vision, hoping no one—or no *thing*—had hitched a ride from Cheshire House. I was relieved to find nothing occupying the passenger seat besides the pile of job-related files and clipboards that I always hauled around with me.

But in the rearview mirror, Emile stood in the middle of the street, watching me the whole way.

*   *   *

Caleb's dad still lived in the pretty Victorian we had once shared on Clay Street. It was less grand by far than Cheshire House, but nonetheless charming and historical. When I lived there, I had painted it in shades of maroon, gold, and dove gray with gold gilt highlights. Shortly after Valerie moved in, she had it repainted in muted tones of taupe and cream, making it blend in perfectly with the staid homes of this affluent neighborhood. Wouldn't want to stand out.

I didn't like coming here. I was slowly—*very* slowly—getting better about not wallowing in the pathos of my failed marriage, but it still felt like a deep-tissue bruise. It might not be noticeable at skin level, but it hurt like hell when you poked it. Seeing this house was a jab with a sharp stick.

I nosed my Scion into the shallow driveway, straddling the sidewalk, and called Caleb. He wasn't ready, of course. His teenage sense of "hurrying" was tortoiselike, at best.

"I'm leaving in five minutes, whether you're out here or not," I threatened. "I am *not* in the mood."

"Yeah, okay," he said, not believing for a moment that I'd leave without him. I'm not nearly as hard-nosed as I try to be.

My heart dropped when a woman descended the steep stairs from the formal front door. Gray trousers with the subtle sheen of fine linen. A fuzzy lavender sweater, probably cashmere. Long black silky hair. Expensive yet understated gold jewelry around her neck and on her fingers. Leggy, svelte, with the hips-forward stride of a runway model. Valerie.

Swearing under my breath, I rolled down the driver's-side window, forced a smile, and kept my tone neutral. "Hi, Valerie. How are you?"

She rolled her eyes and folded her slim arms over her waist. "Adolescents."

I nodded. "He said something about you kicking him out?"

"I told him if he was going to talk to me like that, he should just leave."

"Ah."

"I wanted to ask you," Valerie continued, "do you have more of the original doors for the house stashed anywhere?"

No, there are no original doors floating around that I just didn't feel like putting up, I almost answered in the snidest of tones. But I clamped down on my base tendencies for Caleb's sake. I try hard to be my most diplomatic self whenever I am around Caleb's father or newest stepmother. Since I have no legal ties to the boy, our relationship is sanctioned only by the good grace of his legal parents.

But inside, I screamed. I had sweated blood over the renovation of this house, the first project I had done myself, long before I took over Turner Construction. My father gave me advice and loaned me workers, even pitched in himself from time to time. But I was the one who dug up information at the historical society and the hall of records, talked to elderly neighbors to learn about its recent history, found old photos, steamed and stripped six layers of wallpaper, crawled around on all fours studying the marks on the wood floors to determine where walls had been moved.

At one point the house had been stripped in an appalling effort to "modernize" it, and much of the original charm had been lost. I found reproduction plaster medallions for the hanging lamps, window hardware, and even doors. I made lots of beginner's mistakes. I hadn't understood, for example, that copper and lead pipes can't lead into one another without the proper catalyst. And I replaced several missing fixtures with newly crafted reproductions though I now knew I could unearth genuine articles in thrift shops and salvage yards. Still, I had restored the home as best I could with love and devotion . . . almost as though it were a palette for my marriage.

Looking back on it now, I realized that in some secret corner of my mind I believed that if I could make our home beautiful and harmonious and perfect, our marriage might reflect those qualities. Turns out, that sort of magical thinking doesn't really pan out.

Valerie's dark eyes flickered over my outfit.

After years of dressing in a proper "faculty wife" wardrobe to please Daniel—a professor at UC-Berkeley—I had vowed to wear whatever I wanted, whenever I felt like it. As long as I completed the look with my steel-toed work boots and kept a pair of coveralls handy for inching through crawl spaces, I figured I was good to go. Once the men in my employ realized I knew my stuff—and that it was *my* signature on their paychecks—they accepted my eccentric garb with good grace.

Which was a lot more than I could say for Valerie. Suddenly self-conscious, I started to shift, pulling up the low neckline of today's spangled dress.

"I'm doing a few projects in the house, fixing up some things," Valerie said. "We're going to redo the kitchen."

I bit my tongue and counted to ten.

"And probably the master bath as well."

"Really." I had restored those areas with painstaking historical accuracy. "What are you going to do with the fixtures?"

"Oh, do you want to buy them?"

I already did, I thought to myself. But I just shrugged; no sense getting into this with Valerie.

"So, how are things with you?" she asked. "Still living with your dad?"

"I'm, uh . . ."

Caleb appeared through the garage entrance, heavy backpack slung over one shoulder, computer case in hand, white wires falling from his ears indicating a hidden iPod. My heart swelled a little just to see him, this boy who seemed to be growing up too fast. His dark hair was disheveled, his cupid's bow mouth rosy with the perfect blush of youth. He had a face worthy of one of Raphael's angels, but the sullen air of the privileged American teen. Without saying a word, he opened the passenger door and climbed in.

"Hi, Goose," I said, using the nickname I had dubbed him with, back when we used to pretend–sword fight.

"Hey," he said with an almost imperceptible lift of his chin.

His current stepmother hovered outside my open window. I imagined she was torn between relief that Caleb was leaving and a vague sense of guilt at having kicked the boy out of his own home.

"Say something to Valerie," I whispered to Caleb out of the side of my mouth.

"Something," he said in a loud voice.

"Caleb," I warned.

He rolled his eyes, gave Valerie a wave and a tight smile, hunched over, and started texting someone on his phone.

Valerie rolled her eyes, just like the sixteen-year-old.
"Bye," I said, as we pulled out.

"So how's school?" I asked Caleb as I headed east across
the Bay Bridge. I realized the moment it slipped out that
this was the question dreaded by every high schooler.

He shrugged. "It's school. Whatever. Hey, did you run
that old man down, or what?"

"He finally got out of the way. Oh, don't forget—
Stan's party tomorrow is a surprise, so don't mention it,
okay?"

"No prob."

Caleb listened to rap music on his iPod while I tuned
into a news channel. Traffic was light, so twenty minutes
later we exited the freeway in Oakland. Our neighborhood is kindly referred to as "transitional," which means
there is widespread poverty, a large immigrant population, and a smattering of yuppies redoing the once-grand
old homes. Friendly people and the best Mexican food
in town, hands-down. I love it.

I turned onto a residential street. A clutch of scraggly
plum and peach trees and the neighborhood moniker of
"Fruitvale" were the only signs that this area had once
boasted orchards as far as the eye could see.

Now it was home. Temporarily.

"Hey, look," I said, hoping to wrest Caleb's attention
from his cell phone. "Dad put up the Christmas lights."

"Cool," he mumbled out of duty more than interest.

As we got out of the car, a barking bundle of brown
fur barreled toward us. My dad must have heard my car
pull up and had released the hound.

Dog came flying down the pathway, joyous at our re-
union. The canine was happy to see me, but went bananas

greeting Caleb. He twisted around so far that his shaggy, wildly wagging tail whapped his head repeatedly.

"Hey, boy, I missed you!" Caleb said, dropping to his knees to hug the ecstatic dog. His teenage ways were so typically monosyllabic that it warmed my heart to see him gush unabashedly when it came to Dog. "Do you have a name yet?"

"Not yet," I answered for the dog. "You know how we are here at chez Turner. We've had the poor mutt for months now, and he still has no name."

I glanced up at the second-story window sashes that were sagging. Back in the day, my father would never have put up the Christmas lights without first attending to the broken windowpanes or the detached gutter . . . or the hundred other things that needed fixing. Since it didn't seem like he'd be stepping up to the plate anytime soon, I would have to take this never-ending project in hand one of these days. But for now the old farmhouse was like the proverbial cobbler's child, running about town without shoes.

Dog, his tail held high, led the way along the broken flagstone path to the back door, the entrance used by friends and family. A small mudroom opened onto a big old-fashioned kitchen that tonight smelled of meat, gravy, and Parker House rolls.

Dad ruled with a wooden spoon at the antique Wedgewood stove.

"Hi, babe. Heya, kid," he greeted us.

"Hey, Bill," Caleb replied. "Hey, Stan."

"Caleb, my man, long time no see. What's up?" Stan replied, rolling over in his wheelchair.

A couple of years ago Stan Tomassi had one moment of sloppiness and slipped off a second-story roof, fracturing several vertebrae. Single and alone in the world, he had no one to care for him when he was released from many months in rehab. So Mom and Dad built a ramp onto the old farmhouse, revamped a downstairs room to Americans with Disabilities Act standards, and moved him in. Not long afterward Mom passed away, and Stan helped my dad through the dark times. Now the two men were like an old married couple: bickering good-naturedly over politics, sports, and what to watch on the massive big-screen TV.

Stan and Caleb did an Oakland-style hand slap, up high, down low, fist bump, finger clench. Then Stan handed me a freshly made margarita.

"Thanks, Stan," I said, leaning over to give him a hug.

"Smells good," I said, kissing my dad on his whiskery cheek. He smelled of gravy and tobacco. "We having salad tonight?"

"Nope. That rabbit stuff you get at the farmers market is a rip-off. This is real food. It'll put hair on your chest."

Caleb and I shared a smile. When Caleb was younger, he would always reply, worried, "But I don't *want* hair on my chest!"

"How's work, babe?" Dad asked. "Caleb, the table needs setting."

"I might have hit a snag in the Cheshire House project," I said, watching as Caleb took four mismatched plates from an antique pie cupboard. The plates reminded me of my mother, who always insisted she would never have a matched set of china because she didn't want her children to live in fear of breaking one. "Katenka Daley seems to think that we're stirring up some trouble with our renovation work."

"Trouble with the neighbors? Told you those Union Street folks were touchy." Dad deftly transferred a pot roast onto a big platter, then surrounded it with piping hot potatoes, caramelized pearl onions, and glazed carrots.

"No—actually, yes. One guy in particular—an upholsterer. Looks like he's been there a long time. Emile Blunt?" My dad and Stan had worked high-end construction in San Francisco for so many years that they knew a lot of people.

Dad shook his head and glanced at Stan, who shrugged.

"Doesn't ring a bell. I take it he's a PITA?" PITA was code for pain in the ass. It was a useful term on job sites.

"You could say that. I might ask you to talk to him at some point," I said. "I have the sense an old coot like you would understand him better than I."

"'Old coot'? How d'ya like that?" Dad said to Stan, pretending to be outraged, but enjoying the teasing. He pulled a pan of hot rolls from the oven and transferred them, barehanded, to a cloth-lined basket, singing *"Hey hot ho hot"* and silently whistling. I used to think his reaction was silly, until Caleb pointed out I do the same thing.

"By the way," Dad said, "you should take Dog with you tomorrow. I got him a new supply of carsick pills."

"You want to come to work with me, Dog?" I asked.

The mellow canine glanced at me and flicked his tail, a duty wag, before his soulful brown eyes—and full attention—slewed back to the roast sitting atop the counter. When I first saw the dog—a skinny, scraggly, stray brown mutt hanging around a work site—I figured he was a construction pup. But no one ever claimed him, and once I brought him home and fed him, I didn't have the heart to kick him out. Besides, he was the only living creature—besides me—who had seen the ghost that used to follow me around.

Maybe I should let him look through Cheshire House tomorrow, see how he reacted.

Anyway, now Dog was *my* construction pup. There were only two problems: First, he was yet another speed bump in my long-term plan to run away to Paris; second, the poor canine tended toward carsickness.

"Dinner's on!" Dad called out, even though we were all right there.

We took seats around the scarred farmhouse table in the kitchen and started passing the steaming platters.

"Anyway, it wasn't the neighbors I was referring to," I said as I slathered butter onto a hot roll.

"Then what's the problem?"

I hesitated, took a deep breath, and dove in.

"Katenka Daley thinks the renovation work has stirred up . . . ghosts."

Chapter Four

Three sets of eyes fixed on me. Four, if you counted the dog. But at least the canine's motivations had to do with the possibility of cadging a piece of meat or a dropped roll rather than concern for my mental state.

Dad shot Stan a look before digging into his potatoes.

"I know you heard me," I said.

Dad didn't want to talk about my apparent ability to see ghosts any more than he had when my mother had exhibited the same tendencies. Stan and Caleb seemed more open to the idea—sort of—though more out of their loyalty to me more than any belief in the supernatural. Suffice it to say that none of my current companions was exactly on board with it.

"Something weird's been happening at the job site. That's for sure," I said. "Things going missing, strange noises . . ."

"Sounds more like a disgruntled worker," suggested Stan. "You make anybody mad lately? Or how about that guy from across the street you were just talking about?"

Could Emile have been screwing around with things at Cheshire House? Trying to drive the Daleys out by scaring them, perhaps? I wouldn't put it past him to sneak over at night to dink around with supplies and sabotage power tools.

Still and all, that wouldn't explain what had happened this afternoon. I had seen something in that dining room. Something real.

"I wish I knew more about this sort of thing. I can't even put together a proper history of the place, much less whether it was said to be haunted."

"Hey, last time my sister was in town we went on a ghost tour of Pacific Heights," Stan said. "The guy sounded like he knew a lot about local history, and if I believed in that sort of thing, I guess I would have believed him."

"Ghost tour?"

"Olivier something . . . I forget his full name, but he takes a group out just about every evening from that hotel that's supposedly haunted—what's it called? The Eastlake? French fellow. He's got a Web site."

"You think the guy who cashes in on tourists' superstitions might know something about my house?"

He shrugged and passed the salt to my still-silent dad. "Worth a shot."

"And he's French," Caleb pointed out. "Aren't you looking for a French guy?"

"I want to *live* in France, not get a French boyfriend. Big difference."

He shrugged. "Whatever. Close enough."

"You know, that's not a bad idea, Stan. At least it's someplace to start. Thanks. I'll look him up."

"Which reminds me," said Stan. "There were two phone calls to the office today, asking if you offered ghost-hunting services."

I choked on my water.

"What?" I sputtered. "They wanted *my* ghost-hunting services?"

"That's what they said," replied Stan.

"My *ghost-hunting* services?"

"I told 'em they were barking up the wrong tree, but wrote down their info in case you were opening up a side business."

"I was thinking of having an open house for Christmas Eve," Dad said in a blatant bid to change the subject. "Mel, honey, you see Graham, be sure to mention it, will ya?"

"He's coming tomorrow night, isn't he?" Stan asked.

"Tomorrow?"

"For my birthday party."

We all stared at him.

"Birthday fail," whispered Caleb.

"Was it supposed to be a surprise?" Stan asked.

I cast a dirty look in Dad's direction. He ignored me.

Stan grinned. "Right sweet of y'all. But if it was meant to be a surprise, you shouldn't have given out the home phone as the RSVP. Bill, I got one word for you: E-vite. Been tellin' ya you need to get on the Internet. Password protection, dontcha know."

"Oh, Dad," I said with a sigh.

"Ah well," Dad grumped. "I told you it didn't make sense to try to finagle a surprise party in the man's own house."

"What time you want me back from my weekly chess game?" Stan asked.

"We told everyone to arrive at six, so if you come at six thirty, that would be perfect," I said. "And do me a favor? Act surprised. Real surprised."

"You got it, boss lady." He gave me a little salute and dug into his roast.

Half an hour later, up to my elbows in sudsy water—Stan and Caleb cleaned the table and loaded the dishwasher, but I was stuck with pot duty—I made a mental list of last-minute items for tomorrow's party.

Call about the tamales. Pick up cake by five. Decorate between five and six. Desperately try to ignore the fact that Graham Donovan was coming. Shave legs and wear perfume.

I closed my eyes and took a deep breath. If I was brave enough to chase ghosts, surely I could handle one red-blooded, *live* male. Even a well-built, dark-eyed manly man with a wry chuckle who had a way of looking at me that made a deep, secret part of me start to melt.

Graham used to be an inspector for California's office of OSHA, the Occupational Safety and Health Administration. In fact, he had helped to shut down a job site of mine not long ago. But long before that, Graham worked for my father, and I had developed a mad crush on him while I was in graduate school. He never seemed to return the interest until shortly before my wedding, when he made an entirely uncharacteristic, rashly romantic play for me and tried to dissuade me from marrying Daniel. Our one passionate, out-of-control kiss had been so unexpected and . . . *thrilling* . . . that I had to struggle not to compare all subsequent kisses to it.

Despite such a powerful inducement, I went ahead with the wedding. It didn't take long to realize that Graham had been right about Daniel, a fact that mortified me then as well as now.

Graham had been traveling for the past few months, studying green technology around the world. He was back in town and apparently swamped with all the details involved in setting up his new business. I'd only seen him briefly, by chance. Last time we ran into each other he said he had something to tell me, but we were interrupted by the high-pitched whine of a circular saw and a slew of workers needing guidance. The moment passed.

The thought of what he'd wanted to tell me prompted my mind to cast about in wild speculation. He could have simply called, *would* have called, had it been something business-related. Wouldn't he?

I was trying to convince myself to pull up my big-girl pants and call him. This was the twenty-first century, as Caleb so often reminded me. No reason to wait for the man to ask.

But when it came to romance, my self-confidence had taken a body blow. And it had been a decade since I'd been in the dating world. Still, the party tomorrow was the perfect opportunity. It was about time I moved on, shook off my damned divorce hangover once and for all. Daniel certainly had.

Resolute, I stripped off my yellow rubber gloves, downed the rest of my drink, and headed for bed.

Usually I was up early and on the job site by seven at the latest, but I'd told Caleb I would drop him off at University High School across the bay in Pacific Heights, so I spent the early morning in the home office with Stan, going over the payroll, signing vendor checks, and reviewing client contracts and schedules. After dropping off Caleb, I stopped by city hall to check on the progress of a couple of building permits. Dog waited in the car, greeting me each time I returned as though he'd thought he'd never see me again.

It was past ten by the time I headed to Cheshire House.

Since I hadn't heard from Jim and Katenka, I was determined to carry on as usual. If they decided to sell the house to Emile Blunt, I doubted he would require the further services of Turner Construction. But ghosts or no ghosts, I couldn't imagine Jim Daley abandoning his Cheshire House dream so easily.

But I wasn't able to turn onto Union Street; it was blocked by a police cruiser. A young, fresh-faced uniformed officer was turning away traffic, insisting there was "nothing to see."

Nothing but an ambulance, a paramedic truck, and a half-dozen police cars, red and blue emergency lights flashing.

Right in front of Cheshire House.

Chapter Five

I should have tried harder to convince them to leave last night, I thought as I double-parked and jumped out, taking time only to crack the window for the dog.

Running, I said a flurry of silent prayers that nothing had happened to Jim or Katenka or . . . worst of all, to the baby.

As I pushed my way through the small crowd of curious onlookers, my concern for the young family vied with wondering how to explain this to the police: *You see, officer, there were mysterious footprints, and a shadowlike figure, a strange dark cloud.*

That ought to go over big.

But the stretcher with the blanket-covered body didn't roll out of Cheshire House. It came from across the street—Emile Blunt's upholstery shop.

Relief washed over me. But on its heels came shame.

Could that too-still form on the stretcher be Emile?

What had my parting words been? *"Move it, old man, before I run you down"*?

No matter how obnoxious the old upholsterer was, I should have held my tongue.

And then I saw a familiar face in the crowd near the ambulance.

"Dad?"

To my knowledge, Dad hadn't set foot on a job site since I had taken over the management of Turner Construction two years ago.

I felt suddenly wary. My dad was in his midsixties, but he still had a decent form, wiry and strong. I had never seen him become violent, but if he felt threatened—or more to the point, if he felt his *daughter* was being threatened—he might lash out enough to do some damage. And the truth was that ever since my mom's death, his behavior had been less than entirely predictable. Could he have—?

"I found the poor guy on the floor of his shop," Dad said. "Looked like a bullet wound. Lots of blood, I'm sorry to say."

A woman walked up to us, her head held high, her carriage elegant, as though she'd been trained to walk while balancing a fat book of etiquette on her head. Tall, solid, strong-looking. Regal.

"This is my daughter, Inspector," said Dad. "She's the general contractor on the job site across the street."

"Good morning," she said, flashing a shiny SFPD badge. "I'm homicide inspector Annette Crawford. You're Melanie Turner? Your father tells me you knew the deceased."

"Yes, I didn't know him all that well, but as the neighbor."

"And as a pain in your ass?"

"Excuse me?"

"Homeless fellow over there says you threatened the victim last night."

Dad looked at me, eyebrows lifted. I felt the sting of a blush.

"I didn't threaten him, exac—"

Inspector Crawford glanced at her notebook. "'*Move it or I'll run you over.*' Something like that?"

Dad rolled his eyes.

"Um . . . okay. But I didn't—"

"I'm not accusing you of homicide, Ms. Turner." The inspector paused, and I would have sworn there was a silent "yet" at the end of that sentence. "Just trying to put together the sequence of last night's events."

"Yes," I conceded. "We had words."

"What time was this?"

"I had just left the job site for the day, so a little after five."

"Tell me what happened, as precisely as you can."

I tried to recall our talk. Mostly I remembered being annoyed.

"It was nothing new—we'd had the same conversation a thousand times before. He was complaining about the noise and the mess of the construction project. But I can assure you we're in full compliance—"

"Nothing stood out to you about the conversation?" she interrupted, and I guessed homicide inspectors weren't the same division as the noise police. "Anything different this time?"

"Only one thing: He told me he wanted to buy Cheshire House."

"Is it for sale?"

I shook my head, feeling a sense of déjà vu. Last time I had encountered ghosts, at a once-palatial home on Vallejo Street, a mystery man showed up out of the blue, claiming he had purchased the house—though it wasn't for sale. That had been a case of deliberate malfeasance, however. In this case . . . what could be the explanation? At least Emile Blunt hadn't claimed he *was* buying the house, just the desire to do so. Heck, we all wanted to buy houses all the time, right? And considering how much he hated the construction process, Emile probably wanted to buy it simply to put an end to the noise. Still . . . it was hard to imagine he would have that kind of money stashed away in his broken-down upholstery shop.

"Blunt mentioned that he had spoken with Katenka Daley, one of the owners, and that she had told him she was unhappy," I continued. "He thought therefore she might want to sell."

"Does she?"

"I don't really know. I'm sure her husband doesn't, but . . ." I trailed off. If I told the inspector the whole truth, she'd think I was nuts. I glanced at my dad, who was still standing within earshot.

Inspector Crawford caught the look. She gave a subtle head-jerk toward a beige sedan and we walked over to stand by it, where we had a semblance of privacy.

"You're going to think I'm crazy."

"Try me."

"Yesterday Katenka confided in me that there might be . . ." I trailed off, looking into the homicide inspector's serious, no-nonsense, sherry-colored eyes. No way this woman would believe a word of it.

"Might be . . . what? Out with it."

"There have been some odd events taking place on

the job site recently. Katenka Daley expressed the belief they might be caused by . . . spirits. In the house."

Crawford was silent for a full beat. "House spirits."

I nodded.

"As in ghosts."

I nodded again.

She cleared her throat, took a deep breath, and let it out slowly. Then she rubbed her brow.

"Sometimes I hate my job," she murmured. "Okay, owners of this place think they're being haunted, which leads the deceased, the neighbor across the street who hates the construction noise, to think they'll sell cheap. Did I get that right?"

I nodded.

"After your little run-in with the victim, what happened?"

"I drove over to Clay Street to pick up my stepson."

"Can anyone vouch for you?"

"My ex-husband's wife, Valerie Burghart." The idea of Valerie talking to the police about me didn't exactly give me the warm fuzzies. Still, I gave the inspector her contact information. "And my stepson, Caleb, of course. He's in school. And then we went home. To Oakland. We had dinner with my dad and our friend Stan Tomassi."

"Was your father home all night?"

"Yes, of course he was." Though I had experienced a momentary twinge of doubt when I first saw Dad at the scene of the crime, I felt a flush of anger at the idea that the inspector might suspect him of something like this.

"You all had dinner together, but can you be sure he was in bed all night?"

"I'm a light sleeper. As is Stan Tomassi, whose bedroom is on the first floor. One of us would have heard him leave."

"Your father tells me he owns several guns."

A small arsenal, to be precise. *Please let all the guns be accounted for,* I thought. I nodded in answer to her question.

"All right," Crawford said after eyeing me for another moment. A uniformed cop walked up and whispered something to her. She nodded and he left. "Anything else you can think of? Besides ghosts."

"No, nothing."

"Do you happen to have an employment address for your client, Jim Daley?"

"He works at Integrated Networking Systems. Their offices are downtown, on Sansome."

While the inspector wrote down the name, I glanced over at Cheshire House. Katenka stood at the foot of the limestone steps, leaning against the front balustrade, holding Quinn awkwardly on her hip. The baby was not yet a year old, but he looked about half as big as she, as though Katenka were a child herself, babysitting a younger brother. She wore a long, crocheted sweater, but her gossamer dress blew in the chill wind, wrapping around her bare legs.

When I turned my attention back to Inspector Crawford, I noted her gaze had followed the direction of my own. I had the sense the woman didn't miss much.

"We're finding Ms. Daley less than cooperative," she said.

"It could be a language problem. She's from Russia."

"Yeah, I figured that part out already. I'm a homicide inspector; I have a sixth sense about these things."

It took me a second to realize Crawford was joking. I gave her a weak smile.

"If you think of anything else, you be sure to let me know." She handed me her business card and headed back to the upholstery shop.

I squeezed through the crowd of onlookers to greet Katenka.

"How are you holding up?"

She shook her head.

I held my hands out in a silent offer to hold Quinn. She surrendered him and rubbed her upper arms as though her muscles were sore from his weight.

Quinn had his mother's big hazel eyes, but his were unguarded, open to the wonders of the world. Reveling in his fresh infant scent and the warm weight in my arms, I bounced a little and made funny faces as he gurgled happily. I felt a palpable sense of relief, knowing he hadn't been harmed in the night.

I could do without the crying and diapering, but babies sure are cute.

"So, no visits from ghosts last night?" I asked Katenka.

She shook her head. "I told you: with the amulets, we are safe."

The scene unfolding before us was horrifying, but ultimately it had nothing to do with any of us—unless, of course, my father was actually accused of something. But I refused to entertain that thought at the moment. I had come this morning intending to talk some sense into the Daleys about the apparitions, and the project. "Did you talk to Jim about—"

"He is at work already. He went in early today." There was alarm in her pretty eyes. "But, Mel, listen: The *police* say they need to speak with Jim."

"It's all right, Katenka; it's just standard procedure."

"You don't understand." Her voice dropped and she

glanced around the crowd. "Emile came to the door. Jim told him to stop bothering us. He raised his voice."

"When was this?"

"Last night."

"Were—" The baby put his pudgy little hand on my mouth as though to silence me. I leaned my head back. "Were you with him?"

"No, I stay with Quinn. But then Jim followed Emile to the upholstery store."

"Did you tell this to the police?"

"The *police*? You are crazy."

She looked shocked, and it dawned on me: Katenka was Russian. I had lived in enough different countries and environments to know that not everyone grows up with the concept of Officer Friendly. In a lot of the world the corrupt and violent local police force was about the last organization you would turn to for help.

"Katenka, you need to be honest with the officers. The inspector's no fool; she'll probably figure it out anyway, and if you don't tell her first, it will seem suspicious. Since Jim didn't do anything, he doesn't have anything to be afraid of." I hoped.

She shook her head and took little Quinn back.

"Did you speak to Jim about the renovation project last night?"

"No. I was going to, but Jim was busy with baby; then Emile came to the door. And he was upset, so I wait."

I nodded, unsure how to proceed. "So, shall I continue the job? If your home really is haunted, the ghosts will remain whether or not I do the renovation. Don't you think it's best, for you and Jim and the baby, to get rid of the ghosts?"

She sighed. "Maybe."

"Still, it would be great if you could move out in the interim . . ." I had to try, one more time. The idea of the baby in this house with a possible paranormal presence made me very nervous. "Just for a couple of days? If you don't have anywhere else to go, maybe you and the baby could come stay at my house, even if Jim won't."

"I tell you already, this is not possible. Jim will never agree to it."

"Will you at least think about it?" I handed her my card and wrote my home address on the back. "I'm meeting with someone today at lunch that might be able to help. She knows a lot about ghosts and spirits and houses."

"She will chase the ghosts from the house?"

"I'm not sure if she knows how, but I'll bet she can give me some names, at least."

Katenka looked doubtful. "There is too much to be afraid of. I go call Jim, warn him of the police."

She went into her house, using the basement-floor access door to the left of the main stairs.

I wondered if I should pass on what she'd said to the police. I'd had a less than satisfying interaction with a cop myself not too long ago. But I got no such vibe of incompetence or self-interest from Inspector Annette Crawford.

Still, since they knew his place of employment, the police would find Jim easily enough, and Katenka's knee-jerk secrecy would be a moot point. And I *really* didn't want to be in the position of tattling on my clients. My very well-to-do clients, who provided me and mine with a living.

"Poor bastard." Dad's voice interrupted my thoughts. He had come to stand next to me, watching the commotion with his arms folded over his chest.

"What are you doing here, Dad?"

"Last night you mentioned I might be able to talk to your neighbor, man-to-man." He shrugged. "Thought I'd give it a shot."

"Speaking of shooting . . . you left your guns at home, right?"

"You think I shot an unarmed man?"

"No, of course not, it's just . . . the inspector seemed suspicious."

"That's her job. She has to consider us all suspects until she starts ruling people out. It'll all get sorted down the line." My dad had a lot of faith in authorities, and believed that "the truth will out." I wished I shared his confidence.

We fell silent for a moment, watching as grim crime-scene personnel unloaded bags of equipment and carried them into the upholstery shop.

"You've taken on a lot, sweetie," Dad said, his voice serious, low. "The business, all that and more . . . I want you to know that I know it."

My throat swelled, robbing me of speech.

Here was the sensitive New Age version of my father. Theoretically, I appreciated his newfound soft underbelly. But where was the cantankerous, emotionally distant former marine I had known, loved, and railed against my whole life?

When my mother passed away, Dad, who had remained unflappable through two tours of Vietnam, fell apart. And I mean he totally lost it, was unable to function without his trusted partner in business, love, and life. As much as I wanted to run away to Paris and hide in some obscure Left Bank garret after my divorce, I couldn't bring myself to abandon him, or the construction business he'd built up over the past thirty years, or his cadre of loyal employees. So I moved back home and took the reins for "a couple of months." Months had turned into years, and since then Dad had made no mention of my stewardship of his business, much less of his making a move to come back to work.

We stood there awkwardly for a minute, not meeting each other's eyes, instead looking around at the hustle and bustle.

"All set for Stan's party tonight?" Dad broke the silence.

"Yeah, sure. I'll pick up the cake and should be home a little after five. Could you and Caleb start decorating when he gets home from school?"

He gave a brusque nod and walked away. I watched as he spoke briefly with Inspector Crawford, then strode off toward his dented Ford truck, climbed in, and drove off.

Chapter Six

Turning my back on the crime scene, I took a moment to look over the exterior of Cheshire House.

Like most Queen Anne Victorians, it showed its best face to the street. Tall and elegant, two turrets of differing heights and stepped-out features gave the house asymmetrical charm. A flight of stone steps led to a heavy oak door topped by a stained-glass transom. Jigsaw-cut gingerbread woodwork—some of which I had to have remilled—embellished every eave, corner, and window frame. Multicolored decorative shingles—many of which needed to be replaced—formed an intricate pattern on the steeply pitched roof. And a wrought-iron widow's walk sat atop the highest turret, just for show.

Curved leaded and colored glass sash windows marched up one turret; two of the openings were temporarily covered in plywood, as they had slumped so badly they were currently being restored by a talented stained-glass artist in Carmel. The exterior paint was peeling, and scaffolding had been set up on one corner to accommodate trim repair and painting prep. The small front yard was a disaster area of dirt, weeds, dust, and a few hopeful bushes that were struggling to survive.

To my eyes it was one big, gorgeous project.

I moved my car to a legal space and brought Dog back to Cheshire House with me. Katenka and Jim didn't mind having him on the job site, as long as he stayed in the messy construction areas. As soon as we entered the house and I undid his leash, Dog barreled past me and up the stairs, barking at something I couldn't see.

Knowing Dog as I did, I realized this wasn't necessarily indicative of ghostly activity. He ran after nothing all the time, in what I assumed was a bid to seem useful and on the job.

The real fellow on the job at Cheshire House was Raul Ramirez. Raul was smart, competent, and almost preternaturally calm in the face of construction mishaps. He had failed the contractor's exam, undoubtedly because of his limited English writing skills, not a lack of knowledge. He was taking classes at City College and planned on retaking the test. I wished Raul only the best, but if I were completely honest, a part of me was relieved that he wasn't yet licensed. Good foremen were worth their weight in gold, and I knew how lucky I was to have him. He kept the subcontractors in line, and everyone on task and on schedule. He was also blessed with people skills, which was important because he interacted with the clients on a daily basis. Having a foreman like Raul freed me up to move around, keeping several jobs in various stages of completion going at once.

Or investigating ghosts, as the case might be.

True to form, Raul wasn't impressed by the crime scene across the street, and made sure the crew kept their minds on their work. According to our schedule, the final in-wall electrical and plumbing was to be completed today so that the walls could be repaired. Then the last phase of the painting prep—patching and priming and sanding—would begin. The finish painting would start after that, presuming I could pin down Jim and Katenka on their final color choices.

Raul and I went over the schedule and the thousand details that come up every day on a construction project, and then I took a walk through the house, checking in on the various workers. A small crew was removing paint and shellac from the original redwood wainscoting and crown moldings that featured egg and dart, acanthus leaf, and dentil designs. Once it was stripped back to the original wood, we would dress it in a mahogany stain. Victorian architecture could be rather gloomy inside with all the dark trim, but the wood was too beautiful to cover up. Since Jim was willing to foot the bill for the laborious process of stripping, I was more than happy to oblige.

Besides, Katenka had showed a definite taste for the gloomy in her design decisions. She might be afraid of ghosts, but she had had no qualms when faced with one of Cheshire House's more unusual features: The repeated motif of acanthus leaves surrounding winged skulls topped by angels holding scythes, as though snuffing out life.

This sort of design used to be a reminder of the sanctity of life, a warning to be good and pure while you could, because you never knew when your time would be up. It was a holdover from an era when death and dying took place at home, surrounded by the living, rather than in sterile environments, dealt with discreetly by hospital workers and funeral homes, the way it now was for most of us.

One of my favorite features of the house was its five fireplaces. In the finest Victorian tradition, the hearths were not meant simply to provide heat and a cheery blaze. They were robust combinations of display shelves, seats, decorative panels, and works of art, a complex ensemble that served as a room's focal point. Though distinct, each was adorned with glazed tiles with relief decoration, an over-mantel with a paneled frieze, a mosaic hearth, and a fire-back, a thick iron plate placed at the back of a hearth to protect the wall and reflect heat into the room.

Two of the fireplaces had their original firebacks, with the acanthus leaf motif, but the other three were missing. Searching Craigslist, I had found some possible replacements. The seller had identified them as "old fireplace things—thick sheets of metal with embossed designs." Worth a look.

"Mel, you got your coveralls with you?" asked Andrew, the plumber.

"Always," I responded. I might traipse around in skirts and dresses, but as a contractor I was always prepared to crawl through cobwebs. "What's up?"

I crouched down with him and looked through a gaping hole in the corner of a third-floor bedroom, where his crew had removed a small corner sink. Back when the building was used as a boardinghouse, each renter had his own sink in his room, while sharing the toilet and bath down the hall. Katenka and Jim had decided to remove the sinks in favor of more traditional bedrooms.

"What do you want us to do with the pipes left in the

walls? Easiest thing is to just cap them and leave them," said Andrew. By "easiest," he meant "cheapest."

"Let me take a look."

I donned my coveralls and crawled through the hole in the wall, then squeezed under the eaves to check out where the old pipes connected to one another. Could some of the troublesome knocking and banging be coming from them? Old houses didn't need ghosts to make strange sounds at all times of day and night—that's just the way they were. Some called it character.

One reason Turner Construction was in demand was that we did the job right, not only by meeting code requirements and following basic installation guidelines to the letter, but also by not leaving a mess, even if it was unseen, in the walls or crawl spaces. You never knew when those messes would come back to bite you.

"No, go ahead and take them back to the junctions with the new copper pipe, and remove all of these old lead ones. Abandoning them isn't a very elegant solution," I said.

Andrew barely refrained from rolling his eyes. He was two days behind on the job here, which meant he was now operating on his dime rather than the Daleys', since the delay was his own fault. He was anxious to move his crew on to the next paying gig. I understood, but I wasn't willing to cut corners for the sake of anyone's schedule, not even my own.

As I walked down the third-floor catwalk, a hallway with a railing open to the floor below, I thought I heard something overhead. A scratching, whispering noise.

And the metal-on-metal scraping sound of a heavy bolt unlocking.

There was no one in the attic. The hatch was closed.

I stood still and held my breath, straining my ears, trying to tune out the saws, banging, and radio noise of the workers throughout the house.

More scratching. That could be rats. Or the cat Katenka thought she heard.

But whispers?

Dog ran up next to me, barking and whimpering, agitated and intrigued, the way he was when he treed a raccoon.

After another moment of hesitation, I reached up, grabbed the string, and pulled open the attic access door. The whispers grew louder.

Was it . . . could it be *calling* me?

"Mel?" The voice startled me. It was Raul, coming up the stairs. All sounds from above ceased.

"Hey, Raul."

"Before you go today we need one of the Daleys to sign off on the paint schedule."

"Right," I said, glancing back up into the dark nothingness of the attic.

"What's up, puppy?" he petted Dog, then addressed me. "Something wrong?"

"What? No, nothing's wrong," I fudged. "I was just about to check the insulation."

"Newspapers."

I nodded. Back in the day, newspapers were a common form of insulation. And as free materials go, they weren't bad. As any homeless person could tell you, they're cheap and effective. Newspapers pulled out of walls and ceilings of old houses could also help date a home, and made fascinating reading.

I had been in the attic before, several times. When I first took on the project, I looked through every nook and cranny of the house, and I had returned to the attic with the electrician, the structural engineer, and a city inspector. Each time I was up there I felt a strange, otherworldly sense of the weight of a gaze upon me, a tingle at the back of my neck. But for all the attention I paid to my peripheral vision, I had seen nothing, heard nothing I could pinpoint.

At first I ascribed the feelings to the usual spookiness of attics and basements, those liminal areas between the everyday and the unusual. The parts of the house that were not regularly filled with human life and breath. But now . . .

"I'll go talk to Katenka," I said. "I'll try to get her to make a decision."

As I closed the attic door, something fell. I jumped out of the way as it clanked to the floor. I scooped it up. It was a rusty metal ring, holding half a dozen very old keys.

"Where'd that come from?" Raul asked, looking overhead.

"Must have been stuck in the recess, somehow. The door felt hard to pull open; maybe the keys were lodged in the frame."

Raul looked at them with interest. "Be nice if they'd open some of the old doors in this place, so we don't have to take the locks apart. I like the look of them."

"Me, too. I'll have to check them out, and then I'll see if Katenka wants to keep them, along with the old locks. If not, I'll split them with you."

Raul smiled. "You can keep 'em. I've got dozens."

"So do I."

I took the sheaf of spreadsheets from him, grabbed the book of color samples, and headed downstairs, hoping I could convince Katenka to either state her own color choices or go along with mine.

We were at the point in the renovation where the Daleys needed to make a thousand and one aesthetic choices. Unfortunately for me, they refused to hire an interior designer. I couldn't really blame them—personally, I disliked the sort of cold, overly designed look of so many professionally "done" homes that appeared as though they were laid out for an *Architectural Digest* photo shoot rather than ready to live in. In such places a bottle of dishwashing detergent left out on the pounded copper countertop looked like sacrilege.

Still, interior designers had staffs and schedules and budgets, so they were simple for a general contractor like me to work with. Having to decide on every interior decision, from grout color to stain tone, made the average homeowner want to tear their hair out in a matter of days . . . or hours.

Which reminded me—Katenka and I needed to make time to visit what was referred to as "the wailing wall of knobs" in the San Francisco Design Center.

I was almost to the main floor when I heard something. A moaning sound?

Relief washed over me when I realized it was accompanied by the crackle of a baby monitor. Katenka was in the dining room, the receiver clipped on to her belt. The "moaning" I thought I had heard was simply Quinn, lulling himself to sleep with a cooing sound. My imagination was running rampant.

Katenka stood next to the horsehair settee, looking down at it.

"Katenka?"

As I approached her, she spoke without looking up. "Emile was going to reupholster this. Who will do it now?"

"I'm sure we can find another upholsterer," I said, wondering why she was focusing on this, of all things. "This place won't be ready for nice furniture for a while yet."

She seemed to shake it off. "You are right."

"Hey, look what we just found up in the attic." I held up the old key ring.

She wrinkled her nose. "Is rusty."

"True." It always amazed me when people didn't get excited around such discoveries. This was the fun of old houses, the traces people left behind. In my time I've found everything from perfume bottles to personal papers to old celluloid collars. The homeowners rarely wanted to keep them, which was one reason my bedroom was beginning to look like a museum. Most of us in the historical renovation biz become rabid amateur historians . . . sometimes exhibiting a little hoarder mentality when it comes to old stuff.

"We were going to try the keys in some of the old locks, see if they work," I said. "Or, if you'd rather, we could just change out all the old locks for new, as we'd originally decided to do."

"New is better, I think."

"So you don't want the keys?"

"Why would I?"

"As a memento?"

She just stared at me. I was going to take that as a no. On to the next order of business.

"I'd like to get a final decision from you on the paint colors so we can order supplies and be ready to go next week."

She held out her hand for the samples. Traditionally, houses of the Victorian era were covered in wallpaper from head to toe, in a riotous blend of patterns and designs that extended onto the ceilings. Modern sensibilities tended toward a simpler palette of colors. Still, because most Victorians feature high ceilings, ample windows, and often more than a foot of wood trim at base and crown, in addition to wainscoting, they can handle strong interior colors.

Last week I had painted three-by-three-foot patches of different paint hues on the walls and evaluated how they looked under all kinds of conditions: mellow pink morning light, harsh afternoon sun, a gray foggy day, incandescent bulbs in the evening. I had narrowed the color palette down to creams for most of the painted woodwork, a saffron yellow or wine red for the dining room walls, a grayish violet for the front sitting room, and everything from sage green to buff caramel for the bedrooms. For Quinn's room, I had chosen a mellow green-blue shade that would provide a nice backdrop for his shelves of books and toys. All Katenka had to do was agree.

She flipped through the samples without enthusiasm, pausing on the ones marked with a sticky note.

"Is fine," she said, listless.

"You sure? If you don't like it once it's up, we'll have to repaint, which means a change order, which puts us over budget." I'm always careful to warn clients of potential cost overruns. Usually they ignore me until they get the bill.

"Is fine," she repeated, signing her name to the paint schedule.

"We also need to go to the Design Center for knobs

and tiles, make a few decisions. Is there a good day this week?"

Katenka sighed. "Friday?"

I checked my schedule. "Great. Friday it is. Is late afternoon okay? That way I can send the men home with their paychecks, and you and I won't have to rush back."

"Okay. I get my friend Ivana to take baby. Make it easier." She gestured to the only personal picture I had seen in the house, pinned to the corkboard in the kitchen. It had a number and address scrawled underneath it in a loopy hand. Katenka gazed at the photo for a long moment, then sighed again. "She never answer the phone, so I walk over there. She lives in house with golden lions outside. You like lions?"

"Sure."

"I think maybe we need lions here. As people walk up, on either side of door. Very elegant."

"I . . . um." This was the hard part for me: letting people have their own taste. "Why don't we finish up with all the painting details, and see what you think then?"

She shrugged. "Friday, four o clock?"

"Sounds good," I said, then hesitated. "Katenka, are you all right?"

She seemed particularly listless, but it was hard to tell with Katenka. She had such a serious, tragic way about her at the best of times. Perhaps if I ever saw her happy, I could better note the contrast.

Just then there was a knocking sound directly above us. And a faint, eerie mewing in the walls. Dog came running down the stairs, barking. I grabbed him by the collar and shushed him.

"I am so tired of this," said Katenka.

"Is that . . . a cat?"

"I told you, I think there is a cat here, perhaps from before. Or is cat ghost."

"I'll check it out. There might be an access point along the foundation."

"Okay," she said, moving toward the basement door. "I go take a nap before Quinn gets up."

After going over the final paint decisions with Raul and the painting crew, I checked my watch: noon.

Time to see a lady about a ghost.

Chapter Seven

The first time I met Brittany Humm I disliked her on sight, and it still took me a moment to get over myself. Brittany was my high-school nightmare come to sparkling life: Vivacious and outgoing, she was also slender and blond, several years younger than I, and sported an ostentatious diamond engagement ring.

But the truth was, she was a lovely person. Even if she did get a little too excited about ghosts.

"This is great! I wondered when you'd have another experience!" she gushed as she dipped only the tips of her fork's tines in the cup of Caesar salad dressing on the side, then nibbled on a leaf of romaine.

"Problem is, this time it's no one I could possibly have known." I dug into my full-fat version of the salad, complete with anchovies. "I'm afraid my clients are on the verge of shutting down the project if I don't find a way to stop the activity."

"Lingering spirits don't like having their surroundings disturbed."

"So I've heard."

Brittany laughed. "Anyone ever tell you you're hard to please? At first you hated the idea of seeing ghosts—"

"I just want to be left alone. Is that so much to ask?"

"And then you get impatient, waiting to see them again."

"It just seemed sort of . . . odd that I realized I could see ghosts, but then nothing came of it. Don't you think that's odd?"

"And now that you've seen another apparition, you're unhappy about that, as well."

"This one's not like the last one. This one gives me the willies."

I wouldn't say I *liked* seeing spirits, but once I got over the fear that I was losing my mind, there was a certain allure. Who among us hasn't wondered whether there is, in fact, life after death? As a former anthropologist, I know there is no known culture without some concept of the beyond—*and* the belief that under the right circumstances, a spirit might return to earthly life for a day . . . or forever. Prior to my supernatural experience, though, I had rather enjoyed not thinking much about an afterlife; there was comfort in agnosticism. Thinking about the beyond made me wonder whether I was doing such a bang-up job with my current shot at life. I was pushing forty, and though I enjoyed my work, I had been in a bad mood since my marriage started circling the drain. I dreamt of running away to Paris to lick my wounds in some fourth-floor Left Bank garret for a year or ten . . . but I wondered what I was doing, in the big picture, to improve the world.

New Year's resolution: I was going to look into volunteering. Surely I could give something back, somehow.

"Anyway, I'm not sure how sensitive I am in this case. The woman of the house, Katenka, saw the thing as well. She's scared, and I can't say I blame her. A black shadowy figure is . . . creepy. The ones I saw before looked like people. Like you and me, only . . ."

"Dead."

"Right. So did you look into the listing? Was it said to be haunted?"

She shook her head. "It wasn't in the Bay Area haunted house database."

"There's a Bay Area haunted house database?"

"Oh sure. A couple."

"I don't know why this still surprises me."

"The Cheshire Inn wasn't listed as haunted, but as you know, it was said to be a cat-hoarder house—pretty trashed, and therefore a tough sale. How bad was it?"

"It had been emptied before we started the job. It was smelly, but no trash or anything left around. Even the garden had been dug up, which the landscapers will appreciate."

Though I usually enjoyed seeing houses in their inhabited state before starting a project, I had been glad this house had been cleaned out by the time Katenka and Jim hired us. Turner Construction did mostly high-end stuff now, but back when my dad was flipping houses with a crew of forced labor—me, my mom, and my two sisters—we had cleaned out plenty of buildings.

Emptying out a lifetime of accumulated junk isn't pretty. Besides ruining one's appetite, it can be depressing as heck. Seeing other people's detritus always motivated me to clean out my own room, for fear I'd be hit by a truck on my way home and some poor slob would have to go through my things, making judgments about me based on the sketchy items in the drawers of my bedside table, or the many months of accumulated dust and hair behind the claw-foot tub.

"Okay, here's what I've dug up on the house so far." Brittany took a sip of her unsweetened iced tea and opened a folder with a number of computer printouts. "It was built in 1891 by Dominga Carter after the death of her wealthy husband. She moved into the city from the 'country,' which in those days meant down near Palo Alto."

"Palo Alto was 'country'?"

"Back then they referred to Stanford University as 'the Farm.'"

These days the cities of the Bay Area reached out and touched their neighbors, the transition from one to the next marked only by a faded road sign. Hard to imagine the days before automobiles and bridges, when setting out for another point on the Bay was an excursion involving boats and/or changes of horses.

"Dominga Carter had two sons, Charles and Andre. Charles married a young woman named Luvitica, and all four moved into Cheshire House together."

"Dominga and Luvitica? Where were these people from?"

"From here," Brittany said, daintily picking the croutons out of her salad with a spoon. She had gone "wheat-free," she'd explained to me as we ordered, to lose those pesky extra five pounds. I needed to lose an extra-pesky twenty pounds or so, but I wasn't ready to give up bread. Not here, in the land of sourdough. "It was a long time ago, when people had names like 'Grizelda' and 'Abernathy.' Anyway, Dominga and Luvitica were known to be at odds with one another."

"They didn't get along?"

"Not one bit. The strife centered around Charles. In the vernacular of the era, he was described as a 'mama's boy' and 'henpecked,' poor guy."

"You found this in the public record?"

"There was a little gossipy article on the family that was cited in one of the real estate transactions. But I don't suppose it was much of a secret. San Francisco was a pretty small town back then."

"Hey, how did you find all this out? I tried to do some research down at the California Historical Society and found nothing on the place—not a single newspaper reference."

"Hmm." Brittany tilted her head. "Well, I looked up the real estate listing, and then I did a simple Google search. Took me all of, oh, four seconds. You should give it a try—I know you prefer old-school methods, and it's true that there's a lot of ephemera that can only be found in musty libraries. But you never know what Google will dig up for you."

I used the Internet for all sorts of things, from tracking down vintage items on Craigslist to comparing lumber prices. But when it came to investigating the area's historic homes, I was steadfastly old-school in my approach: I went straight to the California Historical Society. It had never occurred to me I could get much useful information online.

"Here's what I downloaded." She handed me a short stack of papers. "The Carters sound like a *charming* family: The two women were at each other's throats so much, Charles must have decided he needed a break.

He boarded a ship bound for South America without his wife."

"Where was he headed?"

"Chile. His brother, Andre, had invested in a sugar plantation there."

"Chile? That seems unusual."

"Actually, a lot of early immigrants to San Francisco were Chilean. The shipping routes ran up and down the western coasts of the Americas, connecting the two. Ghirardelli came from there."

"As in Ghirardelli chocolate? I thought he was Italian."

"He was, by way of Chile . . . or maybe it was Peru. Somewhere down there. Chocolate wasn't a sweet food, traditionally. But he figured out how to extract the cocoa butter to make chocolate candy."

"Good man."

Like most locals, I avoided the famous tourist triangle of Fisherman's Wharf, Ghirardelli Square, and Pier 39 like the plague. Still, some of my happiest memories were visiting the area as a child with out-of-town relatives. We inevitably stopped by the Ghirardelli chocolate factory tasting room, and I would always double back to the end of the line to get more free samples. Speaking of chocolate . . . dessert was sounding good about now. I wondered if Brittany would consider splitting a piece of the flourless chocolate cake à la mode. After all, it was wheat-free.

"So," I said as I wrested my thoughts from dessert I didn't need, "Charles Carter abandoned Leviticus?"

"Luvitica."

"Oh, right. Wonder what they called her for short."

"Right? Anyway, this article said that Charles died of

kidney failure during the sea voyage. And get this—the sailors put his body into a keg of rum."

I choked on my iced tea. "Why would they do that?"

"It wasn't unheard of at that time. It was hot on those ships; the alcohol preserves the body. They threw the 'unimportant' people into the sea if they had the misfortune to die aboard, but Charles was a wealthy man, so I guess they needed to send him home."

"Seems like a waste of good rum."

"Yeah, really. Anyway, the keg was returned to the family at some point."

"Wow. So the women and Andre continued living in the house?"

She shook her head. "Andre disappeared sometime after Charles left, and was never heard from again."

"So Dominga lost both her sons? And continued living with the daughter-in-law she despised?"

She nodded. "One son dead; one who disappeared. Luvitica gave birth to a baby boy a few months later. That son, who they referred to as Junior, grew up in the house. As an adult, after his grandmother and mother passed on, Junior needed money and turned the home into a boardinghouse."

"When was that?"

"In the twenties. He ran it for the next forty years, believe it or not. This area wasn't as posh as it is now, and there was lots of labor needed in the early years of the city. Junior died in the sixties, shortly after selling the house to Hettie Banks, who continued to operate it as a boardinghouse, though she liked to call it a 'bed-and-breakfast.'"

"I take it you quibble with that term as applied to Cheshire House?"

"There were beds, and I guess there was breakfast,

but with all those cats . . . It doesn't sound much like what one expects from a San Francisco bed-and-breakfast. But you know how men are—they'll live anywhere and never notice the toilet needs cleaning."

I smiled and thought about my dad, who'd become a rather fussy housekeeper.

"And Jim and Katenka bought it from Hettie Banks," I said, and did the math. "So we're looking at nearly a century of being used as a boardinghouse. That's a lot of souls coming and going."

"But as far as we know, only one body," said Brittany.

"What are you saying? That Charles Carter is haunting Cheshire House?"

Brittany leaned back in her chair and shrugged. "I don't know, Mel. I just do research, remember? But it makes for a great story, doesn't it?"

I wondered if a rum-pickled ghost would look different from any other. I could imagine that. It would explain the bare feet, perhaps. What I couldn't fathom was how or why it might wander around in the form of black smoke. But were the footprints connected to the black figure? They had seemed like two distinct entities, to the extent I could tell.

As Brittany signaled the waiter for our check, I glanced around the restaurant. Brittany worked in Walnut Creek, on the other side of the dreaded Caldecott Tunnel, so we had split the difference and met in Oakland at the Den at the Fox, a new restaurant in one corner of the old Fox Theater building, an incredible Moroccan-themed single-screen venue that dated to the 1920s, the heyday of historic theaters. The restaurant was done up with holiday decorations Bay Area–style, which meant lots of red and green garlands, a few nods to Hanukkah and Kwanzaa, but nothing explicitly about baby Jesus, as though Christmas were a sparkly winter holiday consisting primarily of lights and tinsel. I wondered if this was why Halloween was taking over as the locals' favorite: There weren't many folks who couldn't get behind a costume- and candy-fueled good time.

"I think what I need is a ghost buster. Do you have a recommendation?"

Brittany gave me a peculiar look. "With your third eye, or ability to see, you're the kind of expert other people bring in."

"I might be able to sense ghosts—sometimes—but I don't have the first idea how to get rid of them."

"You did a pretty good job at the Vallejo Street house."

When the ghost of a man killed on the job site at a Beaux Arts mansion started following me around, I wound up tracking down his killer and digging up—literally—evidence of an old murder, as well. By the time all was said and done, I had laid to rest at least a couple of the old mansion's ghosts.

"That was mostly accidental," I said. "Once I figured out what had happened, the ghosts left."

"It works that way sometimes. Oh, I should tell you, your fame is growing."

"I have fame?"

"Somebody wrote up the story and named names."

"You've got to be kidding me."

"It wasn't me," she said, holding her hands up in innocence. "You asked me to keep it quiet, and I did. But I kept hearing rumors, and recently I came across this article about you."

She pulled another photocopy from the folder, and I

read it with dismay. The only sort of fame I was interested in was Turner Construction winning the American Institute of Architects' award for historical renovation. I didn't like people talking about me, much less seeking me out to answer questions about ghosts.

The article wasn't long, but gave the basic rundown of what had happened at the Vallejo Street house, a project Turner Construction was still finishing up:

> *Melanie (Mel) Turner of Turner Construction was able to make contact with the ghost of the recently departed Kenneth Kostow, and with his help unearthed the truth about a long-ago murder, resulting in the riddance of two entities. As far as this reporter was able to investigate, it was a genuine spirit encounter, the first for Turner.*

"I can't believe this," I muttered. "Who would have had this kind of information? Where is this from?"

"*Haunted House Quarterly*," Brittany said.

"There's a publication called *Haunted House Quarterly*?"

Brittany grinned. "Sure, gotta keep up with the latest news in the industry. Haunted houses are big business, as I keep telling you. And before you say something you'll have to apologize for, you should know that I'm a regular contributor. Anyway, this issue just came out. I wouldn't be surprised if you start hearing from people."

"Great." That explained the phone calls Stan fielded yesterday.

"Maybe the same thing's happening with this house. Which is good news, right? All you have to do is figure out who the ghost is, find out what he wants or needs, and tell him to leave the house."

"It's not that simple, Brittany."

"Hmm, I see what you mean. With a threatening black shadow figure you might need some bigger guns. I'm sorry to say, though, that I don't know anyone. The folks I know are *looking* for ghosts, not trying to get rid of them."

"Why are they looking for them?"

Brittany sighed. "You still don't get it: A lot of us feel it's a privilege to meet someone from another dimension. Many attempt to document the phenomenon, using special cameras and recording equipment and the like."

"But if you did want them to leave, how would you go about it? "

"You might try a botanica, ask for a *limpia*."

I nodded. That had occurred to me as well. Botanicas are traditional Latino stores full of herbs, candles, teas . . . and all the sorts of items used in cleansing houses of spirits.

"Or you could call the ghost society," Brittany continued. "Or how about that ghost-tour guy?"

"The French guy? Someone else mentioned him."

"It couldn't hurt."

"If only that were true."

I paid for lunch, thanked Brittany for her time and information, and we parted ways. Leaning against my dusty car, I looked at a faded poster advertising hair extensions in the beauty shop across the street. Like my neighborhood, this was an area "in transition." I looked up at the intricately tiled Moorish facade of the Fox Theater and thought a place like that must have a ghost or two roaming its bowels. I wondered if I could go to a show there without meeting up with one.

Brittany was right: I didn't find it particularly exciting to be able to sense ghosts. On the other hand, I was no longer freaked out by it. It was only recently, after my mother's death, that I learned from my father she had possessed a similar ability, and in a way it linked me to her. After I saw my first ghost I was afraid I'd see dead people everywhere, like the boy from that movie a few years ago. I was enough of a misanthrope to worry about that—my long-term goal was to spend time alone, not to be saddled with the souls of all who had passed. But it hadn't happened. True, when I entered historic buildings I sensed where things belonged, how they used to be. Given my line of work, that was an asset.

But it seemed as though there were ghosts in Cheshire House, and whether I liked it or not, I was the logical person to respond to them. I wanted to wrest back control of this construction project, so I needed to talk to my ghosts, or find someone who could. And then I had to find someone to help me get rid of them—these home-owners didn't seem like the type to consider supernatural apparitions as "added value" for the property. Finally, I would have to convince Katenka the ghosts were gone so the renovation project was worth completing.

But before I did any of that, I wanted to talk to the last living owner of the cursed house to learn what, if anything, she had experienced.

I returned several work phone calls, then placed a few more: Raul assured me all was progressing well at Cheshire House; I spoke with the head of the painting crew finishing up the Vallejo Street project; checked on an order of reclaimed barn wood for the floor in a client's den; and confirmed with Stan that everything was set for this Friday's payroll.

Finally, I headed back over the Bay Bridge to San Francisco and across town to the neighborhood known as the Western Addition, to the address Brittany had written down for me. Next up was a quick chat with the cat lady.

Chapter Eight

Hettie Banks didn't have many visitors.

She seemed pleased to invite me in and spent a few minutes cleaning off a stool for me to sit at the kitchen counter, tossing a small stack of newspapers and two plastic bags full of who-knew-what into an already junk-filled corner.

But her watery blue eyes flashed with fear when I asked her whether she ever . . . sort of . . . experienced otherworldly weirdness in her former boardinghouse.

"They might kill me, just for talking about them," she whispered as she poured Diet Coke into two chipped coffee mugs that sported corporate logos—Microsoft for me, Google for her.

"These are ghosts we're talking about?"

She nodded. Her pink scalp showed through the strands of thinning white hair, cut in a short, masculine 'do. She wore an oversized men's T-shirt advertising the services of a Mission Street auto care service, and scratched tortoiseshell glasses from which hung a bright, beaded chain that draped around her neck.

"I don't understand," I continued. "Why would they want to kill you?"

"Just for knowing about them, I guess. I think they want to be left alone. . . ." She waved a hand and got up to open a can of cat food for a fat orange tabby, which she spoke to in a high-pitched baby voice. She spooned the smelly food onto two small china plates decorated with pink and yellow flowers, tapping the spoon against the plates with a series of sharp *tinks*.

At the sound, another cat ran into the room and leapt onto the counter. This one had long white hair and deep blue eyes.

I might not have found any information about the history of the house itself, but I had read several articles about Hettie Banks's arrest and sentencing for animal hoarding, and knew she wasn't supposed to own any pets, much less cats. It was part of her probation agreement. When she was found to be keeping a multitude of felines in the garbage-strewn Cheshire Inn, Hettie had been taken into police custody and charged with cruelty toward animals.

After nearly four decades running the fifteen-room Cheshire Inn as a boardinghouse, Hettie sold the place to the Daleys and was now living in a two-bedroom condo. She told me she spent her days watching reruns of *M*A*S*H*, building a dollhouse reproduction of the Cheshire Inn, carrying on an Internet romance with a man half her age who lived in what she referred to as "the former Yugoslavia," and, it seemed, flouting the conditions of her probation and the condo association's no-pets clause.

I wondered why. The sale of a beautiful, well-located Queen Anne Victorian—even one that was run-down and redolent of too many cats—should have netted Hettie plenty of money to buy a big spread in the country where no nosy neighbors would spot her cat colony. Had she switched from hoarding pets to hoarding money? Sent it to her friend in the former Yugoslavia? Gambled it away in Vegas? Not that it was any of my business.

"I was hoping you could fill me in on the history of the house," I said. "Usually I can learn a lot at the historical society downtown, but not this time. There's nothing in their records on the house."

She grinned. "There wouldn't be, now would there?"

"Why not?"

"I destroyed it all."

I waited a moment before I spoke. I couldn't fathom people destroying irreplaceable historic items.

"Why would you do such a thing?"

"The gal told me to."

"What gal?"

"The ghost."

"A gal ghost?"

"That's right. I went down to the historical society and when the librarian answered the phone, I took the file and left, just as neat as you please."

Wait a minute. The historical society required photo IDs before one could view their materials, to avoid just such a thing.

"Why didn't the historical society come after you?"

She laughed. "I didn't use my own driver's license. I had one that belonged to a friend. She passed on a few years ago, bless her heart. I kept her driver's license for just such an occasion. People always said we looked enough alike to be sisters."

One mystery solved. Hettie was more than a little odd, and obviously cunning.

"So a ghost actually talked to you? A girl ghost?"

"One of 'em. Maybe two. It's hard to tell."

"Did they look like a person, like you and me?"

"You believe me?"

"I do. What else can you tell me about them?"

She sat down in a folding chair, pulled the plump tabby onto her lap, and stroked its ginger coat while she talked.

"At first it was little things . . . There were places in the house that were always freezing—a spot in the second floor walkway and one corner of the entryway."

I had noted those, as well. I had the heating people out, and checked everywhere for possible sources of downdrafts. Nothing.

"Doors opened and closed on their own, dead bolts locked, and heaven knows I'd lost those keys *years* ago. Lots of knocking and scratching throughout the house. Real annoying."

"And did you see anything?"

"You mean—whaddayacall 'em—applications?"

"Apparitions?"

"No, not really. A shadow sometimes. Over my shoulder, like." She looked into her soda. "That one bothered me. It made me feel . . . just awful."

I knew the feeling. "Did anyone else see any of this?"

"Oh sure. Not all of 'em, but boarders came and went; it's the nature of the business. I had this one fellow . . . he was in the attic once, with my daughter. He swore he saw something, some sort of fight between ghosts, I guess. He moved out the next day. Janet denied it, though."

"Janet's your daughter?"

"Yep. Anyways, the ghosts used to scare my cats, too, but they still protected me. Soon as the law took my cats away, there was nothing standing between me and them. That's what did it, why I moved. Well, that and the whole arrest thing." She tugged on her oversized T-shirt and ran her tongue around in her mouth, as though poking at dentures. "I would never hurt the little kitty-witty-woos."

She seemed to be reaching for dignity. It was the least I could offer her.

"Tell me about your cats."

"This one here's Horatio," she said, picking up the orange cat. "Found him in an alley behind the Safeway. Heard him crying all the way from the parking lot. Scrawny little fella. But he's real purty now."

"He is," I said, scratching the friendly tabby under its chin.

"And there's another round here, white with long hair. That's Pudding."

I feared I was already carrying a good deal of Pudding's long white hair on my black sweater.

"I understand you had a number of cats in the Cheshire Inn."

She jutted her chin out like a stubborn child. "Most ridiculous thing I've ever heard. . . . Me? Cruel to my babies? Someone called the animal control on me, but I wasn't like one of them people you hear about. Yes, I buried the cats in my yard when they passed away, but what am I supposed to do? Pay for a pet burial plot somewhere? I don't have that kind of money. Besides, this way I got to visit them. Planted daisies on their graves. The law came and dug it all up. Dug everything up. It was a disgrace."

"What do you know about the man you bought the house from? Junior?"

"A grown man who referred to himself as Junior—let's just start with that. He was real old when I met him. One foot in the grave. Guess he lived there his whole life. Told me only to rent to men, and he was right about that."

"How do you mean?"

"I had my girl there with me. Janet. That was a mistake. The ghosts don't like girls."

"Did they do something to her?"

"At first she hated it there. Said they pulled her hair. But then she started to love the place, maybe too much. She didn't want to go when I sent her away to live with her daddy, when she was in high school. Never did have no problem with men—least not most of them—but the ghosts were meddlesome around girls. Locked doors, ran the showers."

"Do you think I could talk to your daughter?"

She looked at me suspiciously. "What for?"

"Just to hear what her experiences were."

"I guess it'd be all right. . . . She works over to Emeryville, on the other side of the bridge. She drives the . . . whaddayacallit? The shuttle that takes people from the BART station to the stores. She came to see me the other day, so I don't expect to see her again for a while. But sometimes she's at the animal shelter. So when you go ask them about me being some crazy lunatic animal hoarder, maybe you can talk to her right there and then."

"I don't think you're a crazy lunatic animal hoarder, Hettie."

"You don't?"

I shook my head. "Janet's an animal lover, too, then?"

"Don't know if I'd call her that, exactly."

"No?"

She shook her head, but didn't elaborate.

"Hettie, do you know who turned you in?"

"Anonymous, they said."

"What about the boarder who moved out? The one who said he saw ghosts in the attic? Do you have any information on him?"

"That was ten years ago, maybe more. He used to work for a lumberyard in the East Bay; don't know if he's still . . ." Her pale eyes narrowed. "Hey, why you looking into this? I thought you said you were renovating that old place; you were a lady builder."

"I am, yes. I'm the general contractor on the job. But I thought that while I looked into the architectural history, maybe I could find out something about the less savory aspects of the place, as well." I chose my words carefully. "Did anything bad ever happen in the boardinghouse while you were there? Was anyone hurt? Did anyone pass away?"

She stuck her chin out a little and shook her head. "I took good care o' my boarders. Even the spirits were just annoying. Mostly, I let 'em have the attic to themselves. That's why that one fella got so scared: He and Janet went into the attic. I never went up there, never used it."

"Katenka Daley, one of the new owners, thinks she's being menaced by a ghost. Or several ghosts."

"I guess she is, then. I told that man, the guy who

bought it, not to bring his wife and child into that house. But he didn't listen."

"When was this?"

"Before he bought it. My Realtor showed me the offer, and I said I wanted to meet the buyers. Couldn't let 'em walk into that without a warning, could I? Wouldn't be right."

"Did the new owner, Jim Daley, say anything to you?"

She shrugged and hugged the cat closer to her plump chest. "He laughed at me, same as the others. But that little gal who bought it, the Russian? She came by and said she heard cats in the walls still. But that's not possible, is it? I would feel terrible if we left one behind. I was in jail at the time, or I woulda helped to gather them all up, find 'em homes. But my girl was there, at least."

"You mean Janet?"

"That's right." She got up and gestured for me to follow her. "You know, if you want to talk about the house, you should check this out."

Hettie had re-created a Cheshire Inn in miniature. It was an amateur effort, closer to a dollhouse than a precise architectural model, but it was a beautiful rendering of the house, using dark woods and patterned wallpapers, all the fireplaces built with tiny tile facades. It was helpful to see a three-dimensional rendition of the place, and to talk about the structural changes Hettie knew about. Junior had operated the place as a boardinghouse pretty much as-was, but when Hettie and her husband took the place over, they added small sinks in each room. The bathrooms were precisely that: rooms with only baths in them. The toilets had only toilets.

In the attic, I noticed Hettie had misrepresented one

area—I recalled the layout well enough to remember there was something different there.

"Do you know what this is, here?" I asked as I pointed to a line in the interior that didn't match up with the exterior, as though there were a void in the wall.

She hesitated before shrugging her shoulders. "Like I said, I didn't really go up in the attic much, so I sort of fudged it."

Then she fixed me with a steady gaze. "Be careful there, Mel. They don't like young women."

"One more question," I said. "Did you know the neighbor with the upholstery shop across the street, Emile Blunt?"

Her eyes seemed to flash, but she averted her gaze and looked down at her cat.

"Emile? A little."

I hesitated. "He passed away this morning."

Her pale eyes flew up to mine. "*Emile?* How?"

"It looks like a burglary. He was shot."

She took a deep breath, shook her head.

"What are you thinking?" I asked.

"The ghosts. They didn't care for him, not one bit."

"Why not?"

"He lived at the Cheshire Inn for a couple of months when his plumbing busted. Seems like they took a shine to him. They wanted him to stay."

"To stay?"

"Like, for good. Forever."

Chapter Nine

I left Hettie's condo with a whole new set of questions, plus the contact information for her daughter, Janet, and the name of the lumberyard where Dave Enrique—the boarder who claimed to have seen ghosts in the attic—worked, last Hettie knew.

Why would the ghosts have wanted Emile Blunt to remain at the house? Did that have anything to do with his desire to purchase it? And could they have killed him in his shop across the street? Could ghosts kill people? Could they even cross streets?

I closed my eyes and blew out a breath.

Within the last six months I had gone from denying the existence of ghosts at all to wondering if they could roam the streets and handle a gun.

Perhaps the real question I should be asking was, Why should I take the word of a crazy old cat lady?

I had looked up the ghost tour leader, Olivier Galopin, on the Web last night. When I called the number listed, an upbeat, French-accented voice on the answering machine said it would not take any messages but that tours left every night except Thursday at eight, rain or shine, from the haunted hotel at the corner of Steiner and Pine. I hung up, frustrated. I didn't want a ghost tour; I just wanted to talk with the guy.

After returning a few professional calls, I rang the San Francisco Ghost Society. They told me they record evidence of paranormal phenomena, but don't perform cleansings. For that, they referred me back to Galopin.

I sat in my car, frustrated. All these phone calls and I hadn't really gotten anywhere. What was I doing? If Katenka and Jim didn't want me to finish the job, perhaps I should just let it go. The haunting was not my concern if I was no longer renovating the historic house. I had other jobs I could be working on, projects that were starting up that I could push. Running a construction company meant scheduling—and rescheduling—jobs according to permits, architectural drawings, environmental reports, and the availabilities of subcontractors. It was a juggling act, and the general contractor who let one or two items spin out of control found herself booed offstage and out of work. I'd proven very good at keeping my employees working and Turner Construction in the black, and at transforming crumbling, abused structures like Cheshire House into showcases of craftsmanship.

On the other hand . . . even if I figured Katenka and Jim could hold their own against the ghosts, could I abandon baby Quinn to the strange happenings? If a ghost had actually murdered Emile Blunt, and I was one of the few people around who might be able to communicate with the angry spirits, could I live with myself if I just walked away?

And finally, what if my father really was named a suspect? After all, he had found the body . . . and I myself had been overheard threatening to run the old man down. I cringed, once more, at the memory.

My phone rang, interrupting my thoughts. It was the foreman on the Vallejo Street job, the house where I had encountered my very first ghost.

Good. Work I could handle. And I knew for a fact the ghost haunting the Vallejo Street house wasn't out to hurt anybody.

My first ghostly project was a fine Beaux Arts mansion, one of a pair built by a man made wealthy during the gold rush. It featured broad, low arches and monolithic rather than fanciful details. In marked contrast to Cheshire House, the only frilly trimmings were the wrought-iron balconies on the front of the building, which had been reworked by a brilliant metal artist who based the design on a Greek-inspired laurel-wreath frieze we copied from one of the carved fireplace mantels.

My friend Matt, who was supposed to be "flipping" this house, recently had been offered his own reality show, to document the life of a washed-up musician who was still good-looking and slightly outrageous, and who surrounded himself with good-looking, outrageous friends. With the exception of me, of course. I was happy for Matt at this unexpected turn of events, but it was annoying to have to deal with cameras and sound people every time I wanted to talk with him.

"Mel! Great to see you, pet!" exclaimed Matt in his British accent. Matt gushed like Old Faithful at the best of times; now, with the camera documenting his every move, he was eternally pumped up. "Graham and I were just discussing the range of paints that aren't off-gassing, which if you ask me sounds a little like what happens after a midnight trip to the taco truck, am I right?"

I smiled. An old joke, but we were on camera, after all.

"Great news—I might not try to flip this house after all," said Matt. "With the show and all, I might be able to buy out the investors and keep the place."

"Matt, that's great," I said, wondering how he could stand to live in a house where a friend had been fatally injured. On the other hand, it was an incredible home, a grande dame in the best sense of the word. And the renovations had been so extensive that very little had remained of the original walls, floors, and ceiling where Kenneth Kostow's messy death had occurred.

Still . . . another ghost lingered in this home. I felt his presence from time to time, smelled the smoke from his pipe, heard the rattling of his newspaper. But he was a forlorn, sad ghost, not at all like the more powerful sensations I felt in Cheshire House. This ghost wouldn't bother anyone. And in any case, Matt was not the most astute fellow when it came to the subtle sensations around him, living or not.

I met with the faux finishers and the painters, making sure all the details were coming along well. This was the fun stage, when months of hard work, scheduling and rescheduling, and juggling came together in the finishing touches. The exterior had been done in integral color plaster, which meant never having to paint—though you had to be okay with the plaster discoloring here and there due to water runoff, and, in earthquake country, the occasional crack. But in general the final result was a mellow, multihued finish reminiscent of historic homes.

Each room here had a different theme, but they were united by complementary colors. In Cheshire House they would all be variations of Victoriana, since the designs of those houses dictated the internal design. But Matt's house was more open, a conglomeration of styles. While I was there I spoke to the faux finishers about coming by Cheshire House with some books and sample portfolios of classic Queen Anne designs. The head finisher, Dallas Finkel, was a hardheaded businessman who brought the work in on time and up to my standards. All his artists were women, because according to Dallas only women could be trusted not to make a mess and to get the job done. I tried not to think in gender terms, but I had to agree with Dallas on this one. The construction site was dominated by testosterone up until the finishing artistic touches, which were often completed by women.

As I looked around, I sighed in pleasure. The building had reclaimed its original character, in the graceful bones and elegant lines. No wonder Matt wanted to stay here.

I was just wrapping up with Dallas when Graham Donovan walked in.

"Graham." I nodded, hoping I didn't sound as breathless as I felt.

"Mel. Nice to see you."

"You, too.

As usual our gazes held a little too long.

Matt noted the interaction with interest. Ever since we'd become good friends, Matt had been trying to set me up on dates. I hoped to keep my history with Graham under wraps, but among the workers were a few who had known me and my dad for fifteen years or more. And construction workers were gossips of the highest order.

I pulled Graham outside, where the narrow passageway between the houses gave us a little privacy.

Unfortunately, this meant we stood close to each other. I hadn't been much good at chemistry in high school, but I sure seemed to be experiencing a lot now. Whenever I was within ten feet of Graham my hormones shifted into overdrive. He looked good, and smelled better. But he was cautious in the romance department. Welcome to the club.

This annoyed me. Or maybe I was just feeling generally jumpy, what with ghosts on my job site and all. Whatever the cause, rather than ask the man out as I'd coached myself while washing dishes last night, I snapped at him instead.

"Hey, what's with jumping into the Cheshire House job without consulting me?" I said.

"Remind me?"

"You have so many jobs you can't tell them apart? It's a fabulous Queen Anne on Union Street. Jim and Katenka Daley are the owners. Surely you remember which of my jobs you're poaching?"

"I'm not poaching your jobs."

"I'm the general contractor. You go through me."

"Whoa, back up, Mel. Jim Daley called me in for a consult. It was only after I arrived that I realized it was your job site." He smiled down at me. "I planned on speaking with you, as I would with any general, but I assumed I'd see you today. And here you are. Hey, maybe *I'm* psychic now."

"Think so? Can you tell what I'm thinking right now?"

"Anybody ever tell you you're cute when you're mad?"

"No, because I'm always mad. And I'm rarely cute."

"Okay, you're not cute. You're very scary. Intimidating. I'm quaking in my work boots."

I tried, unsuccessfully, not to smile. "So what's Jim looking to do? Can you give me the abridged version?"

"Basic stuff mostly, things you're no doubt already planning to incorporate: insulation and double-paned windows. That sort of thing . . ."

I nodded. "And?"

"And what?"

"Graham . . . beans. Spill."

"He wants solar. He'd prefer wind if we could get the permits, but I don't imagine his neighbors would go for a windmill in the backyard."

I blew out a frustrated breath.

"It's not that bad."

"Easy for you to say. *You're* not the one who has to deal with the decorative shingle patterns on the roof."

Some of the most effective green technologies, like solar and wind power, are wonderful ideas in the abstract, but play heck with trying to accomplish historical restoration while maintaining a modicum of aesthetic sensibility. Like many fine Victorians, Cheshire House was roofed in shingles arranged in a decorative pattern. Covering them up with massive shiny solar panels hurt my sensitive feelings no doubt about that. Other green techniques, such as using sustainable and reclaimed woods and other building materials and incorporating water-saving devices were no problem at all.

"Sorry," I said after a moment when I realized Graham was waiting for me to say something further. "I was hoping—"

"I wanted to talk to you about—"

We began talking at the same time and then paused, each waiting for the other to finish.

"Everything okay out here?" Matt interrupted, the cameras tailing him loyally.

Relationship, Interrupted. Story of my life.

"So I *have* to know," Matt said under his breath a few minutes later. "What's going on with you and Graham?"

"You don't *have* to know anything, and nothing's going on. Do you want semigloss or high gloss paint on the bathroom woodwork?"

Matt and I were flipping through paint chips, and I was forcing him to decide, once and for all, on the paint schedule. The schedule was a flowchart of what paint type, gloss, and color goes where, which was very useful when painting an entire house. Trim, walls, doors; things like mantelpieces and special transoms—everything needs to be thought out. In Matt's house I was excited about a wall of silver gilt in the master bedroom that was to be hung with beautifully framed original drawings from an art deco dress-design book. Last month Matt had acquired the antique book from, and paid a nice commission to, my friend and personal costume designer, Stephen.

"Whatever you say. Semi is fine." Matt dropped his voice again. "So this thing with you and Graham. Is this a past tense situation?"

"No tenses, past, present, or future."

He raised his eyebrows and cocked his head, signaling that he didn't believe me.

"Could I ask you something, Matt?"

"Anything, pet."

"If I did have something I didn't want to talk about,

what would possibly make you think I'd say it in front of the cameras?"

"Hmm, I see your point. Boys, why don't you take a break?" He ordered the cameras away. "Now tell me. What's going on between you and Graham?"

"Nothing," I repeated with a smile.

He gave a dramatic sigh. "You're as bad as Graham. He won't tell me a bloody thing. The pair of you should be working for the secret service. Mark my words: I'm going to get one or both of you drunk one evening and worm the truth out of you."

I smiled some more as I filled in details on the paint schedule. Matt and I had met some time ago—his son, Dylan, is a good friend of Caleb's. But since working together on his house, not to mention our adventure with murder and ghosts, we'd grown closer. He was impulsive, overly dramatic, and a tad self-obsessed—like most celebrities I'd met—but was also profoundly sweet and kind.

His determination to fix me up, however, might strain that relationship.

"Anyway, it's just as well. I have someone I want to introduce you to. He's a brilliant fellow—I really think you'll like him."

"Why would I like him? I don't like anybody."

"You like Graham," he said with a wicked smile.

"Matt, seriously, keep out of it."

"And you like *me*."

"Your word against mine."

"I know you like to think of yourself as a loner, but it's not so."

I refrained from grunting. Barely.

"Just meet him for a drink tonight."

"*No.*"

"Why not?"

"Because we're giving a party for my dad's friend Stan tonight. And besides that, I don't go on blind dates. Plus, I dealt with a murder this morning. It's been a long day."

"You dealt with a *what*?"

"It was the neighbor across the street from a job I'm working on."

Matt looked at me, his blue eyes worried. Unfortunately, he was no stranger to violent death. "Are you okay?"

"I'm fine. Thanks. It had nothing to do with me," I hastened to add.

"And there's been no . . . aftermath?" Matt asked. I had told him an abridged version of the ghosts I had seen in this house, months ago.

"I haven't seen the victim, if that's what you're asking. But . . . I'm afraid there may be *something* in the Daleys' house, though it's not the location where the murder occurred. So I doubt the ghosts had anything to do with that, right?"

"I have no idea. But if you're thinking there are malevolent spirits, shouldn't you walk away?"

"I can't. There's a young family living in the house. And besides, I guess I'm supposed to communicate with these things. Maybe that's why they're appearing, because they know I can see them."

"You really think so?"

"Truthfully, I have no idea. I'm making this up as I go along."

"Hey, have you heard of the ghost-whisperer guy who leads tours out of the Eastlake Hotel?"

"His name's come up a few times recently. Do you know him?"

"A little, only through TV connections. He's been working on getting a series himself, so he came over once to check out what it's like to live with cameras. Seemed like a good guy. He might even be on the up-and-up. Oh, hey," Matt added with a light in his blue eyes, "he's sort of cute, darling accent . . . and I think he's single."

"See you later," I said, gathering my notes and giving Matt a hug and a reluctant smile. "You matchmaker, you."

Chapter Ten

I sat behind the wheel of my car and pondered.

It was only four fifteen, but I wasn't kidding when I told Matt it had been a long day. Hearing Emile Blunt was murdered. Finding that my father had discovered the body. Being interviewed by the police. Still not knowing what was happening with my clients. And plagued by a strange sense that Blunt's death had something to do with the ghosts on my construction site. I couldn't explain why I felt that way—but then I couldn't explain why I saw ghosts, either.

I had to pick up Stan's cake by five, and leave myself enough time to get in a festive mood. Maybe allot a few minutes to panic over talking to Graham about something other than business . . .

Get a grip, Mel. You're not sixteen years old.

But if I left now, I could make it over to the animal shelter, which was kind of on the way home. If one thought creatively.

I would really love to see whether Hettie was the monster the press made her out to be. She didn't seem like it, one-on-one. On the other hand, if her current cats were in danger, I would have to turn her in. I hated the thought of it, but somebody had to do it. Animals couldn't advocate for themselves.

I drove out to the San Francisco animal rescue center.

The shelter was located across from a mediocre Mexican restaurant where I'd eaten once, years ago, when I accompanied Caleb's third-grade class on a field trip to the animal shelter. Caleb's teacher confided later, over margaritas, that the trip had resulted in more tears than any other school outing and, she said with a conspiratorial smile, half a dozen pet adoptions. Eight-year-olds and abandoned animals were a potent combo.

When I walked into the animal shelter, I noted a distinctive scent: animal and cleaning products squished together on the bottom of a rubber-soled shoe. I could hear the muffled sounds of dogs howling and cats mewing in the rooms beyond. I was suddenly in touch with my inner eight-year-old, and tried to harden my heart, doing my best to ignore them.

After all, not so long ago I had adopted Dog without ever intending to. Despite my protests that all I wanted to do was to rid myself of baggage, I had acquired a construction company, a teenage boy, and a dog. One of these days I was going to have to take a good, hard look at why my actions didn't match my words.

For the moment it was easier to wallow in the conviction that the world was out to get me.

A few minutes after I told the receptionist what I wanted to talk about, a stunningly beautiful woman came out to meet me. She wore no makeup and didn't need to. Her skin was otherwordly, pearlescent; her brown hair long and shiny; her lips a natural rosy red. But when she turned to address me, her left eye wandered off to the side, and then down, giving her an off-kilter look.

"I'm Mel Turner," I said, trying not to look at the wandering eye.

"Eva Briggs. You had some questions? I'm happy to answer them, but do you mind following me around while I multitask? It's a busy day."

"Of course. I know that feeling," I said, trailing her down a narrow corridor. "I wanted to ask you about a woman named Hettie Banks."

"The crazy cat lady?"

"Um . . ." For some reason I thought the shelter folks would be more sensitive. I stepped aside to let a plump teenage girl pass; she was leading a limping collie on a leash.

Eva ducked into a cubicle, dropped two folders on a generic metal desk, and took a seat. Her eye skewed off to the left and up toward the ceiling, but when she smiled, the effect was dazzling.

"Have a seat. I'm sorry if I was rude. In this line of work we have a rather dark sense of humor. It comes from dealing with tragedies like that every day. I could tell you stories. . . ."

"Please don't. I'm about at my limit for the day."

She smiled. "So yes, we handled the Cheshire Inn cats. The Cheshire cats, as we called them. It was a big deal because the media jumped on it. They love all those stories of mummified bodies and hoarders and whatnot."

"So I hear."

"For a few days we could barely get past the cameras to get to work. We try to use those occasions to highlight the need for loving adoptive parents, for people to come to us when they're looking for pets, rather than to puppy mills or breeders, but it still made it hard to get work done."

I nodded and waited while Eva reviewed a dog food order with a young employee.

"But here's the weird thing," Eva said, turning her attention back to me. "The Cheshire cats were actually well taken care of. They might have had a few issues, but Hettie Banks wasn't the horror show they were always talking in the news, some poor person whose neglect was essentially cruelty."

"Then why did the police get involved? How many cats can a person legally have?"

"The law's not clear—it's supposed to be three within the city limits, I believe, but unless someone's really bothered, no one's going to complain if you go one, or two, or even five cats over the limit."

"Do you know who turned her in?"

She shook her head. "It could have been anyone. One of the neighbors, probably."

I thought of Emile, who also referred to Hettie as a crazy cat lady.

"How many cats did she have?"

"I can't remember offhand exactly how many there were. I'd have to look through the paperwork, and frankly, I'm swamped. Does it matter?"

"I guess not."

"I do know the daughter helped to gather the cats, so she might know."

"In the news they always report sixty or seventy," I

said. "But I didn't see a final number in the article I read."

"It must have been bad in the house; that's all I can imagine. Since they pressed charges and everything. I know they found a number of bodies buried in the yard."

"Is that unusual?"

She shrugged. "Lots of people do it—I grew up doing that for my pets. It's only recently, and in specific urban areas, that people pay for pet cremation or interment. Tell half this country they have to pay to bury Fifi when she goes, and they'd call you certifiable."

I nodded, remembering Dad taking our beloved pup out to the woods and burying her.

"Look, I don't know what else to tell you," Eva said, grabbing a stack of files as she moved from the office into a small conference room cramped with cardboard storage boxes in all the corners. "Sorry about this place—there's too much need and not enough money. One thing I'll say for Hettie Banks: She's more than made up for her hoarding ways."

"How do you mean?"

"She gave a huge grant to our feral feline rescue group. The fix and release program. Her daughter, Janet, is part of that."

"What does the program do?"

"Folks go out and catch feral cats, and we spay and neuter them, give them their shots. Then they're released back into their territory."

"You don't keep them, try to find homes for them?"

"We do with the kittens, and an occasional adult. But the mature cats are rarely socialized to humans, and it's tough to rehabilitate them. We're overwhelmed as it is with domesticated animals needing loving homes. We're nowhere near able to take them all in. It's a very effective program; within three generations we can reduce the feral population dramatically."

Before I left, I wrote the shelter a large check. My inner eight-year-old was appeased. For the moment.

My next errand was to pick up Stan's birthday cake from Neldam's Danish Bakery; then I hurried home.

Passing through the kitchen I was glad to find the tamales had been delivered, and Dad had huge vats of beans and rice simmering on the stove. A couple of our workers' wives, who had been hired to help for the evening, were making guacamole and fresh salsa. The scents of lime and cilantro filled the air. Caleb and a couple of other friends were taking care of the decorating. They had already hung streamers and tacked balloons to the walls.

One nice thing about living in a house with patched walls in need of paint, and wood floors begging to be sanded and refinished, was that we didn't worry about pinholes or tape marks.

I set the cake on the round dining room table, which was dressed up with a clean, snow-white tablecloth, and headed upstairs.

"What do you need to get changed for?" Caleb called after me. "With your sparkles, you always look like you're on the way to a party."

"Yes, well . . ." The truth was that I wanted to shower off the job site, and then magically transform myself into a woman who would inspire Graham Donovan to spit out the words and ask me out, or else into a woman brave enough to ask *him* out. No way was I going to try to explain that to my stepson. "I want something new. Girl stuff."

He rolled his eyes.

Unlike the rest of the house, my room was beautifully finished—it's my sanctuary. I faux-finished the walls in an ochre evocative of Venice, and one wall was lined with floor-to-ceiling bookcases that held not only books but also salvaged and junk-store finds. A bunch of old skeleton keys rested in a carved brass Moroccan bowl. An antique mannequin stood in one corner. A hat with ostrich feathers hung on a hook. A mobile of old crystal doorknobs, many of which had turned differing shades of violet from exposure to the sun, turned lazily in a slight breeze from the open window.

A big cherry armoire held my assortment of dresses, most of which were every bit as sparkly as Caleb had claimed. After a quick shower I tried on one after another, calculating the effect in the freestanding antique mirror. By the time I was done the room looked as though a bomb had gone off in a craft store, with feathers, spangles, and shimmers everywhere.

If you aren't careful, Mel, old girl, you'll wind up as eccentric as Emile Blunt.

I heard the revelers start to arrive and decided Dad could handle it. They were mostly his and Stan's friends anyway, as well as a lot of the crew.

Back to the business at hand. What do you wear to a party to look special when your everyday clothes are so over-the-top?

I got so frustrated I ended up putting my original spangled outfit back on, dressing it up with nylons and strappy heels, a step above my usual work boots. I piled my hair on top of my head, letting curls dangle. Added shoulder-sweeping crystal earrings. Applied a little makeup. A couple of necklaces. Made it three. Took one off and changed the crystal earrings for smaller hoops.

Yelled at myself for being so *lame*. Enough already.

I was just about to go when I noticed my grandmother's wedding ring, a plain, thick band with the mellow gleam of old gold. The ring reminded me more of Mom than my grandmother, and it made me miss her with a visceral yearning. I thought of the moment she placed it in my hand and gave an almost embarrassed laugh, suggesting I might want to wear it when I got married. "It will be a talisman for you," she had said, cupping my hands in hers.

I was feeling in great need of a talisman. I hung it on a thin black satin ribbon, tied it around my neck, and went downstairs to join the festivities.

Since the guests thought the party was a surprise, they made sure to arrive on time. In honor of the occasion we greeted them at the front door instead of the kitchen entrance. By six fifteen everything was ready. Stan's friend Angelo had taken him to play chess at the Union Hall; he promised to call when they pulled up so we could be poised to yell.

I was arranging appetizers on the food table when I looked up to see Graham walk in, wearing a camel hair sports coat over a white shirt, new Levi's, and brown leather boots. He had a blue wool scarf tied at his neck, against the December chill. He was so tall, broad-shouldered, and handsome, it made me happy just to look at him. He smiled at me, and I smiled back.

Until I saw the woman who walked in right after him.

She was pretty. Elegant. Thin yet curvy. Not flashy, just stylish and sleek where I was peculiar and . . . not sleek.

"Who's that with Graham?" Dad growled.

"How should I know?"

Dad glared at me, as though I were somehow responsible.

My stomach churned and my mouth went dry, as if I were back in the middle school cafeteria when Chris Marriott, who had *kissed* me behind the bleachers, walked right by me to sit with my archenemy Candy Grayson. Or worse, as if it were the day my now ex-husband walked into our divorce "mediation" with Valerie on his arm, a massive diamond on her finger and a superior smile on her face.

And all because of a man who had been emotionally distant with me, and then was absent for months. Had I really expected a good-looking, sexy, smart guy like Graham Donovan would remain unattached in a place like the Bay Area?

That did it. I was getting on that plane for Paris, come hell or high water. And soon.

I needed a drink. Maybe a few. I started for the bar.

Too late.

"Mel, Bill, I'd like you to meet Elena Driscoll. Elena, this is Bill Turner, an old friend of mine. And this is Mel Turner . . ."

Graham's dark eyes were unreadable.

". . . Mel runs Turner Construction."

"So nice to meet you both." Elena leaned in and gave us each a gracious shake of the hand before allowing that same hand to rest on the small of Graham's back.

So much for the slender hope that Elena was Graham's sister or a casual acquaintance.

"When I heard the party was for the famous Turner Construction crew, I *insisted* Graham bring me along.

We've been seeing each other for *months* and I have yet to meet most of his friends. Can you imagine?"

"Tuesday's your yoga night," said Graham, his voice quiet. "I didn't think you'd want to give up downward-facing dog for a bunch of sweaty construction workers."

I felt vaguely insulted. Elena laughed, high-pitched and nasal. Grating. But now I was just being mean.

"What's everyone drinking?" Dad asked, and before I could offer to go, he took our requests and hurried to fetch the drinks.

Elena turned to me.

"I understand you're working on the Daley house on Union Street?"

I nodded, but avoided making eye contact.

"Charming place, loads of potential," she said. "Katenka Daley's such a sweetheart. And her darling baby, of course."

"You know Katenka?" I asked, glancing at Graham. Now he was avoiding *my* eyes.

"She spoke to me about throwing a party."

"A party." Where was Dad with those drinks?

Elena laughed, for no apparent reason. I took a deep breath and counted to ten.

"A holiday-themed event for her son's first birthday," she said. "Sort of a Russian New Year Tree party, though a bit early. I just adore Russian cultural traditions, don't you?"

"Oh sure, who doesn't?" I checked my phone to see if I'd missed a call. Why did it not ring? It always rang.

"The tale of Snegurochka and Ded Moroz . . . no? The Snow Maiden and Father Frost? I'm a professional party planner, so I know a lot about different cultural traditions. Wonderful inspiration."

"How interesting," I said, wondering what Elena-the-wonder-planner thought of our green and red crepe paper streamers, which had been put up with much more enthusiasm than skill and were already sagging. I imagined we were a little lowbrow for her tastes.

"You have *no* idea the fascinating people I meet in my line of work."

"I'll bet." Where the hell was Dad? I *really* needed that drink. Was I becoming an alcoholic?

"The thing is, I was thinking about staging it in the house. Maybe use the construction as a transition theme. Children just love Bob the Builder."

I was only half paying attention, distracting myself with anything at hand. At the moment I was analyzing the line of the crown molding in the parlor—was it my imagination, or did it bow out just slightly?

Until her words registered. . . .

Chapter Eleven

"Wait—you want to throw a party on my construction site?"

"I think it's a splendid idea."

"A *party*? With, like, *children*?"

I gaped at Graham, expecting the former safety inspector to step in and rescue me. He just smiled and gave a little half shrug. So much for gallantry.

"I'd love for you to take a look at the plans as they develop," Elena said. "Obviously we'll work around you."

"Just when is this shindig supposed to take place?"

"Next Monday—Quinn's actual birthday. That's why she asked for my help. She couldn't accomplish what she wanted in such a short time frame. I happened to be available—I'd just had a cancellation—and this will be a small affair, and after all, who has a party on a *Monday*? And we really just clicked, so it all fell together. I know it's a bit unorthodox, but you'll see. It'll be fun!"

First ghosts, then a neighbor's murder, now a children's party. What had happened to my job site? I glared at Graham, who looked relieved when someone called his name. He hurried off. Coward.

Elena smiled, her teeth so white she looked like a toothpaste ad. "Isn't Graham darling? So manly. Not exactly tuxedo material, but I'll rectify that soon enough."

"Think so?"

"You wait and see."

At long last, Dad returned with a Chardonnay for Elena and a vodka martini for me.

"Lovely to meet you, Bill. And so nice to meet you, too, Mel. I'm looking forward to our working together."

She drifted off to join Graham. I downed a good portion of my martini.

"What the hell happened?" Dad said. He'd been angling for me and Graham to get together ever since Graham shut down one of my job sites months ago. "How'd you let him get a girlfriend?"

"I was supposed to keep him locked in a tower? I'm not in charge of the man's love life, Dad."

The house phone rang just then, signaling Stan's imminent arrival. Dad, Caleb, and I rushed around switching off the lights, and the guests scurried to hide behind sofas and chairs. When the door swung open and Stan rolled in, everyone leapt out and yelled "Surprise!" Stan faked having a heart attack, a big grin on his face. I had to hand it to him: He did an admirable job of pretending to be shocked.

After greeting his guests, Stan came over to me. "Great party, Mel. Much obliged for all the trouble you went to, and I mean that. Soooo, who's the woman with Graham?"

"Party planner."

"She planned this party?"

"No, that's what she does for a living."

"Okay, let me rephrase: What's she doing with Graham?"

"I don't want to think about what she does with Graham, if you don't mind."

Stan let out a silent whistle.

Caleb joined us. "Who's the ho with Graham?"

"*Caleb*, that's not nice."

"So who is she?" he asked, helping himself to a root beer.

"Party planner," said Stan.

"What's he doing with a party planner?" Caleb said. "I thought *you* liked him, Mel."

"Why do you all think that I'm the man's social secretary?" I could hear a screechy note in my voice. This whole situation was rapidly veering toward the pathetic.

I refreshed my drink, found a spot partially hidden by the arched entrance to the living room, leaned against a wall, and observed the party. Luckily for me, Stan's friends didn't require a hands-on hostess, and Dad was there at the ready to keep everyone happy. They ate and drank and traded stories, filling the old farmhouse with energy and life.

Good thing they weren't depending on me to set the tone of the evening.

Just then my friend Luz arrived. I love Luz, but she's the type of woman who arrives late to surprise parties. After dropping a small gift on the pile in the dining room, giving Stan a big kiss, and, after flirting with a blushing Raul, she got herself a drink and leaned against the wall next to me.

"So. Who's the chick with the Louis Vuitton handbag?"

"I wouldn't know a Louis Vuitton from a Louis L'Amour, as you well know. "

"Okaaaay," she said, looking at me sideways, holding back a smile.

Luz and I met years ago, when she took my course on anthropological field methods. The anthropology didn't stick, and Luz pursued sociology instead, where she didn't have to get her hands dirty. She now taught social workers at San Francisco State. Luz knew everything there was to know about psychological conditions and how to treat them. She didn't have clients, though, because she didn't like to hear people "whine about their problems." Luckily for our friendship, she made an exception for me.

"But if you're asking about the only woman under sixty at this party besides you, me, and the women steaming tamales, she's Elena Driscoll."

"And this Elena Driscoll is with . . . ?"

"The man standing next to her."

"Ah. The man you were going to make a play for tonight."

I sipped my drink.

"Graham," she clarified.

I sighed.

"You're mooning," she said.

"I'm not *mooning*. I'm contemplating the joys of a solitary Left Bank existence."

"Not that old saw again. Face it, Mel, you are *not* moving to France."

"I am. Just as soon as things settle down around here, I am."

"Uh-huh." Luz scored a plate of tamales from a man

passing them out and dug in, gesticulating with her plastic fork. "You do realize, don't you, that things will never 'settle down.'"

"I'm not listening."

"She's pretty enough," Luz said in a thoughtful tone, taking a big bite. "Probably smart, too, if Graham is with her."

I glared at her.

"I mean, we don't like her. Obviously."

"Obviously."

"What's to like?"

"Thank you."

"You know who you should go after? That Zach guy."

"*Zach*? Zach Malinski? The man who kidnapped me six months ago?"

She shrugged. "Kidnap's a little strong, isn't it? I'm just saying, he was pretty cute. I liked his energy. And he sure liked you."

"He liked the gun. Anyway, even if he weren't a criminal, he's nine years my junior."

"So? My mom's fourteen years younger than my dad. How come it's okay when the guy's the older one?"

"Because men are generally less mature than women? I don't know. I'm not sure it *is* okay. I'm just . . . I can't imagine going out with someone not even thirty."

"I can't imagine walking on the moon. Doesn't mean I wouldn't try it if the situation presented itself."

"I'll be sure to let NASA know you're ready to go."

"I've heard younger men have certain advantages that older men lack."

"Experience not being among them."

Luz laughed. "Okay, *chica*. I just hate to see you grumpy. That's all."

"I'm always grumpy. Besides, at the moment I'm more pissed than grumpy."

"At Graham?"

"At myself."

"Give yourself a break. You've had a few things going on. As my papa used to say, '*mejor un pedo entre amigos que el cólico solo.*'"

"You lost me after '*mejor.*'"

"It means . . . actually, it's better in Spanish. Seems downright rude in English, now that I think about it. Point is, enjoy your friends and relax. Don't worry so much. It'll all work out in the end."

"Think so?"

"I'm a mental health professional. I know these things. Oh hey, is that Caleb? I'm going to go say hi."

I meandered into the kitchen to fetch paper party plates and plastic forks for the cake. Then it dawned on me: I'd forgotten to get birthday candles. *We must have some around here somewhere . . .* I started yanking out drawers, searching them, and slamming them back. The near-violent level of force felt good.

"You okay?" I looked up at the sound of the voice. Graham.

"Sure. The party's going well, don't you think?" I was determined to keep things light between us. What was I going to do at this point—confess to a little-girl crush? "Did you try the tamales?"

"Had to stop myself at three."

I slammed another drawer shut.

"You sure you're okay?"

"Why wouldn't I be?" I yanked open one more drawer, pushed a bunch of junk around, and voila, five little birthday candles in a very old box. I put them into the cake.

"I heard about what happened across the street from the Daleys' today." He searched my face. "This isn't the first time this has happened to you."

As unsettling as it was to talk about murder, it beat discussing romance, I thought. Or was that weird?

"It didn't happen 'to me.' I had nothing to do with it."

He nodded. Our gazes held for too long, as they almost always did. *This is ridiculous,* I chided myself. *Say something real to the man.* I opened my mouth to speak when Caleb stuck his head in from the dining room.

"Almost ready for the cake?" he asked in a loud whisper.

I nodded. "Give me two minutes, then turn out the lights."

He ducked back out.

Graham helped me light the candles.

"So, Graham, a party on a job site? Really?"

He had the good grace to look sheepish.

"I already tried to talk her out of it, but she and Katenka are determined."

"I take it you introduced them?"

"My bad. And I'm sorry I didn't mention her before."

"Why would you? None of my business."

"Maybe I like to think you might be interested in my business."

"I don't tell you about *my* love life." Not that I had one.

Graham hesitated, as though he wanted to say something else. But he didn't.

In the other room, the lights went out and the crowd began to sing "Happy Birthday."

"All right then, tiger." Graham gave me a crooked smile. "Hang in there."

He reached out one hand and . . . ruffled my hair. Swear to God.

"Make yourself useful," I said, since it was either order the man around or inflict bodily harm. "Carry the cake."

I woke up the next morning in a foul mood, equal parts hangover and regret. I took two Excedrin, fended off my father's loving offers of breakfast in favor of an extra-large travel mug of French roast, tossed my satchel and Dog into the car, and tried to throw myself into work.

After the usual round of phone calls I met with the engineer for a hillside project in Marin; the "renovation" had begun with an avalanche of engineering reports and technical drawings. This was earthquake country, after all. The structural issues were beyond the scope of Turner Construction's capability; we did foundation work on many jobs, but this project's steep grade required sophisticated engineering and heavy machinery. I was coordinating the work, helping to bridge the gap between the structural engineers and the architect, all the while keeping in mind the long-term goal of transforming the early 1960s beach shack into a graceful Prairie-style home.

Back at Cheshire House by midmorning, I met with the landscape architect.

Dog, tail wagging, checked out the smells while Claire, the landscape architect, and I stood assessing the backyard. Aside from a row of dusty cypress trees at the back, remnants of an old brick walkway, and a surviving bush here and there, it was nothing but holes, piles of dirt, and whatever hardy weeds had grown since the winter rains. The surrounding wood fence was gray and cracked with age.

"Did they try to rototill it or something?" Claire asked in her smoky voice. She was young, dressed like a tattooed, gothic-inspired hipster, and swore and drank whiskey like a sailor. But she was one of the best landscape designers I had ever met—creative, flexible, and great with clients.

"I was told they dug up some cat remains."

"*Ew.* Why?"

"I honestly don't know."

Did the police use the remains as evidence in their case against Hettie? And what could cat remains tell a person, anyway? Did they even perform autopsies on cats? It seemed hard to believe they would bother, in these days of budget shortfalls. The charges had been reduced to mere probation, so it wasn't as if they brought her case to trial. But Hettie said "the law" had dug up the yard. . . . I wondered if it would sound too trivial if I called Inspector Crawford and asked her about it. Probably. I couldn't imagine cat remains were high up on the list of things to worry about during a homicide investigation.

While Claire took some final measurements, I searched the entire perimeter of the house, looking for small crevices or cracks where a cat might enter the walls from the outside. Dog helped, sniffing along behind me. Neither of us found any access points, much less actual cats.

Claire got the information she needed, said she'd call Jim and Katenka to make an appointment to go over design drawings as soon as she had them, and took off in her beat-up Jeep.

When I opened the door to go back in the house, Dog ran straight for the basement stairs.

"Out of luck, pal. The baby's out with his mom," I called after him, as though he spoke English.

I was about to head upstairs to consult with Raul when I heard Dog barking wildly.

"Stupid dog," I muttered to myself, heading for the stairs to the basement apartment.

If Katenka had returned, she wouldn't be pleased about the noise. Dog barked as much when he was happy as when he was on guard. So I imagined he might have found the baby and would be licking him all over, while Quinn giggled and Katenka ineffectually clapped her hands at him.

Just then Dog came tearing back up the steps.

His tail was between his legs, and he was soaking wet.

Chapter Twelve

"What happened to you, sweetie?"

Panting and trembling, he shook the water off, sending droplets everywhere. Wet dog smell permeated the narrow hallway.

Doors locked, showers ran, I remembered Hettie saying. The back of my neck prickled.

"Katenka?" I called down the stairs, just in case she'd come back and decided to hose Dog down. No response.

My grandmother's wedding ring still hung around my neck, its warm weight reassuring me. I took a moment to stroke it, thinking of my mother. I hadn't known about her abilities until after her death, but one reason I was able to accept my own strange talents was because I inherited them from her. Looking back on it now, her "knack" for finding the right houses to restore and flip was one of those things my sisters and I took for granted as kids. She would sometimes go into attics or basements or other rooms, lock the door, and stay in there awhile, alone. Now I knew she was most likely seeing spirits, perhaps even communicating with them. But I didn't remember her ever being afraid.

On the other hand, my mom had a flair for finding warm, happy homes, whereas my special ability—based on my two experiences with haunted houses—seemed to involve death and mayhem.

I descended the narrow steps.

At the base of the stairs was the door to the basement apartment. I tested the knob. The door was often shut to keep out the dust and noise of the construction work, but to my knowledge had never been locked. But now it was.

I knocked. Silence.

Like many general contractors, I'm good with locks. Keys go missing all the time, especially in older homes. In fact, I had gone so far as to take a few lock-picking lessons on YouTube. Luckily, old locks like this one were the easiest to defeat. But first things first: I would try the old keys, just in case. I pulled the ring out of my satchel and tried one key after the other. The fourth key turned the lock.

I was so intent on what I was doing that I forgot to be nervous, much less consider the moral implications of breaking into my clients' private space. I had been in the basement apartment many times, of course, and I could come up with plenty of legitimate reasons for needing access to it, if I were called on the carpet to explain myself. Still, under normal circumstances I would have asked permission to enter.

But the smell of wet dog spurred me on.

"Katenka?" I called out as I pushed the door in. "Hello?"

The entry led directly into the kitchen. I saw nothing more frightening than the uninspired harvest-gold linoleum and Home Depot pressboard cabinets that I remembered. I was looking forward to tearing all this garbage out of here, once the upstairs was finished. Though there wasn't enough historical detail to be salvaged, starting with a fresh slate could be fun, as well. We would totally redo the apartment, from the wall placement to the finishes.

I peeked into the bedroom, the sitting room, the baby's room. Katenka had decked the place out in Byzantine-style paintings and posters of the Madonna and child, and there were ornate Russian Orthodox crosses on every door. Candles in various colors adorned at least one table in each room, and the whole place smelled like burnt sage.

In the bathroom, the shower stall was wet, but there was nothing more sinister than a little mold patch in the far corner.

And that was about the extent of the apartment. In the storage room I noticed an old pipe organ in one corner, covered with a tarp. Along with the horsehair settee upstairs, a couple of straight chairs, and the old key ring, the instrument was one of the few traces of the former owners left in the house. I was glad Jim Daley had decided to keep it and refurbish it, as he said, "one of these days."

I wandered back into the kitchen, staring for a moment out the window over the kitchen sink. It looked out onto the neighbor's wall, an uninspiring view of dirty beige stucco. I felt strangely let down. Now that I was prepared to see them, I was getting tired of this dinking around. *Bring it on, ghosts. Let's get together and talk, get this over with.*

Dog let out a single bark, and whimpered.

Just as I was leaning down to comfort him, something caught my eye in the barely-there reflection in the window.

A man stood behind me. I whirled around.

Nothing.

I looked down: Footprints. Wet tracks on the linoleum floor.

"Who are you?"

I tried to see him in my peripheral vision, but couldn't catch more than quick flashes.

This was ridiculous.

"Follow me," I said, and headed toward the bathroom. I flipped on the lights and looked into the mirror over the sink.

Lo and behold, there he was.

He looked terrible, even for a dead guy. He was wet, his raggedy linen shirt hung open to show a scrawny chest, and there was a greenish gray cast to his skin. Dark eyes appeared sunken and too-shiny, so I couldn't see his irises.

But worst of all, when he opened his mouth to speak, water came out and he gurgled, making his speech unintelligible.

The strong smell of alcohol assailed my nostrils. Not water, then: rum?

"You must be Charles," I said.

He cleared his throat and spat more liquid onto the floor between us. He looked down at it, as though appalled. Then back up at me.

Confused, I told myself. *Not frightening.* Well, yes, frightening, but still . . . mostly confused.

"I'm Mel Turner. I can see you in the mirror, but not face-to-face."

He disappeared.

"Come back! Charles?"

I heard a woman's far-off laughter. The only woman working on this job site was me, and that sure didn't sound like Katenka.

How is it ghostly laughter can be even more sinister than moaning or chain-rattling?

I stood my ground, checking my peripheral vision but looking into the mirror. "Either talk to me, or go away. Let Charles come back."

The shower came on. Full blast. Hot, steaming water.

Something brushed past my legs. Startled, I jumped back, but as before saw nothing.

Clouds of steam quickly filled the room. I had to force myself to look back into the mirror. It was steamed up; I could tell something dark was behind me, but I couldn't quite make it out.

The shower turned off. All was silent, even Dog.

"Someone's coming!" yelled a woman's ghostly voice.

And whatever stood behind me rushed the mirror. I whirled around and ran, yelping in fear.

Dog and I fled, racing down the short hall and up the stairs.

The eerie sound of a woman's laughter followed us.

As soon as we reached the top of the stairs, all seemed normal. It was a bright, sunny day. Saws whined, men in boots clomped about, and I smelled the familiar, comforting smells of fresh-cut wood, plaster dust, and primer.

Dog and I stood, panting, in the hallway.

Raul came around the corner. His serious dark eyes flickered over me and Dog.

"You two okay?"

"Sure," I said, catching my breath. "Dog got into a little trouble. Didn't you, Dog?"

The wet canine was shivering, rubbing his body against my legs. I reached down and hugged him, wet dog smell and all.

I was shaken, torn between feeling foolish and feeling terrified. But I was also pissed. I had to get Jim and Katenka to move out of the house temporarily, and do whatever I needed to get those things *out* of here.

I dried Dog as best I could with an old towel, then loaded him into the car and drove downtown to Jim's office on Sansome. Though I turned up at the reception desk without an appointment, in my unusual attire, smelling of my close association with a wet dog, I was escorted right into Jim's office, given a cup of coffee, and offered a seat.

"I need to discuss a couple of things with you," I said to Jim. "I'm sorry to intrude on your work."

"No problem."

Jim seemed vague, taking a beat too long to respond. He was absorbed with a pile of yellowed, old papers on his desk, so I wasn't sure my words were registering. It reminded me of dealing with Caleb when he was playing video games.

"Jim? I know you're busy, but I really need your full attention. It'll just take a minute."

"Sure, sure, sorry. You need a check?" he asked, already reaching for his checkbook. His eyes drifted back to the papers on his desk.

"Not at this time. Thank you. Your account's current.

I wanted to talk to you about moving your family off-site, just until—"

He started shaking his head, but I now had his full attention.

"Just until we complete this first phase, get the wiring and plumbing and all attended to so we can repair all the walls and start painting. Just a few days, maybe."

"Absolutely not. I thought we'd settled this."

"Just hear me out. I know you want to stay, but . . ." I was handicapped by not knowing if Katenka had confided her fears to Jim. She had waited for him to leave with the baby before speaking to me about it. I didn't want to make things awkward for her. It always struck me as highly ironic that in my line of work I often mediated between married couples. "I just think it would be healthier for all concerned."

"You said you tested for asbestos, and were taking steps toward lead abatement."

"Yes, we are. We're very safe. But—"

"Wait—does this have to do with my lovely wife's fear of ghosts?"

"I . . . um . . ."

"I let her do a thing with a bunch of basil—"

"A sage bundle?"

"Some herb. And a broom and a bell—she wanted to burn the broom, believe it or not. It was like a freaking exorcism. She put up a bunch of Russian trinkets. She's still not satisfied?" This was the first time I had seen Jim appear less than enchanted with Katenka.

"I don't think it's a matter of being satisfied. She's scared. And there's Quinn to think about . . ."

"Don't tell me you believe her."

"Well . . ." I trailed off. How could I mention what I

had just seen in the basement, without owning up to snooping around in their private space? And even if I did—was there any chance he'd believe me? "I don't know what's going on, but there's something odd happening on the job site."

"How would that be lessened if we weren't on the premises?"

"I just think that with you coming in and out of the job site—"

"Look, Mel, I waited a long time for this house to come along. I used to live just down the street; I always wondered what the Cheshire Inn would be like if it were brought back to its former glory. The minute it went on sale I snatched it up. It's the house of my dreams."

"I know that, Jim. It's an incredible place. But—"

"Our staying there is nonnegotiable. Is that it?"

Jim clearly wasn't going to budge. If Katenka couldn't convince him, what chance did I have?

"One more thing: Did you know Katenka's planning to throw a party for Quinn on the construction site?"

He gave a strange little half smile. "A party, for Quinn? Well now, isn't that sweet?" He got that dreamy look he usually got when thinking of his child.

"I don't think it's a good idea," I said, trying to shake the uncomfortable feeling that I was going over Katenka's head. "Construction sites are dangerous places, and—"

An alarm went off on Jim's watch, one of those European deals with all the bells and whistles.

"I'm sorry. I've got a meeting." He stood and started to stuff papers into a handsome leather briefcase that probably cost more than my car. "If Katenka wants a party, then I'd really appreciate it if you would cooperate, give her whatever she needs to make it a success. I'm happy to pay more if it puts you behind schedule. But you know what they say: The key to a happy child is a happy mother."

What could I say to that?

"I really appreciate your flexibility on this issue, Mel. Turner Construction has been great. Very easy to work with. I'm sorry it's inconvenient for you to have us there onsite, but I'm not willing to own such a lovely home and not live in it. Katenka and I are making a home for our son. Nothing's going to get in the way of that."

As we snaked our way through the office building, Jim pointed out a painting of the Marin Headlands that he liked, and the framed and mounted *TIME* cover story about his company. Before I knew it, we had reached the express elevator. Jim held the doors open for me, leaned in and hit the Lobby level button, and waved as the doors closed between us.

So much for going over Katenka's head.

Chapter Thirteen

After what happened in the Daleys' quarters, I was too nervous to go right back to work. The crew had always been safe enough there, bothered only by pranks, not by threatening images in the mirrors. I must be calling these apparitions, somehow. If only I knew more about them, I would have a better sense of how to approach this whole thing. Maybe. I hoped.

There was someone else who might be able to tell me more about the entities in Cheshire House. I rooted through my satchel, pulled out a slip of paper, and called the cat lady's daughter.

"I don't have a lot of time. I'm at work," Janet said. "But I drive the Emery Go-Round; you could sit on the bus and talk if you want."

"The Emery Go-Round?" I asked.

"It's free and everything."

I looked it up on my BlackBerry. The Emery Go-Round was a shuttle bus that ran from the MacArthur

BART station to the shopping meccas of Emeryville, a small city at the very base of the Bay Bridge that was bordered by Berkeley and Oakland. Emeryville had never met a corporation it didn't like. It was the land of sprawling shopping malls, massive pharmaceutical research companies, and miles of parking lots.

It wasn't my first choice of places to spend time, but I did want to ask Janet some questions. So I drove to the BART station and tried the first shuttle that pulled up, which was driven by a middle-aged African-American woman. I was willing to bet this wasn't Janet Banks.

"Janet's on the next one," she told me when I asked. "Shellmound loop."

"Thanks," I said, wondering what a shellmound loop was. In anthropology, shellmounds are signs of ancient waterside villages, basically ancient dumping grounds for seafood eaters. But whatever Ohlone village might once have flourished here on the banks of the San Francisco Bay had long since been covered over by big box stores and miles of asphalt.

I boarded the next bus that pulled up, introducing myself as I took a seat right behind the driver. I had to lean forward to speak around the plastic partition.

"Just be sure to stay behind the yellow line," Janet said. "Rules and regulations."

Janet wore her dishwater blond hair in heavy braids that hung on either side of her head. She was the St. Pauli Girl's plainer, zaftig cousin, the one who tended the cows. She wore no makeup, a plaid shirt over a white T, cargo pants, and once-white athletic shoes.

"And that guy next to you is Cyrus," Janet said. "He's my most loyal passenger. Aren't you, Cyrus?"

Cyrus nodded. He was as big and strong-looking as

Janet. He stared out the window and spoke slowly. "Can't smoke on the bus."

"That's right: can't smoke on the bus," said Janet. She met my eyes in the rearview mirror. "Cyrus here is my bouncer."

I smiled at him. "Nice to meet you, Cyrus."

"Do you smoke?"

I shook my head.

"Neither do I, at least not here on the bus," Cyrus said.

A group of young teens in huge down coats and sagging jeans boarded and staked their claims to the seats in the very back of the bus. They started goofing around, shoving each other and laughing, getting loud.

"Hold it down back there!" Janet barked, and they did. She glanced at me and winked, then said in a low voice, "They're good kids, just a little rowdy. You talk a tough game, they don't mess with you."

She pulled out from the station, narrowly missing a dented gold Impala. Turning right onto MacArthur, the lumbering vehicle groaned as we accelerated.

I looked at her broad hands grasping the steering wheel. Thin scars covered the backs of her hands, wrists, and lower arms. Some were red and angry-looking, others faded and white.

"Cat claws," Janet said.

"I'm sorry?"

"When you catch cats. They claw you. Even with gloves on, it happens. Their claws are nasty, full of all sorts of bacteria and whatnot." She looked at me in the rearview mirror. "It's not like they're cut marks, or like I tried to commit suicide or anything."

"I . . . uh . . ." I shook my head. "I wasn't thinking anything like that." Okay, it had crossed my mind.

"I belong to a group that captures feral cats. We fix and spay them, give them their shots, then return them to their territory. We don't hurt them. If anything, they hurt us."

"I hear it's a really successful program. Good for you."

Janet focused her attention on her driving, and I noticed her ring full of keys swinging from the ignition. They reminded me of the old key ring weighing down my satchel. Could the keys hold the secret to what was going on in the old house? Had they dropped on me not by accident, but to show me something? I decided I should go through the house methodically, trying each old lock and each key.

"Yeah, whatever." She shrugged one hefty shoulder. "The other women are the real cat lovers. I'm just good at catching them, since I grew up with so many of the things."

"I like cats," said Cyrus.

"Could I ask you a professional question?" I said to Janet.

"Shoot."

"Would it be possible for a cat to have remained in the house, surviving in the walls somehow?"

"Sure. I mean, it could sleep there and go out to hunt at night. That sort of thing. They're clever animals."

"Could you tell me about growing up in the Cheshire Inn?"

She hesitated for so long I thought she might not answer. But after pulling up to a stop in front of Office-

Max, taking on two new passengers, and pulling back into traffic, she spoke in a low voice. "It wasn't much of a home, if that's what you're asking. Mom rented rooms to 'bachelors' mostly, which is code for creepy single guys who didn't earn enough for a decent apartment."

"Did they . . . harass you?"

She shrugged. I waited, but it didn't seem as if she was going to say more on the subject. It was a long time ago and when it came down to it . . . was it any of my business? And what could it have to do with ghosts in the house, or Emile Blunt's death?

"Do you remember a man who lived at the Cheshire Inn briefly who had an upholstery shop across the street? Emile Blunt?"

She tweaked her head in a move that was neither a nod, nor a shake.

"He was killed the other night."

Janet slammed on the brakes as we came to a yellow light turning red. The airbrakes made a screeching sound.

"What are you talking about?" she asked.

"He was found in his upholstery shop, shot to death."

"Wow." The light turned green and she stepped on the gas. "I hadn't heard that. Geesh, I really disliked the guy, but murdered? Wow."

"Why didn't you like him?"

"He was kind of weird. He stole something from me when we lived there."

"What was it?"

"Nothing valuable," she said with a shrug of her plump shoulder. "But the point is, a grown man stole something from a kid. Isn't that kind of weird?"

"Yes, it is," I said. "Could it have been a misunderstanding?"

"Maybe. I don't know. Maybe I was just jealous because of his relationship with my mom."

"What kind of relationship?"

She paused while she turned onto a street called Shellmound. No shells in sight. We headed toward IKEA and the Bay Street shopping center.

"He was more than just a boarder, if you catch my drift."

"Really? But he and your mom didn't seem . . ."

"I know. They had a falling out at some point. But they used to be close. He was the one who gave my mother her first cat. A scrawny little flea-bitten thing he found in the back of the upholstery shop. He didn't want the fur on the furniture, so he brought it over to Mom." She gave a humorless chuckle. "Thanks *so* much for that, Emile."

"Are you and your mother close?"

"My mother is a very disturbed woman," she said.

"I had a nice talk with her yesterday. She seemed okay."

"She told you about the ghosts, though, right? That's not very 'okay,' is it?"

"Well, I guess . . ."

"Do you understand how animal hoarding works? It's a mental condition. She can't help herself."

"Any idea who turned her in?"

She shook her head.

"What about the bodies in the yard? Who dug those up?"

"The police, I guess."

"Why would they?"

"Or maybe she did it herself, to keep them with her or something. Wouldn't put it past her. Like that creepy Emile, stuffing them. Heck, maybe *he* dug 'em up."

"I like digging," said Cyrus. "Janet lets me garden sometimes."

"That's right, Cyrus. You're my assistant gardener."

"I like gardening, too," I said. My father would laugh if he heard me say that. I hadn't spent time in the yard for ages. I liked gardening in *theory*, though.

"When I stopped by the animal shelter," I said to Janet, "the director said the cats taken from your mother's home were in good condition. She said they looked well cared for."

"Doesn't surprise me," Janet said, the sides of her mouth pulling down into a grim line. "She treated those cats like royalty. Better than she treated me, I'll tell you that. When I came home from school I had to change sheets and do laundry and peel potatoes while the other kids went out to play and have a good time. *Hey, you kids, pipe down!*" She glared in the rearview mirror at the teenagers, whose conversation had grown in volume.

I had resented having to work with my dad when I was a kid as well, but now looked back on that time fondly. I learned a lot, not just about construction but also about confidence, responsibility, doing the right thing. On the other hand, both of my sisters ran screaming from anything having to do with working with their hands, citing the trauma of their childhood. Different temperaments.

"Nope, housework was good enough for me. But those cats? They didn't so much as catch a goddamned mouse." Her eyes brightened, and she smiled. "Hey, when you were at the animal shelter did you see that crazy-eyed gal?" She laughed. "I guess the animals don't make fun of her, though, right? At least there's that."

I tried one more time. "Your mom said the cats

helped alert her to anything . . . different. To lingering spirits in the house."

Janet concentrated on driving, remained silent.

"Do you remember a guy who lived there who moved out after seeing ghosts when you and he went up to the attic?"

"Sure, I remember him. Dave Enrique. Creepy guy."

"How was he creepy?"

"Inappropriate. I don't know. Maybe I was imagining things. I felt unsafe in that house, and it's possible I read too much into things. That's what my therapist says, anyway."

"So you don't remember seeing any ghosts yourself?"

Having finished our loop, we were pulling up to the BART station.

"Regulations state that you have to get off the bus once I've made a full rotation," Janet said in a formal voice, though she smiled when I met her eyes. "I'm just kidding, you're welcome to stay if you want. Cyrus stays on all day sometimes. Don't you, Cyrus? But I thought you might be done with your questions, and unless you want to go another full circuit with me, this is your stop."

"Just one more question." Actually, the same question one more time. "Your mom said you left the Cheshire Inn as a teen. Before you left, did you ever see anything odd in the house?"

"*Everything* was odd in that house." A thoughtful look came into her eyes, and she rubbed the scratches on her arm. "I didn't know what normal was till I went to live with my dad. He was a piece of work himself, but at least he didn't have any pets, or boarders."

"No ghosts?"

"I don't like ghosts," said Cyrus.

There was a long pause while the group of teenagers bounced off the bus.

"I'm a grown-up," Janet finally said. "I don't believe in ghosts. Do you?"

"I think I do, yes."

She nodded and shrugged. "To each his own, I guess. Good luck with . . . whatever it is you're doing. Why are you looking into this, again?"

Like mother like daughter. Asking the really pertinent question.

"I think it may be a problem that needs to be laid to rest," I said, surprising myself. "I think something might have gone on in that house that needs to be addressed, and that it might have something to do with Emile Blunt's death, somehow."

The BART train had arrived, disgorging its passengers. People began to climb onto the bus: two gray-haired women walking arm in arm, helping each other to board; a woman burdened with several plastic bags and a toddler; and yet another group of boisterous teenagers.

As he passed by Cyrus, one of the teen boys muttered "retard" under his breath.

Janet surged up out of her seat.

"*Hey!* Off this bus, *now!*" She gestured him up to the front of the bus, then practically pushed him down the steps. "Learn some manners, you little *brat!*"

Everyone on the bus, including me, fell silent, chastened. You could have heard a pin drop.

"Well. Anyway," Janet said as she settled back behind the wheel, "if ghosts decided it was time to take out Emile Blunt, I'd leave them well enough alone."

"I thought you didn't believe in ghosts."

"I don't have to believe to know this isn't something to fool with. I'm not stupid."

Excellent point. "Thank you for talking with me about this, Janet. I really appreciate it."

"Yeah, sure," Janet said. "Good luck, and all that."

As I climbed down off the bus, the steam from a hot dog stand drifted my way, mingling with the diesel of the bus. Urban smells that made me miss the fresh-cut wood smell of the job site. Probably what I should be doing was getting back to work I understood: building things.

My mother used to say, *Don't borrow trouble.* And was I? No, I thought, I didn't have to borrow it. *It* was bothering *me*, in the form of ghostly hijinks on the job site. Plus, I couldn't shake the notion that Emile's death had something to do with the inhabitants—whether real or ephemeral—of Cheshire House. But how does one say such things to the police?

Okay, new plan. While I was in the East Bay, I could make a stop to follow up with Dave Enrique. According to Hettie, the former boarder worked at Heartwood Lumber in San Leandro, which was down the freeway a few exits past Oakland. While I was there I could order some sheetrock we needed for the job site, and then see if Luz would let me bounce some ideas off her in exchange for lunch.

Suddenly I was so hungry that the BART hot dogs were starting to smell good. Clearly things were at a desperate pass.

Chapter Fourteen

When entering an unfamiliar supply yard like Heart-wood Lumber, I sometimes felt like Arnold Schwarzenegger at a quilting bee: My very presence set things abuzz.

My attire probably didn't help. Today had dawned chilly and overcast, so I wore black fingerless gloves, black leggings and matching sweater, a rather short gray skirt, a long, thin red scarf my sister had knitted, all topped by a full-length black leather jacket I bought in Spain a million years ago.

Only my steel-toed work boots marked me as an insider.

Heartwood Lumber was open to the public but was set up for contractors, not do-it-yourself homeowners. There were no friendly vest-clad employees eager to answer questions about which pneumatic drill bit worked best on concrete, or if a synthetic paintbrush could be used with oil as well as latex paint. Instead, behind the cluttered counter were several guys sitting at computer terminals, inputting orders of thousands of pounds of rebar or truckloads of lumber to be delivered to building sites.

As was typical in these sorts of places, I was the only female.

Construction is one occupation that has, by and large, ignored the women's movement. There simply aren't that many of us double-X chromosome carriers with the interest and the inclination—or the training and support—to compete successfully in the trades. Younger women often have to leave if they want to have families, because health and safety standards don't allow for pregnancy on many job sites. And then there was the incessant sexual harassment. But a lot of it was simple tradition: Many construction workers went into this line of work because their fathers were in the trades. Dad was a carpenter, so they were raised to see that as an option, and probably spent many a weekend building things and learning to use tools. Dad was a journeyman plumber, so he helped his son get into the apprentice-training program. No doubt it would change in time, but progress was slow.

In the meantime, I tried to hire and work with women whenever I could, but by and large I spent my days in a man's world. On the upside, I was easily recognized at all of the lumberyards, cement and gravel companies, and hardware outlets I frequented in the Bay Area, not to mention the numerous specialty stores that carried architectural salvage goods and reproductions. Most of the men accepted me when they realized I didn't dink around or play the "girl card" to avoid less savory aspects of the work.

The hefty man behind the counter wore a name tag that read HARLAN LOFGREN, HEARTWOOD ASSISTANT MANAGER. Harlan's watery blue eyes checked me out not in the way of a man appreciating a woman, but as though he was assessing my sanity. But within the first two minutes of our discussion I had thrown in enough information about my current renovation projects that he knew my boots weren't just for show.

I ordered a truckload of half-inch wallboard to be delivered to Cheshire House. Then I requested a catalog of reproduction windows, and a list of current lumber prices. Finally, I asked if I could speak with an employee named David Enrique.

"Sure, go on back. He's on a forklift in lumber. Mustache."

Out in the yard tall piles of different-sized gravel were on one side, stacks and stacks of lumber in metal frames in the covered building to the back. Cinderblocks and pressure-treated wood, rebar, and metal framing supplies were all in orderly sections. The yard smelled of freshly sawn wood, pine dust, and axle grease.

There were several men working forklifts, but only one with a mustache.

I flagged him down.

"Dave Enrique?"

"Ye-e-ah . . ." he said, as though unsure whether he should give away such vital information.

He looked to be anywhere from midthirties to -forties, white T-shirt gone gray, jeans, stocky physique, with the kind of ropey muscles more common to building sites than twenty-four-hour fitness centers. His hair was salt-and-pepper, his heavy mustache more toward the pepper than the salt. It was midday and yet he had a five-o'clock shadow.

"I was hoping to talk to you for just a minute."

He looked around, as though scouting out a supervisor.

"Harlan sent me back here," I said.

Enrique shrugged and climbed down, deliberately stripping off tan leather work gloves, one after the other. A medallion hung around his neck: a symbol of protection. A guardian angel. There was another angel inked on one forearm, an intricate tattoo of a nine-millimeter automatic on the other.

Then he brought out a box of cigarettes with an old-fashioned-looking foreign label. The cigarettes themselves were long and slim and as dark brown as a cigar.

"Can you believe this? Expensive habit already, and I get hooked on the imports."

He didn't offer me one. Not that I would have accepted.

I didn't approve of smoking, and was always bugging my dad to quit. But there was something about the habit that seemed so . . . French. Especially with exotic cigarettes like these. And I was a sucker for anything Parisian. They made me wish I was puffing and drinking espresso and becoming nervous and gorgeous and thin, which is how I'm sure things would be if I ever actually made it to Paris.

He crossed his arms over his chest and leaned back against the forklift. "So are we talking, or what?"

"You used to live in the Cheshire Inn, on Union."

The expression in his eyes morphed from cautious curiosity to cold impatience. It didn't take supernatural skills to pick up on this fellow's mood.

"A long time ago."

"Can you tell me anything about living there?"

"I wasn't there long."

I nodded. "I spoke with Hettie Banks, the former owner. She said you moved out because you thought you saw something strange."

Enrique's dark eyes swept the yard. There were forklifts transferring items onto delivery trucks, gloved and booted men carrying planks on their shoulders. Metal clanged, engines churned, men shouted. The reassuring hustle and bustle of the construction industry.

"Why are you asking?"

"A new couple bought the place, and I'm the general on the renovation. There have been some . . . strange things happening."

He nodded. "That's a bad place."

"What's bad about it?"

He shrugged. "I was sort of kidding around with the girl who lived there once. She was kind of a weird kid, not that I blamed her. Unusual upbringing. Anyway, she used to play up in the attic. We . . . saw something once."

"What was it?"

He hesitated, taking a long drag on his cigarette, and I feared he was going to stop speaking. I had no way to compel him to tell me anything, after all.

"It wasn't exactly clear," he finally said. "First there were voices, then what sounded like a woman crying. But the worst of it was, I felt this . . . rage building up inside me. It wasn't directed at the kid, *gracias a Dios*. It made me want to go after Emile."

"Emile?"

"Yeah, Emile Blunt. This other guy who lived there. Had the room next to mine. Owned an upholstery shop across the way." One hand reached up to finger his medallion.

I felt the urge to mirror him and stroke the wedding ring on the ribbon around my neck. Great. At this rate I would become one of those people who had to tap the plane three times before boarding to ward off bad luck.

"So we were just there, checking out the attic, and it happened. We all three saw it—whatever it was. But the weirdest part was the feelings. Emile had them, too—we talked about it after. And the girl, Janet. It was almost like . . . almost like they were trying to get us to do something."

"What did you mean when you said the girl was 'kind of weird'?"

"I found something, up in the attic. No big deal, just this little piece of metal, with an engraving on it. I gave it to her, but she managed to lose it, and then she totally flipped out about it. Accused Emile of stealing it from her. Strange."

"What did the engraving look like?"

"I think it must've been part of the house; it sort of matched a design that was in other parts of the place. These stylized leaves, and a face that looked sort of like a grim reaper. I'm telling you, that's a bad place."

"I hear Hettie kept a lot of cats."

He shrugged and took another drag on his cigarette. "They were okay. I like animals. I didn't like 'em on the kitchen table, but I never ate there anyway, just grabbed a doughnut and coffee on the way to work."

"Did it seem like she neglected them?"

"Are you kidding? Treated those things like family."

"Can I ask how well you knew Emile Blunt?"

He shrugged and threw his cigarette onto the ground, twisting his boot over the butt. "As well as I cared to. I only knew him as a fellow boarder; we passed in the hall occasionally. Besides that time in the attic, alls I know about him is he spoke Russian, and the jerk borrowed some money from me once, but never paid me back. Why?"

"He passed away."

"That so?"

"Murdered. He was found yesterday."

Enrique made the sign of the cross.

"When was the last time you saw any of these folks?"

"It's been years. And I'd like to keep it that way."

"What about the money Emile owed you?"

"It wasn't that kind of money. I was just as happy to let it go, so long as I never have to deal with any of those people again. Now," he said as he pulled on his leather gloves, "break time's over."

He climbed back up on the forklift and started the engine.

I walked back toward the building, my boots crunching on the loose gravel and broken concrete of the yard.

Funny how neither Hettie nor Emile had mentioned to me that he used to live in the house.

My stomach growled. I couldn't think about all this on an empty stomach. I checked in with my foremen by cell phone, then bought tacos from my favorite parking lot truck and brought them to Luz's place. Wednesdays were her day off from teaching, and she'd been working like mad on her new condo in a 1920s building, out in the Avenues near Portola.

I had sent over Jeremy, one of my carpenters, to help her out today, so I knew she'd be home. Luz would make any excuse to hang out with Jeremy.

The place was tiny, but we were transforming it into a

jewel box. The inspiration came from a castle I had seen while traveling through the Dordogne Valley with Daniel, years ago. We came upon it by chance, and learned that it had once belonged to Josephine Baker. The glamorous American dancer had transformed a section of the castle into a 1920s art deco dream, including a bathroom tiled in black and gold, designed by Givenchy. Gorgeous.

The idea was to gold- and silver-leaf the walls and ceiling, and to upholster with plush velvet and silks, so that it would seem like one was walking into an actual jewel box.

Luz answered the door covered in splotches of red-brown paint. Though *I* spent a good deal of my life covered in paint and dust and plaster, this was a big deal for a woman who usually balked at getting her hair mussed.

"You look like you've been in a knife fight," I said.

"More like a fight with this can of paint, and the paint won," she replied as she led the way into the main room.

"Have you eaten yet? I brought lunch."

"I had a little something, but if those are tacos I smell, I'll eat again. Just let me get washed up. Oh wait, do I have to wash out this brush? It'll take forever to get the red out."

"Use the old painters' trick: Wrap it in plastic." I wrapped it tightly in the plastic taco bags. "As long as it's airtight, the paint won't dry out for a long time. If you want to leave it overnight, stick it in the freezer."

"Like a paint Popsicle?"

I smiled, remembering my mother finding my brushes loaded with any number of colors in the freezer. Problem was, I would forget about them, and even wrapped and frozen, they only lasted so long. Good painters' brushes were not only essential to a good paint job, they were expensive. Thcy had to be treated right.

While Luz was washing her hands, the hammering from the next room came to a halt, and Jeremy walked in. We chatted about the status of the job, and then I offered him lunch.

"Thanks, but I'm meeting a friend to take a run. I'll get a protein smoothie after. I'm on a cleansing diet, detoxing all month. I'll be back in an hour or so."

"Oh, that sounds so much better than tacos," I said. "Have fun."

"He's so freaking gorgeous," Luz muttered, watching Jeremy's fine form as he slipped out the front door.

She and I scooched down to sit on the floor on drop cloths, backs up against the wall. It had turned into a sunny winter's day, and cool, fresh air wafted in through the cracked windows. We could hear the sound of someone strumming on a guitar, and children playing in the schoolyard down the street.

"You do know he's gay, right?"

"That doesn't mean I can't look, does it?"

"I guess not, as long as he doesn't mind. Sexual harassment runs both ways, you know."

Luz sighed and laid her head back against the wall. "There should be a law against a man that good-looking being gay."

"Maybe you find him that attractive precisely because he *is* gay. Ever think of that?"

She frowned. "I reject that theory."

"On what basis?"

"That I don't like it."

"Very scholarly of you."

"Scholarliness is overrated."

"So says the academic. Besides," I said, handing Luz a taco, "if he weren't gay and you started seeing each other, you'd have to go jogging and talk about protein shakes instead of indulging in tacos with me."

"Excellent point." She took a huge bite of her favorite, *carnitas*. Talk about your unnatural occurrences: I would never understand how Luz kept so slender given her voracious appetite.

"What can you tell me about animal hoarders?" I asked as I unwrapped my *pollo asado* taco.

"Like crazy cat ladies?"

"Yes, crazy cat ladies, or deranged dog gentlemen, or whatever else there might be. Women can't be the only ones who own lots of cats, can they?"

"Not at all." Luz chuckled. "In fact, one of my students did a research paper last year on animal hoarding, and its many permutations—it's seen in both genders, all walks of life. But did you know there's actually a group on the Web known as Crazy Cat Ladies? They're trying to reappropriate the term. Like hussy."

"We're reappropriating 'hussy'?" Even when I was young I was always out of touch with the latest trends, and this tendency seemed to be getting worse with age.

"If we're not, we should. It's a good word." She elbowed me. "For instance, if you ever had sex again in your life, you could come in here and I could say, 'You hussy, you.'"

"I'll keep you posted," I said. "So how's the Crazy Cat Ladies Society doing?"

"No idea," she said with a shrug, taking another big bite. "I just thought it was interesting. Anyway, animal hoarding is an actual psychological condition. It's related to obsessive-compulsive disorder, marked by delusions and the inability to judge reality. Animal hoarders tend to believe they can provide proper care for their pets, despite all evidence to the contrary."

"I visited a former hoarder yesterday. She still has a couple of cats, but they seem well-treated."

"That's good. They're usually true animal lovers, you know. The problem is that they can be a bit like alcoholics; it's hard for them to stop at anything like a reasonable number. They get overwhelmed, and then they're afraid to ask for help, even if they do recognize they're in over their heads. Hey, how come *you* got green chile?"

I handed over my foil-wrapped taco. "Here."

"No, that's okay. You should eat it."

"I already had chicken. And I'm saving room for a protein shake."

She took the taco.

"You think I should turn her in?" I asked. "I believe her probation stipulated she stay away from all animals, particularly felines."

"That's a hard call," Luz said, sitting back with a sigh. "It's not like it's a snap to find a good home for another unwanted pet. I'm guessing she doesn't have a lot else in her life?"

"One daughter."

"Are they close?"

"I don't think so."

"Hmmm . . . I presume this is related to the house you're redoing? I thought the cat lady was long gone."

"She is. But there's . . . something from the past, sort of, that's come up with the house."

"From the past?" Luz had polished off the green chile and was munching on chips, eyeing the extra bag of tacos I had brought for Jeremy. She was a phenomenon.

"There have been some odd events, not quite . . . natural, if you get my drift."

"As in . . ." Luz trailed off and fixed me with the kind of look only a close friend could muster, the kind that registered concern, annoyance, accusation, and humor all at once. "Wait, don't tell me: The ghosts are back."

Chapter Fifteen

I blew out a breath, then nodded. "I think so. There were some odd handprints on the ceiling, and footprints on the floor."

"And surely no human could leave handprints and footprints."

"The handprints, possibly, but the footprints appeared right in front of me, while I was watching. No one else was around to leave them. And earlier today Dog and I had a rather interesting encounter with a guy in a mirror. I'll spare you the details."

There was a moment of silence.

"They say ghosts don't like their surroundings disturbed," said Luz.

"Maybe it really could be . . . you know . . . something slightly more prosaic."

"Like . . . ?"

"Do you think someone could want me to *think* there are spirits haunting my job site?"

"Why would anyone want you to think that? Other than your ex-husband, that is. I wouldn't put it past him."

I smiled. Luz made it a practice to lay all manner of sin at the door of my ex-husband.

"I can't imagine he'd bother to arrange such an elaborate hoax," I replied. "But neighbors always hate the noise and mess of construction projects. I thought at first maybe it was that weird guy from across the street, but . . ."

"But what?"

"He was found dead yesterday morning."

Another pause.

"*Please* tell me it wasn't death by nail gun like the last time."

I shook my head. "No, but it looks like a homicide for sure. The police are investigating. In fact, Dad found the body. I'm afraid he might even be a suspect."

"You didn't tell me any of this last night."

"It was a birthday party. Not the place for talking about ghosts and murder."

"It's starting up again, isn't it?" One of the many things I appreciated about Luz was that although she initially thought my previous ghost sighting might have been the result of emotional trauma, she believed me when I told her the whole story. Like me, she didn't understand it, but she believed me. In fact, she had asked me to check out her apartment to be sure it was "phantom-free"—because one of the few things that scared her was ghosts. And clowns. A ghostly clown might just send her round the bend.

"Is this guy following you around now?" she added.

"Who?"

"The dead guy. Isn't that what happened last time?"

"What a horrible thought." I was surprised it hadn't

occurred to me. I couldn't imagine having Emile Blunt, of all people, dogging my footsteps. Something like that might just send *me* round the bend.

"I haven't seen anything yet."

"Good. Let's hope it stays that way."

All this talk of being followed around by spirits made me nervous, so I gathered up our trash, unwrapped the paintbrush, and started in on trim. The standard base paint for gold gilt is red oxide, a deep earthy color that looks a lot like blood. It made me think of poor grumpy old Emile Blunt, lying in a pool of blood in his upholstery shop. Though I hadn't actually seen it, my unruly imagination had taken a stab at re-creating the scene.

"So," Luz said, all innocence, "aren't we going to talk about Graham?"

"What about him?"

"'What about him?'" Luz mimicked. "How about the fact that he showed up to Stan's party with a woman on his arm and you spent the rest of the night moping?"

I blew out a frustrated breath. "I'm beginning to think he went to Europe just to get away from me."

"That's ridiculous. You'd both been in the city for years and hadn't seen each other. Why would he have to leave the country to avoid you? Seems to me he does a fine job avoiding you when he's right here."

I grunted.

"You never slept with him . . . did you?"

"What? No, of course not."

She lifted one eyebrow. "*I* would have slept with him."

"Okay, it's not like I didn't think about it. But no. We were barely in contact for a few days, and if you'll recall, they were very busy days."

"I'm just saying . . . you could have fit in some romance if you'd really wanted to. No wonder he found another girlfriend."

"Yes, thanks, Luz. You're always so loyal. It warms my heart."

She laughed. "I'm just saying. With a man like Graham, there's not a lot of waiting around. One of these days you might just figure out that you miss male companionship, despite whatever shenanigans Daniel pulled, and he'll stop calling the shots."

"Daniel doesn't call the shots." My voice sounded defensive even to my own ears.

"Sure about that? You're making decisions shaped at least in part by the way Daniel treated you. I'd say there's a lot of shot-calling still going on."

Sometimes it was a drag that my best friend was a mental health professional. A brutally honest mental health professional.

"I don't get what Graham sees in her."

She raised one eyebrow. "Oh, don't tell me you didn't check out that perfect hourglass body. She doesn't have to have a scintillating personality when she's got a booty like that."

"What about *my* booty?"

"Your booty's darling, but you don't swing it like she does, is all I'm saying."

"In my profession, you swing your booty too enthusiastically and you might get something taken off with a power tool." I laid a bit more paint onto the trim, taking extra care in the corners. "Anyway, I guess I thought the man might be deeper than that, character-wise."

"You know what they say: When you can't figure out why a couple's together, it's probably due to what goes on behind closed doors."

"I don't want that visual! Why do I talk to you about these things? Now it's worse than before."

"So make a move on him already and stop whining. It doesn't suit you."

"I'm not *whining*," I whined. "Anyway, I missed my chance. He's got a girlfriend."

"Was there a ring on her finger?"

"No."

"Then he's still up for grabs."

"I don't know," I said, stroking on the red paint with a sure hand. "Sounds like work for a professional, and I'm strictly amateur hour. Not even that, when it comes right down to it. I think I should stick to dealing with ghosts at this juncture — I think my odds are better."

"Hey, how come you can paint so fast? It would take me all day to do that much trim, and you didn't even use blue tape!"

"I never use blue tape. It's way too expensive. I haven't kept Turner Construction in the black for two years by overspending on frivolous supplies." Good *lord*, I was beginning to sound like my father. Next thing I knew I'd join the NRA and start watching football. "Besides, blue tape lulls you into a false sense of security with your edges."

"I *like* feeling as though my edges are secure. We don't all have your hand-eye control, you know."

"You know what blue tape's excellent for? Sealing up cabinets when you're sanding. Keeps the dust out. Right tool for the job. Hey, will you go on a ghost hunt with me tonight?"

"Uh, *no*." Luz looked aghast. "I told you, ghosts scare me."

"It's not like there will be real ghosts there. It's just a tourist thing. I think."

"Then why are you going? Besides, I thought you were trying to stay away from ghosts, not hunt them down."

"I don't quite know who to talk to. I need to sort out this ghost situation at Cheshire House. I'm hoping the ghost tour guide might be legitimate. Matt knows him, says he's a good guy."

"Matt? Now *there's* a sound judge of character."

"Plus, the local ghost society referred me to him."

"There's something called a 'ghost society'?"

"Believe it or not." I nodded. "Interestingly, though, they're more about documenting ghosts than running them out."

She started applying blue tape to the bottom edge of the egg-and-dart trim.

"I guess it takes all types. Anyway, you know I'm there for you when you think you're crazy or want to discuss your love life—or lack thereof. But ghosts, *mi amiga* . . . ?" She shook her head. "You'll have to find another playmate for that."

"All right then, how about going with me to talk to someone at a botanica?" I was willing to try just about anything at this point.

"Why?"

"In case they speak Spanish."

"It's good for you to practice."

"I don't want to miss anything. And I don't want to go alone. Do you ever use botanicas?"

"Do I *look* like I frequent botanicas?"

"I have no idea what someone who goes to botanicas

looks like. Come with me tomorrow, and I'll buy you lunch in the Mission."

"It better be a good lunch."

"Have I ever failed you?"

While I was out in the Avenues, I thought I might as well chase the lead from a Craigslist ad for molded iron fireback plates. A fellow named Nelson claimed to have fireplace equipment from the era that Cheshire House was built.

When I talked to Nelson by phone, he had the quailing voice of an elderly man, which was a good sign. Old-timers were by far the best resources for this sort of thing. When I pulled up to the ramshackle house out near San Francisco State University, I wasn't disappointed. The porch and yard were crowded with the sorts of items some people refer to as junk, while others consider them treasures.

The man who met me at the door looked to be in his seventies, wearing suspenders that held up stained jeans far too big for him. He'd either lost weight recently, or he was wearing someone else's pants.

"Guess I spoke to you on the phone," Nelson said. "You the one who called 'bout the fireplace parts?"

"Yes, I'm Mel Turner. Nice to meet you."

"C'mon in. That's Al. He doesn't get up."

Al was sitting in a recliner in front of a large plasma flat screen. True to Nelson's word, Al held up one hand in greeting but didn't take his eyes off the movie on TV. I recognized the music for *The Bridge on the River Kwai.* My father loved that movie, and was probably parked in front of his own massive television right now, sitting back in his recliner and watching it for the umpteenth time.

I followed Nelson through the living room and kitchen, out a back sunporch, and down into a yard that was dotted with dozens of vintage wood-burning and gas stoves under plastic sheets, in varying states of repair.

Under the back porch, which was at the level of a second story, was Nelson's workshop. As a builder, I salivated at the view. This was the sort of collection it took a lifetime to build up—every sort of tool imaginable, vises, cutting tables, and hardware from antique to shiny new.

"Wow, this is great," I said. "My father would be jealous. Heck, *I'm* jealous."

"You in the trades?"

"I'm a general contractor."

"Good for you. Not enough women in the field." Amen to that. "Now, where are those fireplace pieces again . . . ? Oh, right. Over here."

He pulled back a blue tarp, moved a motorcycle frame that had been stripped down to the gas tank, and leaned in.

"They're a little rusty," he said with a grunt as he pulled out a panel and passed it to me. "Need restoration, sure. Meant to get around to it, but never did. We're trying to get rid of stuff if we don't fix it up within five years. New get-organized plan."

I smiled at the idea of this place being organized. Nelson chuckled.

"This motif, the acanthus leaves surrounding a face like this . . ." I said, tracing the relief with my fingers. "There's something very similar in the house I'm renovating. In fact . . . I can't believe how similar it is."

"You said the house was built in 1891? That's the same era as these. There weren't all that many foundries casting this sort of thing, and it was a common motif."

"I hadn't seen it before."

"Probably because most people pulled 'em out later on. Got more superstitious, maybe, or just didn't want symbols of death all over the place. Acanthus leaves themselves are symbols of death, you know."

"I thought they were associated with eternal life."

"Only in the sense that they symbolize rebirth. The natural cycle of death in winter and rebirth in spring. But the way I heard it is that in the early days of Christianity, believers wanted to shift folks to thinking that they would be reborn in heaven, not here on earth. So the acanthus leaves—which are thorny by the way, like the thorny crown of Christ—came to be associated with earthly death."

I love old-timers.

"That's fascinating. I had no idea. And you're right: The house I'm working on does have death symbols all over the place."

"I've got a book. . . . Let me see. . . ." He ducked into the basement, which, quite unlike the basement level apartment of the Daleys' house, looked like a real basement. Musty, dank, and full of scary-looking hidden rooms.

"Here it is." He unearthed a book from a cardboard box. The pages were yellowed and foxed. The spine cracked as he opened it, releasing that distinctive smell of must and mildew, as in used bookstores.

He looked up something in the index, and then flipped to another page.

"Yup, that's what I was thinking of," he said, tapping the picture and holding the book out to me. It was a line illustration of a similar motif. On the opposite page was a paragraph describing the design, and discussing the fascination with death symbols.

"'It was common to invite death,'" I read aloud. "'To observe it and *fear* it as one would God.'"

Our gazes met and held.

"As they said back then," Nelson said, "*Life is uncertain; death is the cure.*"

I cleared my throat. "So how much for the book and the fireplace backs?"

"Fifty for the fireplace pieces, if you take 'em all and get 'em out of my way." He snapped the musty book closed and held it out to me. "And this book is my gift to you. Good luck."

Chapter Sixteen

B ack at Cheshire House, I brought my toolbox in with me. After checking in with Raul, I wanted to examine the fireplaces to see if the newly purchased fire-backs would fit. This might well entail dismantling the internal structure and modifying it to accommodate the iron slabs, since cutting the iron wasn't an option. There was no point in having the pieces restored if they weren't going to work.

I looked up to see Graham walk through the front door.

"What are you doing here?" I asked him as I set my tools on the plywood worktable in the front hall.

"I've got a meeting with Jim tomorrow, and I wanted to check out the insulation potential in the walls, take some measurements, that sort of thing. Do you mind?"

"Of course not. Make yourself at home."

"Cute toolbox. Is that Caleb's handiwork?"

I nodded. All of us marked our tools, since it was so easy to mix them up on job sites, and these are the necessary items to ply our trade. Plus, they were expensive, and many of us got sentimental about our tools, whether they belonged to our fathers, or fit our palm just right, or reminded us of favorite jobs.

But it was always easy to distinguish my toolbox from everyone else's, because Caleb had decorated the side of my toolbox when he was eight: MEL TURNER was written in crooked letters with multicolored magic markers. I got a few looks from some of the men, but it warmed my heart every time I saw it.

I left Graham to wander about on his own—the man knew his way around a construction site—and after speaking to Raul again, I checked in with the carpenters and the paint crew repairing the walls and ceilings. In earthquake country, old plaster had a tendency to crack. A lot. Lumpy, erratic lines showed previous repairs through the years, and often wallpaper was put up to mask this. The painters had stripped seven layers in the living room, ten in the kitchen. They had also stripped the carved wood fireplace mantels of several coats of paint, and the metal of paint and rust. Unfortunately, this made the fireplaces too "new-looking," so after they had been restored and properly sealed, I would bring in faux finishers to place a little fake verdigris on the metal, and darken the recesses of the wood.

On my way upstairs, I gathered bits of the old wallpaper stripped from the walls. Along with progress photos, these mementos would eventually go into the scrapbooks I kept of each house Turner Construction renovated, carrying on my mother's tradition.

Today I also wanted to investigate the old keys, trying them out systematically on all the doors and lockable cupboards in the house. And starting in the attic I would check for rodent activity—and/or cats—as well, just in case the strange noises I heard overhead yesterday were perfectly natural. All seemed quiet so far, but it was early yet.

From the third-floor hallway, I yanked open the access door to the attic and pulled down the ladder. Hesitating for a moment, I took a deep breath and climbed up into the dark space.

Even with the overhead light on, the attic was dim and shadowy. But there was nothing particularly frightening about it, I assured myself. I crouched down to peer at a crack in the wall near the baseboard.

Nothing but dust and cobwebs . . . and a man's voice whispering behind me, low and urgent.

Whirling around, I tripped and fell on my butt. "Hello?"

I looked into the shadows and checked my peripheral vision for ghosts. No one was there.

Another whisper. This time it was a woman. Her voice was harsh and anxious, as though answering the man.

The voices were muffled, and seemed to come from behind a paneled wall.

Slowly, I approached, studying how the walls came together—yes, there could be a void there. I looked closer. The "door" was more like a panel cleverly concealed by molding, with no handle. But there was a very old dead bolt. Recessed, it was almost hidden by the molding, and had been covered in spackle.

My heart was pounding, but I refused to be intimidated by age-old whispers and errant shadows. Not so long ago, I helped figure out who had murdered the ghost who kept pestering me. Surely I could do that again. Or at the very least identify what it was these spirits wanted.

As soon as I started feeling around the door, the whispers stopped.

"I heard you," I said loudly, trying my best to sound confident. "Is there something you want? I can see and hear you a little, but it's unclear."

No response.

"Are you talking to me?" said a decidedly human voice. Graham stood on the ladder, poking his head into the attic.

"*Graham*. You scared me!"

"Then I take it you weren't talking to me," he said, coming up the rest of the way. "Who *are* you talking to?"

"I . . . uh . . . I thought I heard something."

"Something?"

I remained mute. I didn't really want Graham knowing the extent of my visions.

He fixed me with a serious look, halfway between impatient and caring, the one that always made me think of a moment we'd shared in a warm car in the middle of a rainstorm. So many years ago. And which now made me resent Elena the party planner, who otherwise seemed like a perfectly nice woman.

"Have you seen something in this house, Mel?"

"Why would you ask that?"

"Because you look as though you've seen a ghost," he said with a slight smile.

"Maybe."

I turned back to the paneled wall, and started to investigate.

Something had been scratched into the wooden header, then covered with paint. It was faint and hard to make out. I grabbed a carpenter's pencil and a sheet of the paper we put down to protect the floors, and held the paper up to the wood. I rubbed the lead over the paper, as my mother taught me to do with crayons and old headstones at Oakland's historic Mountain View Cemetery.

Words appeared: MEMENTO MORI.

"What does that mean?" I asked.

"You're the Latin expert."

"Spanish."

"Close enough."

"And I speak a little, but I'm no expert. Memento—as in souvenir? And in Spanish, *morir* means to die."

"A souvenir of death?"

I stepped back and looked around, half expecting to see a ghostly presence in my peripheral vision. Was there something in this closet I didn't want to discover? Or was it like the rest of the house, a possibly harmless little obsession with death . . . and therefore, life?

Surely this room couldn't have been locked ever since Dominga lived here. With all the people coming and going in this house it must have been opened—and closed—repeatedly over the years. There wouldn't be, say, an old rum barrel with a skeleton in it? That would be awfully . . . *Pirates of the Caribbean.*

"Mel, you okay?"

"Oh sure, just peachy." Dead bolt or no, I was getting into that closet. I was scared. But I was also pissed off. Who were these spirits to be putting me through this, and to be pestering a young mother? "I'm going to go get my tools."

I descended the attic ladder to the third-floor hallway and started down the stairs, noting a water stain near the ceiling. I really needed to take care of the roof sooner rather than lat—

I suddenly heard something overhead—a harsh scraping sound. I glanced up just as a toolbox fell from the upper floor.

Right toward my head.

Chapter Seventeen

I jumped out of the way, throwing myself against the banister. With a sharp *crack* the railing started to give way under my weight. I grabbed the sturdier newel post and watched, my heart in my mouth, as a section of the wooden banister fell, shattering on the stone floor two stories down.

The toolbox landed on the step below me with a crash, gouging out a chunk of wood. Tools and hardware spilled, clattering and clanging.

Graham grabbed me from behind, swearing a blue streak.

I leaned back against the strength of his chest, and felt the rapid beating of his heart. One muscular forearm was wrapped around me, holding me just under my breasts.

A large metal nut made a *whoosh, clink, whoosh* sound as it rolled down several stairs.

I peered upward, but saw nothing but an empty hallway.

There had been no one there. And no toolbox.

"*Mel!* Everything okay?" yelled Raul as he charged up the stairs, slowing as he took in the tools strewn along the stairs, and the toolbox lying facedown. "What happened?"

"I was just coming from the attic. I have no idea where it came from."

Raul turned over the toolbox. A name was written, clear as day, in magic marker: MEL TURNER.

"It's yours," he said, looking at me curiously.

I nodded.

"Did you leave it on the landing, or the banister?" His voice sounded doubtful. Raul, of all people, knew how safety conscious I was.

I shook my head. "I left it in the entry hall. I was coming down to get it."

He held my gaze for a long moment, then sat on the stairs. I slid down next to him. Graham remained standing, mute.

"Something strange is going on around here," Raul said in a low voice.

I nodded.

"You think someone's sabotaging us?" he continued.

"I don't know . . . but I don't think so. Not a normal person, anyway." I picked up an old adjustable lug wrench and turned it over in my palm, appreciating the familiar weight. Even as a child I used to love the feel of my dad's cold, heavy tools in my small hands. They seemed magical to me, enabling my dad to create houses from a pile of lumber and stone and cement. "Raul, do you believe in ghosts?"

He made the sign of the cross and muttered something in Spanish that I didn't catch.

We sat for another minute. The fear receded, leaving anger in its wake.

"I'm going back in the attic," I said, tools clanking loudly as I gathered them up and put them back into the toolbox.

Raul's eyes held mine. "Are you sure? Maybe . . . maybe you shouldn't."

"I'll go with you," said Graham.

"I . . . Thanks. That would be great." I realized that I liked the idea of Graham having my back, quite literally. "Raul, would you check out the dining room ceiling, make sure the handprints aren't something normal, like grease prints?"

Raul had been a professional housepainter before becoming my foreman and would recognize grease. Like water stains, grease prints would show up, rather ghost-like, through the finish paint. The only way to be rid of them was to use the proper primer.

It wouldn't explain how the prints had gotten up there in the first place, but I wanted to eliminate any possibility of a natural cause.

With a heavy sense of foreboding, I readied myself to return to the attic. Up the flight of stairs, down the hall to the ladder. The square access loomed overhead, dark and yawning, like the mouth of a hungry monster. I swallowed, trying to slow my pounding heart. Still, my fear stoked my determination. I started to climb.

The whispers were louder this time, but again stopped when I approached the hidden panel door.

"Did you hear that?" I asked Graham.

He shook his head. "I don't hear anything."

Turning back toward the hidden closet, I reached out

and laid my palm against the door. Nothing felt out of the ordinary.

"About last night . . ." Graham said. "I wanted to explain."

"There's nothing to explain, and this isn't the time to talk about it anyway," I said, examining the lock. "We aren't . . . whatever it is you think we might be but we really aren't. Hand me that X-ACTO knife, will you?"

I did *not* want to talk about this here, or now. Or possibly ever. Besides, I needed to concentrate.

Graham handed me the knife. Rust and spackle filled the indentations at the top of the lock's screws, and my screwdriver couldn't gain purchase. I started scraping.

"I've known her for some time—"

"I don't want to hear about it."

"But—"

"No."

And then I did the most remarkable thing. I set down the knife, put my fingers in my ears, and started chanting *la la la la la.* Just as I had when I was twelve.

"I'm not listening," I singsonged.

Graham's jaw clenched.

"Talk to me, dearest," he said, his voice gravelly.

"Dearest"? What kind of game was he playing?

I unplugged my ears. "I *said,* I do *not* want to talk about it."

His dark eyes were velvety black in this light. I noted the strength of his jaw, the stubble sprinkled on his cheeks, the scar bisecting one eyebrow.

"Then we understand one another?" he said.

"We understand nothing. Because there is no 'we.'"

He took a step toward me, and I moved away to keep

a distance between us. We started circling one another, our booted feet clomping on the broad wooden planks of the attic. I could have sworn I heard far-off music, a mournful sound like a church hymn. I thought of the old pipe organ sitting in the corner of the basement storage closet, covered in a tarp. It used to have pride of place in the parlor, and looked like it had been there for centuries, though the date on it was 1896.

I felt an overwhelming rush of déjà vu. I had been here before, said these lines before, to a man such as Graham.

"I had to escort the lady to the ball," Graham said. "And after all, you were there with your 'husband.'"

He said "husband" with great disdain.

"Why did you fawn all over her? Was it to make me jealous?" I replied. "Charles would never have noticed. You know how he is, thick as molasses in January. Be gone, sir. Your lady friend requires— "

Graham closed the distance between us in a single stride, grabbing me by the upper arms and pulling me to him.

"I can't stand that he gets to touch you," he growled. His mouth moved toward mine. His lips hot, demanding . . .

A loud crash resounded from below, and the surreal moment was over.

"Who's Charles?"

"What 'ball'?"

We stared at each other. I was shaking more now than when I'd nearly fallen from the stairs a few minutes ago. What had just happened? *What* were we talking about?

More whispering noises came from behind the door. Falling to my knees, I grabbed the screwdriver, determined to open the hidden door. This time the screwdriver gripped, and I applied as much force as I could muster. Slowly, the rusty old screw began to turn.

From below came another sound: a man crying out.

Another shouting, "Call nine-one-one!"

I dropped the screwdriver and leapt to my feet. Graham beat me to the attic ladder and headed down the stairs, taking them two at a time. I followed close on his heels.

The men were crowding into the dining room, talking excitedly. I noticed an extension ladder propped against one wall.

"What happened?" I asked.

"Raul fell off the ladder," Bertie, Raul's young assistant, said, looking stricken.

The men stood aside to let us through. Raul was lying on the floor. Graham and I knelt on either side of him.

"How did this happen?" I asked Bertie.

"I don't understand," he replied, shaking his head. "I was right there, holding the ladder. It didn't shift or bow, I swear. But he fell off anyway. Landed on his side. We already called nine-one-one."

"How far did he fall?"

"He was at the top. Almost ten feet."

Fortunately, Raul had landed on a wood floor covered in cardboard and paper. As bad as that was, I thanked heaven he hadn't fallen onto stone or concrete.

"Raul? I'm going to check for injuries, okay?" I probed him gently, relieved to find no signs of blood. Raul just grunted in the ugly, strange way of someone who has had the breath knocked out of him. Or whose ribs were broken. And then there was the possibility of internal damage. I said a quick, silent prayer that the EMTs would arrive soon and that a bad bruise would be the worst of it.

Then I saw the unnatural angle of Raul's elbow.

"Looks like a broken arm," I said, glad to see that color was returning to his face. "Raul, can you tell us where it hurts?"

Construction is dangerous work. I once fell from a ladder myself, though not from such a height. So I knew that having the wind knocked out of you is frightening, not to mention physically uncomfortable. The lungs seem to freeze up, as if they've forgotten how to breathe. It's a bizarre sensation, but it's temporary.

Raul started to suck in air, and after a moment he spoke. "I think I'm okay, except for the arm." His voice was shaky, but he managed a small smile. "I can wiggle my toes, and everything."

The men uttered a collective sigh of relief.

"Do you feel any chest pain or dizziness?" I asked.

"No. I'll be all right."

"Lie still. An ambulance is on its way. Let's see what the doctors say."

He glanced at his ashen-faced assistant. "It's not your fault, Bertie. It was me—an accident."

"What happened?" I asked.

"I was looking at the ceiling, and I . . . I thought I saw something. I yanked back, and fell." He whispered, and I leaned in to hear him. "This sounds crazy, Mel, but . . . handprints appeared. Right in front of me. Dragging through the paint like it was wet, only it wasn't."

I nodded. "I believe you. And I'm so sorry."

Rage surged through me. If these ghosts wanted war, so be it. I'd find a way to banish the supernatural horrors, come hell or high water.

They had messed with the wrong general contractor.

Chapter Eighteen

We insisted Raul remain where he was until the paramedics arrived. I could probably have gotten him to the hospital faster if I had driven him there myself, but I had learned enough about spinal injuries in first aid courses to know it was best to let the trained professionals handle it.

While we waited, Raul asked me, "Do you think it was just an accident?"

"Sure I do," I said. "Just like my toolbox nearly falling on me was an accident."

Our gazes held.

"Mel, the other day, Katenka Daley asked me about performing a *limpia*."

"A *limpia*, as in a cleansing of the house?"

He nodded. "Like a psychic cleansing, sort of. To chase off spirits."

"What did you tell her?"

"I don't know that much about those sorts of things,

but I gave her the name of a botanica in the Mission called El Pajarito. That's where she got the sage. But to tell you the truth, I think it made it worse."

"Do you know who she talked to there?"

"I don't. I've never believed in this sort of thing. My wife, a lot of the people I know do, but I never . . ."

Deafening sirens announced the arrival of the paramedics, and we all stood back to give them room to work. They did a quick assessment of Raul's condition, fitted him with a neck brace, and transferred him onto a stretcher.

As we watched them load him into the ambulance, Graham came to stand beside me.

"I have to go with him, see what the doctors say," I said. "Would you do me a huge favor and be my foreman? Settle everyone down, have them wrap up early for the day, then lock up."

"Of course. I'll take care of it."

I handed him an extra set of keys to the front door.

"And would you take Dog with you? I don't know how long I'll be at the hospital."

"Sure. Call me later and let me know what the doctors say. And Mel—at some point we have to talk about what happened in the attic."

"I know. Do me another favor? Stay clear of there for a while?"

Graham nodded and I ran out to chase an ambulance.

As I followed the paramedics to the hospital, I admitted to myself that I was out of my league. My first ghost had been annoying but ultimately benign. These ghosts were dangerous.

As I sat in the ER's waiting room to hear what the doctors would say, I made phone calls until Raul's wife came to be with him. I told her what had happened, and assured her that all Raul's needs would be covered by our health insurance, and workers' comp, if necessary. At the very least, they wouldn't have to worry about the financial ramifications of a job site accident. Before we were finished talking, Raul's grown daughter arrived with her husband and children, and then Raul's brother joined them.

I was leaving him in good hands. My time would be better spent figuring out how to banish these phantoms.

Looked like I was going on a ghost-hunting tour tonight. I wouldn't have minded having someone strong and capable to accompany me, but if I asked Graham, he might bring Elena. I was not in the frame of mind to deal with a ghost hunter and Elena at the same time. So I called someone not nearly so strong, nor as capable, but a far sight more open-minded: Matt.

"Want to go with me on a ghost tour tonight?"

"Is this a trick question?"

"Don't all the girls ask you to go ghost hunting?"

"Only if it's a euphemism."

"Not in this case."

"Didn't think so. I'm not really up for a ghost hunt, Mel. Call me crazy."

"It's with your buddy Olivier Galopin. You said you knew him from the reality TV business, remember? Please?"

Matt sighed. "On one condition: If I go, you have to tell me about you and Graham."

"Deal. The whole sorry saga," I said, mentally crossing my fingers. No way would I tell Matt about our latest adventure in the attic. I could barely bring myself to think about what it might mean. The memory of the brief kiss, before we were interrupted, made my heart race. But . . . it had been Graham, but he was acting completely out of character. "Fair warning, though: There's not much to it."

"I'll take my chances. Where and when?"

"Meet me at the Eastlake Hotel a little before seven," I said. "On the corner of Steiner and Pine. Oh, and don't bring the cameras," I hastened to add.

"Not even my digital?"

"Oh, yeah, sure. But lose the camera crew."

When I arrived, Matt was waiting outside the hotel, wearing a big puffy parka and boots, shifting from one foot to the other, as if fending off a blizzard. The temperature was in the low fifties, which would not strike many as particularly frigid, but we Bay Area folks are weather wimps. If the thermometer drops below the midsixties, we freeze; when it rises above the low eighties, we wilt; and when it has the nerve to rain, we bemoan our fate.

"It's cold out here," I said. "Why didn't you wait for me inside?"

"I'm scared to go in alone."

"It's a hotel, Matt, full of people. Not an abandoned factory."

"Ghosts give me the creeps," he said, hunching his shoulders. "I'm highly suggestible."

"You *are* aware this is a ghost tour, right?"

"I'm also highly bribable."

"Some badass rock-n-roller you are," I said with a smile, pushing the door open and leading the way in.

"Yes, well . . . don't believe everything you read on the Internet."

I walked around, studying the faded grandeur of the Eastlake Hotel's antique-filled, red velvet–curtained lobby. As a sumptuously decorated Victorian building, it was a wonderful inspiration for the Cheshire House renovation. Every corner was filled with ornate carved chairs, fringed lampshades, and gilded frames. Enclosed bookshelves were nestled on either side of the fireplace, and brocade settees flanked a grand piano. An impressive staircase led upstairs to guest rooms and, I presumed, more antiques.

Matt picked up a pamphlet on the building's history from the marble-topped reception desk and read aloud.

"It says here that at one time this place was Miss Mary Lake's School for Young Ladies. Some guests in the hotel claim to sense the ghost of Miss Mary, saying she covers them up with blankets at night."

I was surprised that a hotel would embrace its reputation for being haunted, but then Brittany Humm would remind me that there's a premium on haunted real estate, at least among some people.

"See, Matt, nothing's going to hurt you," I said. "Miss Mary just wants you to be warm and comfy."

Matt gripped my arm. Eyes wide, he nodded toward a shadowy nook where a woman sat on a fringed bench. Her hair was short and bobbed, and she was dressed in a cloche hat and coat from the 1920s.

"It's a ghost," Matt breathed, ducking his head as though afraid the spirit would read his lips. "I can't believe it; it's sitting right here. Am I the only one who can see it? I'm looking at . . . a *ghost*!"

As I watched, a young man walked up to the woman and handed her a steaming teacup. They exchanged pleasantries.

"Seems your ghost is on a date. No wonder it's hard to find an eligible bachelor in this town." But I breathed a quick sigh of relief. For a moment there, Matt had me going. "She's just wearing an old-fashioned hat, is all."

"Oh. Well, she could have been a ghost."

"I need a drink," I said.

"Me, too. Too bad I don't drink anymore."

"It's a moot point anyway, since there's no bar. And I forgot to slip my flask into my garter before leaving home."

"You wear garters?"

"No. But then, I'm not a ghost." I poured two cups of tea from the urn by the fireplace.

"With your outfits I wouldn't put it past you," said Matt, helping himself to an oatmeal chocolate chip cookie from a delft platter. He pointed toward an old-fashioned doll propped in the corner. She wore a bonnet and crinolines, and stood about three feet tall, her green glass eyes staring into space. "Now *that's* scary."

"Gotta agree with you there," I said.

The woman behind the reception desk announced that everyone waiting for the ghost tour should congregate in the dining room. We funneled in and sat at round tables in the otherwise empty room. Most in attendance appeared to be out-of-town tourists. There was a group of giggling college-age women, two middle-aged couples, a father with his teenaged son, and a young couple from Australia, with the cool affects and clothes of world travelers, talking about the spirits they had seen in Thailand and Quebec.

The lights went out, plunging us into darkness. When they returned a few seconds later, our host stood in front of us dressed in a vintage green velvet coat over a vest and breeches. Black boots and an old-fashioned lantern completed the costume. He was more interesting-looking than handsome, with blue-green eyes and dark hair buzzed close to the skull.

"Welcome to the world-famous San Francisco Ghost Walk!"

Olivier had a great voice, deep and resonant, and he spoke with a lovely French accent. Perfect for storytelling. But the community-theater aspect of the evening was already embarrassing me. I'm not what you'd call big on public scenes.

After spinning a few tales of ghostly goings-on in the neighborhood, our tour guide went over a few logistical issues, then recapped the story of Miss Mary Lake's supposed haunting of Eastlake Hotel. Olivier did his best to get us in the mood, warning us that some people do see spirits when they're on the tour, though "most likely they won't appear, since they prefer to come to people who are alone."

"Very convenient," I whispered to Matt.

"Be nice," Matt whispered in return. "For all you know he'll be the next Mr. Mel Turner."

Before beginning our outdoor ghost walk, Olivier led the way up the three flights of stairs to the room of the former headmistress, Miss Mary Lake. Matt and I caught up with him by the second story.

"Olivier, remember me? Matt Addax, from the TV filming?"

"Of course! I am so happy to see you here!" said Olivier. "But I thought you were afraid of ghosts?"

"I brought a very brave friend along. She swears she'll protect me. Mel Turner, this is Olivier Galopin."

"So nice to meet you—Mel? Unusual name."

"It's a nickname," I said before Matt could tell him my full name was Melanie. I've never felt like a Melanie.

"It is a pleasure. And now we have arrived at Miss Mary Lake's bedroom." Olivier turned and addressed the group. "Please remember that Miss Mary is a friendly ghost. Let us all gather within and remain very still, and if you are sensitive, perhaps you will feel vibrations from beyond, or a cold spot."

We all shuffled into the small but gracious room, beautifully furnished in antiques of the era.

"I definitely feel something," said the Australian woman.

"Do you consider yourself sensitive?" Olivier asked.

"Oh yes." She nodded enthusiastically.

"Are we allowed to take photos?" asked the man with her. "I reckon they'd show orbs."

"Of course," said Olivier. "Feel free. And if they do show orbs, which are a sign of spirits present, please e-mail them to me so we can put them up on the Web site."

Most in the group seemed so earnest and . . . gullible . . . that I found it hard not to roll my eyes. Since my experience at Matt's house six months ago, I had come to believe in the existence of spirits from a different dimension. But this tour felt like nothing more than making money off the titillation provided by the idea of a ghostly presence. I supposed there were worse ways to make money, but it felt unseemly, somehow.

Things improved as we left the hotel and walked the neighborhood. Olivier spun a fascinating tale, and clearly knew a lot about San Francisco history. We heard about scandals and tragedies, and numerous possible spirits and hauntings. Finally we paused outside two houses connected by a breezeway that belonged to sis-

ters who grew to hate each other. Olivier told us a lunatic cousin had been kept in the attic but broke out one
day and killed a woman visiting in the front parlor. The
houses operated as a hotel for a while, but the guests
complained of horrifying apparitions.

"Now, though, we must only look at it from this side
of the street, for the current owner does not like the fact
that he is a stop on the famous Ghost Walk tour."

The crowd tut-tutted their disappointment, but I sym-
pathized with the homeowner. I could imagine spending
millions on a house only to have the local ghost groupies
hang out in front, oohing and aahing and talking about
lunatic murderers and lingering spirits.

"I found this key in an antique store, and the amazing
thing is that it once belonged to this very house. Now, if
you hold it in your flat palm, it will sometimes move toward
the house."

The group gathered in a circle around Olivier, watching intently, hoping to see the key turning in his palm.

"How does he know the key belonged to this building?" I whispered to Matt. "It's an old skeleton key. I
have a dozen of them at home, and a few in my satchel."

"Because he's psychic?" suggested Matt.

"And why would a key point to a building, anyway?"

"Because he's pushing it?"

I smiled.

"It's a nice night for a walk, in any case," said Matt,
lifting his face to the stars. "Except that it's flipping
freezing out here."

Several stops later we circled back to the Eastlake
Hotel. Matt and I hung around until the crowd dispersed.

Olivier met my eyes, and gave me a small, ironic
smile.

"I take it you're not a believer?" he said.

"What makes you say that?"

"You rolled your eyes with every story I told."

I blushed. "I'm sorry; that was rude. I didn't mean to make you feel—"

He gave a very Gallic shrug. "Not a day goes by that someone doesn't denigrate me. Comes with the territory."

"I wouldn't say I was denigrating you."

"What would you call it then?"

"Sincere skepticism."

He laughed. It sounded genuine, and the twinkle in his blue-green eyes was hard to dismiss. He wasn't all that good-looking, but there was something about him . . . probably that voice.

"But I must ask: Why take my tour?"

"I was hoping to ask you a few questions, in private. The ghost society referred me to you. Could I buy you a drink, or hire you for an hour or something?"

"Hire me?"

He looked surprised, and I was afraid he misunderstood.

"I'd like some advice and I'm happy to pay for it. That's all I'm saying. . . ."

"Mel and I want to take you for a drink," Matt interrupted. "She wants to ask you some questions about ghosts."

Olivier nodded, looking intrigued. "I would love to take a glass with you. There's a nice bar on the corner. *Allons-y.* Let's go."

The lounge was upscale and mellow, a slight murmur from the patrons vying with a recording of Nat King Cole crooning "The Very Thought of You."

We scooted into a plush upholstered booth.

To my surprise, Olivier ordered not wine but a tumbler of Macallan, a single malt scotch. Suddenly that seemed like a great idea, so I followed suit. Matt ordered a Sprite. Olivier raised his eyebrows at Matt's order, but said nothing.

"You know your scotch, I see," I said to him.

"It is in my blood. My mother was Scots, my father French. I'm a Channel baby."

"Wouldn't that be a 'Chunnel' baby?" I asked.

Olivier laughed, and looked from me to Matt.

"Just FYI, Mel and I aren't together," Matt said.

"Matt's friends call him Mr. Subtle," I said.

"Ah?" Olivier said, looking confused.

"Mel and I are strictly platonic friends. Though I'm half in love with her, like all the men she knows. And you, Olivier, are you married?"

Olivier smiled, but didn't answer. Instead, he looked me in the eye and held my gaze, the way European men do. It made me nervous. I became fascinated by the amber depths of my scotch.

"Coincidentally, Mel's been planning to move to France," Matt said.

I felt myself blush. Though I kept insisting that was my plan, the more it became widely known, the more embarrassing it felt that I didn't either up and leave, or drop the whole thing.

"Is that right?" Olivier asked. "Which part?"

"Paris."

"A beautiful city, but of course I must love it, because I am French. Though myself, I am from Normandy. What will you do there in Paris, Mel?"

"Nothing much. No definite plans, I mean. I thought

I'd find a cheap apartment somewhere on the Left Bank and just hang out for a while."

"I hate to tell you this, but the Left Bank has been 'discovered.' I'm not sure you could find anything cheap there these days."

I shrugged. "At the rate I'm going, I won't get there until it's fallen out of favor again, anyway. Guess I'll cross that *pont* when I get to it."

"Oh!" said Matt as he scooted out of the booth. "I just remembered something I have to do. So sorry to leave you two alone. Have fun without me." With an obvious wink to me, he abandoned his Sprite and hurried out the door.

"I apologize for Matt," I said to Olivier. "I don't know how well you know him, but his enthusiasm tends to overwhelm his good sense."

Olivier smiled. "He's charming. So, Mel, what can I help you with?"

I leaned toward him and spoke in a low voice.

"When you said earlier that I wasn't a believer . . . That's not entirely true."

Chapter Nineteen

"No?"

"I've seen things that convinced me there are, in fact, people . . . or beings . . . or whatever, on some different plane maybe, and they visit us. . . ." I stumbled over my words. I didn't have the ghost lingo down.

"What have you seen?"

"Some months ago I saw an apparition of an acquaintance who had recently died. But once I got over the shock of it, he didn't try to harm me in any way. He was confused . . . and annoying, to tell the truth."

Olivier nodded and sipped his scotch. "That's typical, actually. It is only human to react with fear, but most spirits aren't out to hurt us."

I wasn't quite so sanguine about the brief, odd glimpses and sensations I'd had from the ghosts in Cheshire House.

"But now I'm working in a house where there's something . . . wrong. I can feel it."

"What has happened?"

"It started out with things going wrong as the house undergoes renovations. Handprints appearing on the ceiling; equipment starting of its own accord; things being moved. Rusty old dead bolts that lock and unlock by themselves. And earlier today, I thought I heard whispers behind a wall. And then someone was hurt falling off a ladder, and my toolbox was pushed off a ledge. It barely missed hitting me on the head."

Olivier frowned, shook his head, and took a sip of scotch. "That sounds more like an unhappy human than a spirit. It is rare for a ghost to attack someone, and it's difficult for them to manipulate physical items."

I nodded. "I haven't completely ruled out human mischief. But in the closet in the attic, where I thought I heard whispers, I saw something written on the wooden panel that serves as a door: *Memento mori*. Do you know what that means?"

"'Remember you must die.' Or 'remember to die.' Depending on your interpretation."

"That sounds like a threat."

"Not at all. It used to be a common inscription on tombstones and that sort of thing. Have you seen any actual apparitions in the house?"

"I saw footprints in the dust right in front of me, as if someone was walking toward me. And a figure in a mirror. But the worst is a dark, amorphous figure, like a shadow or black cloud. The woman of the house says it hovers over her shoulder sometimes when she tries to enter the baby's room."

Olivier's nostrils flared slightly as he inhaled deeply, nodded, and released the breath.

"What do you feel when you are in the presence of this shadow?"

"Rage. Fear. Even . . . desire, lust. I didn't feel this way with the first ghost I met, at least once I got over the shock. This time it's . . . more disturbing."

A group of twentysomething hipsters started laughing loudly in the next booth, their rambunctiousness seemingly at odds with the subdued tone of the lounge. Olivier leaned toward me and spoke in a low voice.

"What you are describing sounds like a shadow ghost. They appear darker than their surrounds, and are often experienced as a barely-there figure, or a column of smoke."

Great. I was already searching my peripheral vision; now I had to scope out shadows for something darker than dark?

"Some believe they are more dangerous than other ghosts, that they remain in the shadows out of guilt, or shame, or the fear of being revealed. What you may be feeling is this fear, this shame."

"How are they different from other ghosts?"

"Many spirits are trying to reveal themselves, which is what allows sensitive people to see them from time to time. It is why you saw your friend before. They may need something from us, or may simply not understand where they are and what is happening. And so they wish to interact with the living. But shadow forms . . ." He took another sip of scotch, sat back, and shook his head. "They're usually not benevolent."

"Can they actually hurt us? Or do they just make us so jumpy that we end up hurting ourselves? I mean . . . how can something immaterial, ghostly, affect the material world?"

"Do not discount the power of emotions. You have no doubt heard of people who, when faced with a grave crisis, find strength they do not normally possess? A mother seeking to rescue her child, suddenly able to lift a heavy weight?"

"Sure. The fight-or-flight response to threat. The mother's body releases adrenaline when she sees her child in danger, and it pumps up her muscles. But a ghost doesn't have either muscles or adrenaline."

"Of course it does not. But, Mel, it is the mother's *emotions* that release the adrenaline, yes? What if that emotion had no body to be released into, to channel it? Who knows what effect it might have on the surrounding physical world?"

"Wow. I . . . I guess that makes sense."

The increasingly raucous group at the next table called to the waitress for another round, making me realize I had gulped down my scotch. I contemplated ordering another, but I was driving. And considering the circumstances, it was probably best if I kept my wits about me.

"This sounds silly, but could ghosts have been responsible for a murder across the street from where they usually live—er—reside? A man was shot."

"Ghosts don't shoot people. However, a powerful ghost might inspire someone to shoot someone else."

"Are you talking about . . . possession?"

He gave a one-shouldered shrug, sticking his chin out slightly. "Not in the way it's portrayed in movies. It's more that their emotions can influence others, particularly if a situation reminds them of a critical time in their own lives. They sort of . . . what is the word . . . pigbacky?"

"Piggyback?"

"Yes, piggyback on the living person, enhancing the living person's guilt or anger. Or even lust, desire, jealousy."

That sounded bad. Really, really bad. I didn't want to think too hard about what had happened in the attic with Graham.

"So how do I get rid of them? My client says she lit sage and asked them to go, but now it seems worse than before. I . . . I know this is asking a lot, but would you be willing to come to the house, see what you can see?"

"I would be honored." He held my gaze again, sipped his scotch, gave me a crooked smile.

Is he flirting with me?

"I will have to charge you a small fee, I'm afraid."

Strike that. He was just happy to meet another sucker he could soak for money. "I'll talk to the owners, make sure it's okay with them."

He nodded. "May I ask you a sincere question, Mel?"

"Shoot." I signaled the waitress for the check.

"Why are you so worried about this? It is not your home being haunted."

"It's my job site." *Duh.* "And it's just plain wrong."

"Ah, you are very American!" He smiled. "You think everything should be sweetness and light all the time. But that is not life. If you move to France you must embrace your dark side. There is beauty and romance in the darkness, no?"

I wondered if I could leave Jim and Katenka with that insight. *"No worries,"* I'd tell them as the black cloud appeared and footsteps marched across the floor. *"Just embrace the beauty of the dark side!"* Then again, I imagined Katenka was no stranger to the "life is pain and then you die" school of thought.

Feeling a headache coming on, I sighed and rubbed my temples.

"Headache? Allow me," Olivier said. He reached across

the table and encircled my head with his large hands, his thumbs on my forehead, the fingertips holding the back of my neck, at the base of my skull. He pressed hard, rubbing slightly. I studied his face; his eyes were closed.

After a few moments the ache receded, just like that. He sat back and smiled. "Better?"

I nodded. "What are you, a healer of some kind?"

He laughed. "It's a trick my mother used on me when I was a child. It only works if you catch the headache when first it starts."

"Well, thanks. And thanks for your time, as well. I'd better get going."

Olivier insisted on walking me to my car. The fog had rolled in, thick and cold. A foghorn sounded in the background, low and mournful.

"Have you eaten?" he asked as we walked.

"I, uh . . . had a samosa from the lunch truck on the way here."

"*Bof!* That is not dinner. You need real food to function properly, especially if you are to have the fortitude to go up against ghosts, no? Yesterday I made an amazing osso buco. Do you cook?"

I shook my head. "My dad's the cook in our family."

"Ah, this is how it should be."

"You and my dad would get along. He insists the best chefs in the world are men."

"I did not mean that in a sexist way. I meant only that cooking is the least we can do, since the women do so much more."

"Uh-huh," I said, unconvinced.

"At least I believe it is true for the French. Cooking a beautiful meal, awakening the senses through taste and aroma, is a wonderful way to please a woman."

"In America we say that the way to a man's heart is through his stomach."

"Perhaps so. But I am not interested in men."

"This is me," I said as we arrived at my boxy Scion. "Oh, what's the best way to get in touch with you? Your answering machine doesn't take messages."

He pulled out a business card and wrote a phone number on the back in curvy, French-style writing, then handed it to me.

"I'm available tomorrow night. Nighttime is better, because the vibrations are clearer." He gazed at me for a long moment, the streetlight bathing the planes of his face in an amber glow. "Perhaps together we will vanquish these ghosts, and find you and your friends some peace, yes? And then I will cook for you."

The jury was still out on that last part.

"Thanks again, Olivier."

"I will see you soon, then. I look forward to your call."

"Hey!" the homeless man shouted at me the next morning as I walked toward Cheshire House. "You're the one who yelled at Blunt the night he died, right?" He was sitting on the sidewalk in front of Emile's shop, his back against the wall below the grimy display window.

"Um . . . yes," I said, blushing. It wasn't among my proudest moments.

"Some lady just threw me outta the doorway. Why can't I sit in the doorway? Man's already dead—what does he care?"

"Who threw you out? The inspector?"

He shook his head. "Old lady. She's in there now."

The crime-scene tape was torn and hung limply on

either side of the shop door, waving lazily in the light breeze. Last night's fog had become this morning's deep mist, and the mournful foghorn lent a mysterious note to the scene.

Stepping over the cracked mosaic at the entrance of Emile's shop, I pushed on the door, which was slightly ajar. I recognized the old woman inside the shop.

"Hettie? What are you doing here?"

"This here's my place now."

Chapter Twenty

"Your place?"

"That's right. Emile left it to me in his will. Don't that beat all? Maybe I'll hire you to fix it up for me."

"I'm . . . surprised," I said, recalling what Janet had said about Hettie and Emile. It was hard to imagine them being amorous toward anyone, much less each other, but as I kept reminding myself, I was no expert in the ways of love.

Heck, I was no amateur in the ways of love, either.

"Will you look around with me?" Hettie asked, tucking a big black patent leather pocketbook securely under her arm. The formality of the purse contrasted sharply with her oversized T-shirt. This one was black with bold yellow lettering, and advertised a local supermarket chain. "I'm afraid the ghosts will figure out I'm here and come on over. Or do you think they're stuck in Cheshire House? But then, if they're stuck there, how'd they kill Emile?"

"I, uh, really don't know." I thought of last summer's apparition. He hadn't been limited to one location, that's for sure.

I glanced around the shop. It felt strange to be here, on the site of a murder.

Dozens of footprints and scuff marks, no doubt belonging to emergency personnel, were visible in the thick film of lint and dirt on the ugly linoleum. The crime scene itself had been cleaned of blood. The seven-by-four-foot patch was the only clean spot in the room.

I felt a pang of sadness. Curmudgeon or not, Emile didn't deserve to die like this.

"Hettie, the last time we talked you didn't sound very fond of Emile. And frankly, he didn't exactly speak of you in glowing terms, either. Why would he leave his place to you?"

"We go way back."

I waited for more. Looked like I had a long wait.

"I guess he could leave it to whoever he wanted to," Hettie finally said, peering into the cupboards along one wall.

I noticed white hair on one side of the burgundy moiré sofa. I remembered Emile telling me he didn't keep cats because of the risk of getting fur on the furniture. So where had this hair come from?

"Were you here that night, Hettie?"

"What night?"

"The night Emile was killed? Did you stop by to see him?"

"I don't know what you're talking about." She played with her dentures a minute. "Place is a dump anyway. Not much of value here." She pointed to the stuffed cat I'd noticed on my previous visit to Emile's shop. "Maybe

I'll take the cat, at least, give it a proper burial. Never did like how he did that, stuffed them. Why'd someone want to do that to a kitty?"

"I think he meant well by it," I said halfheartedly. Then I noticed that the cat's rhinestone collar, the one that held the charm, was no longer around his neck.

"Have you taken anything from here?"

She looked surprised. "No."

"Because the shop's not yours yet, you know. The police have to release the crime scene, and then the actual transfer of ownership will take a while."

"I know that. Wasn't born yesterday, you know. I just wanted to see if it was worth anything, is all. Maybe I'll do what I did before, and donate it to the shelter. That way I don't have to mess with it. And I don't want to deal with any more ghosts, anyway."

"Hettie, I wanted to ask you something. The other day you mentioned one of your former boarders, Dave Enrique? Remember?"

Hettie nodded.

"What was his relationship to Janet? Or Emile's for that matter? Janet mentioned that Emile took something from her."

"I don't know anything about that."

"No idea what went on that time up in the attic?"

Hettie smoothed her T-shirt, and poked her dentures with her tongue. "I expect it wasn't anything good. Grown men and a young girl. After that Janet seemed different, changed. I sent her to live with her daddy after that. Better that way."

When we left, the homeless man was still sitting on the sidewalk, talking to himself.

"Got a dollar for the hobo?" Hettie asked.

"I'm not sure 'hobo' is the best term. . . ." I said out of the side of my mouth as I scrounged in my satchel for a dollar.

"Actually, I prefer 'hobo,' come to think of it," the man said with a lopsided smile. "Sounds more adventurous, doesn't it? I'm not lacking a home; I'm on a grand adventure." He pulled a fifth of some kind of liquor out of his coat pocket. "Bon voyage to me!"

As we left, we heard the man singing to himself.

"Ever notice how now that regular folks walk around with their phones in their ears, talking out loud 'bout this and that, the crazies on the street don't seem so crazy?" said Hettie. "You gave that feller some clean clothes and . . . maybe a chair to sit on instead of that piece of old cardboard, and people'd assume he's talkin' to his stockbroker 'stead o' being nuts."

"You might be right," I mused. Seemed like a social experiment worthy of one of Luz's graduate students.

I walked Hettie to her car, a dented avocado-green gas guzzler that must have dated back to the seventies.

"You think you could fix the place up for me, I decide to keep it?" Hettie asked as she climbed in.

I paused. The truth was the building didn't call to me, and besides, I wasn't sure how much time I wanted to spend with Hettie the cat lady. And anyway, where would she get the money to fix it up? In my business I had to make quick judgment calls about clients' ability to pay, and my ability to work with them. Hettie failed on both counts.

"Why don't we cross that bridge when we come to it?" I said as I closed her door for her. "Give your cats a squeeze from me."

She laughed, a kind of hoarse chuckle. "Will do, lady builder. That much, I can do."

Hettie fired up the car's engine and roared off, her driving style as unrestrained as her personality. She flapped one arm out the window, waving good-bye, and screeched around the corner, narrowly missing a stop sign.

Time to go back to work.

But . . . Emile's place was wide-open. What could it hurt to have a more thorough look around? I didn't know what I was looking for, but maybe I would discover something that would connect Emile's murder with the ghostly goings-on across the street. Inspector Crawford probably wouldn't approve but . . . I promised myself I'd be extra careful not to interfere with any possible evidence, and headed into the shop.

I didn't see anything else out of the ordinary, except for the hair on the sofa. That bothered me. I noticed a pad on Emile's desk. *K. Daley, 2 pm* was written in blue ink, but there wasn't anything suspicious about that. Katenka mentioned to me that she was going to have him reupholster her settee.

Had this really been a simple break-in that had turned lethal? Could Emile's spirit be hanging around, angry that his life ended so horribly?

If so, perhaps I could communicate with him. Then I wondered if I *wanted* to communicate with Emile. I hadn't liked him when he was alive. Why would I like him any better as a mad-as-hell ghost? And if I did manage to reach him, could he even tell me what had happened? Did I want to hear it?

Impatient with my own doubts, I forced myself to stand on the clean spot, where Emile had died. I took a deep breath, focused, and called to Emile with my mind. I waited.

Nothing. No tingle at the back of my neck, no sensation of being watched. All I felt was depressed.

The shop was quiet as a tomb. I took in the mess, the gloom, the gazes of forlorn creatures. *Reason #348 why I don't want to be a taxidermist: The risk of spending my last moments on earth like Emile, prone and injured, surrounded by dead animals, their glass eyes unblinking, hungry . . . vengeful.*

I squeezed my eyes shut, cursing my overactive imagination.

"You are *so* busted," a voice said from the vicinity of the door.

"*Graham!* You scared the *daylights* out of me!" I clapped my hand over my heart in a dramatic gesture. "I swear: you're committed to giving me a heart attack."

He remained in the doorway. "Maybe you're jumpy because you're snooping around a crime scene where you have no right to be. Come on out, before you get busted for breaking and entering."

"I have a right to be here," I insisted, but I joined him at the door. "Sort of."

Graham just raised his eyebrows.

"Hettie Banks says she inherited this place, and she might hire me to redo it."

"Does she have that kind of money?"

"Not to my knowledge," I admitted as we left the shop and I closed the door behind us. "Anyway, the crime-scene tape's down."

"She probably took it down herself. Doesn't mean you can go poking around someone else's property."

"I just . . ." As we crossed the street toward Cheshire

House, I wondered whether I should tell him the truth, that I was trying to conjure Emile's ghost. That sounded crazy, though, didn't it? "I was wondering if Emile's death might be linked to the strange things going on at the Daleys."

"Linked how?"

"I have no idea. But I . . . I seem to have some sort of connection to these . . . entities. Spirits. Whatever."

"So you *did* see a ghost."

"Maybe."

Graham leaned back against his truck and crossed his arms over his chest. I could see his jaw clench, but he said nothing.

"What," I pushed, "are you going to pretend you didn't feel something up in that attic?"

"I felt something—that's for sure." His gaze flickered over the length of me, then returned to mine. When he spoke again, his voice was very quiet. "I felt like kissing you. And a whole lot more."

"I . . . I think maybe the ghosts sensed something between us and piggybacked on our emotions, ratcheted things up."

"Or maybe it was just high time I kissed you."

I swallowed, hard, and tried to keep my mind on the supernatural, rather than the very real chemistry I felt whenever I was anywhere in the vicinity of this man. "I think it had more to do with ghosts than with . . . with you and me. It was like they took control of our conversation, remember?"

"Okay," he said. "For the sake of argument let's put aside everything science has taught us for the past century and pretend you can talk to the dearly departed. What makes you think you're qualified to deal with them?"

"Who else is there?"

"Surely there's someone who knows more than you about this sort of thing."

"I'm working on it. I met a guy last night who might be able to help. He leads ghost tours out of the Eastlake Hotel. If Katenka agrees to hire him, he'll come take a look at the house."

Graham let out an exasperated breath and pinched the bridge of his nose as though fighting off a sudden headache.

"Olivier something? French guy?"

"You know him?"

"He came to Matt's house once, shadowed the film crew. He's an actor, Mel, out to fleece the tourists. Get serious."

"If you have any other suggestions, I'm all ears. I'm skeptical of Olivier, too, but what are my options? There's something strange—and maybe dangerous— going on with this house. I don't know if I'm supposed to find a priest to conduct an exorcism, or contact a Mexican *limpiadora*, or what. But I need help, and it's not like there's a section for 'ghost busting' in the Yellow Pages."

"Have you looked?" Graham smiled. "This is the Bay Area, you know."

Actually, I hadn't. I ignored this. "I've seen things, Graham. I can't pretend I haven't."

"That's what worries me. If this is true . . . Has it occurred to you that you stir them up? Maybe if they couldn't sense that you can see them, they'd go away."

"And how do you propose I do that? Spray myself down with a can of Ghost-B-Gone?"

Graham didn't answer for a moment. I avoided his eyes, but I could feel him studying me.

"I've never thought of you as a woo-woo Berkeley type," he said at last.

"I'm not." I shrugged. "But ever since what happened at Matt's place, and even before that, with my mother . . . let's just say that I have a whole lot of questions and not many answers. At the very least I keep my mind open."

He nodded. "Listen, I hate to change the subject, but Elena's inside talking to Katenka about the party. I saw you going into the crime scene when I pulled up, and figured you might want a say in the matter."

"Graham, seriously, can't you use your masculine wiles to put a stop to this stupid party?"

"Sorry. Must've left my wiles in my other truck."

We found Elena and Katenka in the kitchen laughing like old friends as they pored over Elena's portfolio and a stack of design magazines. Smiling and talking, wearing a floaty yellow dress, Katenka looked like a girl, perfectly at ease. She never acted like that around me, I noted sourly. Katenka wasn't my favorite person, either, but at times like this it struck me that being able to make a perfect miter cut didn't make up for all the things I was bad at.

"Mel!" said Jim, the baby in his Snugli kicking his legs. "Glad you're here. Graham and I wanted to include you in our discussion about some of the green techniques we'd like to incorporate into the house."

And why did I always get stuck talking with the men? How come the men never huddled in the kitchen talking about party favors while the women were designing the solar heating system? But then I might as well ask why I was one of only a handful of female general contractors in the Bay Area, arguably one of the least sexist places on earth.

"How's the design coming?" I asked the men.

"Jim and I have come up with a plan. I'd like to go over it with you in detail, when you have a chance," Graham said. Was it my imagination, or did his eyes rest on me just a little too long?

"Sure," I said. The idea of "going over designs" with Graham, just the two of us, was very distracting.

"Mel, what you think?" Katenka asked.

"About what again? Sorry, I lost track of the conversation."

"For the party, we'd like to have things more or less like they are now," Elena answered. "Would it be a problem to work on another part of the house for a while and leave this area pretty much as is?"

I felt the words bubble up, tried to suppress them, and failed.

"Want me to take out everything we've spent the past three months on, make it look like it used to?"

"Oh, I don't think that's necessary, do you?" Elena said.

Katenka might not be fluent in English, but she sure spoke body language.

"Is joke," Katenka said to Elena, her tone conciliatory.

"Besides," Elena continued, "that would be prohibitively expensive, don't you think? There's no call for such a thing for a baby's birthday. Unless, of course, you'd like to, Katenka."

I felt Graham's hand on my shoulder, giving it a squeeze.

Elena continued, oblivious. "Or do you think you

could have the place done for the party? I know! If you can finish up within the week, we could go the other way, have a lovely Victorian-themed tea party with lace ta-blecloths and cucumber sandwiches—"

"We're three months into a six-month rehab, Elena," I said through gritted teeth. "We can't 'finish up' in a week."

"Oh, I see," she said, gathering together her portfolio. "That's fine, just fine. I'll figure something out."

Katenka was avoiding my eyes. I thought of how happy and easygoing the two women had seemed before I arrived on the scene. *Make an effort, Mel, or you'll become as churlish as Emile Blunt, the pooper of every party.*

"I'm sorry, Elena. Why don't you and I go into the front room and you can explain what you have in mind. I'm sure I can find a way to work with whatever Katenka wants."

Jim and Graham beamed at me approvingly, and I had to stifle the desire to do something with a nearby rotary sander that would violate numerous safety regulations.

"One problem is the kitchen," Elena said as we went into the front parlor. "The caterer simply can't cook in the kitchen the way it is."

"We could expedite delivery of the new stove and in-stall it, if necessary. But it doesn't make sense to change out the counters yet, as the new cabinets aren't finished. What will you be cooking?"

"Katenka tells me the Tree party traditional meal is an apple-stuffed goose, sausages, mayo-based salads, salted fish, cheese, caviar."

"Seriously? This is a birthday party for a one-year-old

child, right?" I glanced over at Katenka, thinking she should be in on the menu planning. But she, Jim, and Graham were discussing something, heads together as though in a huddle.

"Parties for children this age are more for the adults than for the children," Elena said.

"Okay . . . but what are the children going to eat?"

"Mel, I appreciate the concern, but why don't you concentrate on what you do, and I'll take care of the party planning. I've found a wonderful caterer who specializes in the traditional salads, which include dill, peas, carrots, and potatoes. Lots of mayo, I'm sorry to say. And *kalach* sweet bread, and *sbiten*, which is a hot honey drink with herbs."

Once again I looked over to Katenka, hoping to catch her eye. What were the three of them talking about so intently?

"Babies aren't supposed to eat honey," I said. "Because of the allergies. Or something."

"Do you have children, Mel?"

"A son."

"Caleb? I thought he was your stepson."

"He is, yes."

"And you were with him since he was a baby?"

"No, but I can read. And babies aren't supposed to eat honey."

Jim's angry voice floated over to us.

"Get your hands off her."

Chapter Twenty-one

Katenka was resting her hand on Graham's forearm as she leaned in to ask him a question.

She looked at Jim, guilt in her big hazel eyes. What did she have to feel guilty about? I might be a failure at male-female relations and not have a clue about the workings of a man's mind, but I knew one thing with great certainty: Graham was not fooling around with this wisp of a Russian.

"*Jim*. Don't make scene."

"Jim, I wasn't—" Graham began.

"I know what I saw," Jim said, jutting his chest out and glaring at Graham. "She's a beautiful woman—it's no surprise. But understand this: You ever get any closer to her and I'll make you regret it, hear me?"

Graham nodded, calm and composed, as though pondering a mathematics problem. "Of course I do, Jim. How about we go outside for a minute, talk in private?"

After a tense moment, Jim relaxed, ran a hand

through his hair, and blew out a breath. "I'm sorry, I . . . I must have overreacted. I haven't been sleeping well lately."

"I hear a baby'll do that to you," Graham said.

Jim gave a rather mirthless chuckle. "Yeah, I guess so. Hey, no hard feelings? I'm really sorry . . . I apologize."

"No problem," said Graham, shaking his hand. "Mel, shall I stop by tonight after work to go over the solar design plans?"

I checked my BlackBerry. "Make it a little on the later side, okay? Seven?"

"See you then," he said, and he and Elena left.

Jim muttered something about changing the baby and went downstairs.

"I don't know what gets into him," Katenka said, watching her husband retreat. "He get like that sometimes, jealous."

"Was he always like that?"

"A little. He seems very easygoing, so it's surprising. But you should see the men in the town I come from — they are crazy jealous." She smiled, just a wee bit pleased.

"Katenka, has Jim been spending any time up in the attic?"

She nodded. "He was looking around up there last week — he found some letters. He showed them to me."

"What letters?"

"Love letters, very old." Her nose wrinkled. "Dusty. Maybe from people who live here before. They are hard to read, but Jim is trying."

"Could I see them?"

"Jim has them somewhere."

"Will you try to convince him to let me take a look at them?"

"Okay. Anyway, I think party will help," Katenka said. "With the . . . entities."

"Nice word."

"I learn it in class yesterday." Katenka was taking English as a Second Language at City College. "Is good word. Useful."

Is it ever. "Katenka, did Emile speak Russian?"

"Oh, a little. *Terrible* accent." She shook her head. It seemed a bit cheeky of her, considering her own strong accent in English. Katenka's language skills had improved considerably in the short time I'd known her, but she still sounded as though she were swallowing all the vowels at the back of her throat, and her "th" sound was a decided "ze."

"And he spoke to you about selling the house to him?"

"He was to redo this settee." She gestured to the horsehair. "So, you think maybe the party will frighten the ghosts away?"

"I wish I could say. It's possible the activity will stir them up more." I would just have to be darned sure no one ventured into the attic. These ghosts were not exactly standard party entertainment. I was pretty sure even Elena would agree with me on that one.

"Last night I met someone who knows a lot more about ghosts than I do," I said. "He agreed to come check out the house, for a fee, if you agree."

"I cannot let Jim find out," Katenka said. "But I would like this person to come, yes. I do not care about the cost. Sooner, the better."

"I'll arrange it."

"If he come tonight, it would be perfect," said Katenka.

"Have you been seeing something?"

"Not since you were here. But . . . Jim is out tonight."

She seemed to be holding back. "What is it, Katenka?"

She bit her lip and played with the medallion around her neck. "The more he reads those letters, it is like he can't stop thinking about this place. Like he is . . . how you say? Owned?"

"Do you mean possessed?"

She nodded.

"Yes. *Possessed*."

With Raul off the job, it fell to me to touch base with all the subcontractors to be sure everyone was still on schedule. First I caught up with the carpenters building bookshelves in the library, and the painters finishing up stripping and sanding. Then I signed off on the workers' time cards and checked on the plumber's final work.

But however busy I was, I couldn't shake the idea that I should inform the police of the details I noticed this morning while I was in Emile's shop.

After some deliberation, I found Inspector Annette Crawford's business card and gave her a call.

"This is Mel Turner, the general contractor across the street from Emile Blunt's upholstery shop."

"Yes, Ms. Turner. Do you have some information for me?"

"Possibly . . . could I ask, is it true Blunt left his building to Hettie Banks?"

"Who told you that?"

"Hettie."

"You sound surprised," Inspector Crawford said.

"I am."

She waited.

"It just seems strange. The last time I talked to Emile he referred to Hettie as 'that crazy cat lady.' And she spoke of Emile with about the same degree of fondness."

"It happens," the inspector said, and I could almost see her shrug. "According to Banks, she and Blunt were close at one time. Maybe he never got around to changing his will. Is this why you're calling me?"

"No. I was wondering, did you notice white hair on the sofa in Emile's shop? Cat hair, maybe?"

"What about it?"

"It wasn't there earlier in the day, when I was in his shop."

"Are you sure? Would you remember a detail like that?"

"I think so, yes. Emile told me he couldn't have a cat because he had to keep hair off the reupholstered furniture."

"Maybe a customer who came in later transferred the hair to the sofa. We see that all the time."

"Maybe. But I also noticed that a rhinestone collar from the stuffed cat is missing."

"It sounds like maybe you were wandering around my crime scene. Ms. Turner, I sincerely hope you haven't been wandering around my crime scene."

"I . . . uh . . . ran into Hettie Banks, and she asked me to go in with her," I fudged. "She said the police tape was down and she was inheriting the place, so it was okay."

"Uh-huh. Trust me, it's not okay."

"I'm sorry. But I thought you should know about the hair, and the collar. It seemed important."

"As a matter of fact, forensics took a sample of the hair on the sofa as part of the investigation. But it's good to know it wasn't there earlier. And I'll make a note of the missing rhinestone cat collar."

"One more thing?" I said. "Who dug up the yard, and why?"

"Someone dug up Emile Blunt's yard? Did he even *have* a yard?"

"No, sorry. I'm talking about Hettie Bank's old house across the street. The house I'm working on."

"Is this related to my crime scene?"

"Not in so many words . . ."

"Then how do you expect me to know, and why would I care?"

"Someone dug up Hettie's old yard to disinter cat corpses."

"And . . . ?"

"I have a feeling Emile's murder is connected with the strange events at Cheshire House. With the . . . ghosts."

"Ghosts."

"Yes." I waited. "Inspector?"

"I know this is wacky San Francisco and all, but I don't do ghosts, Ms. Turner. I solve crimes the old-fashioned way. I appreciate your interest in the case; if you learn anything relevant, give me a call back. But please, don't hassle me about ghosts or UFOs or anything else of that ilk. Get me?"

I was glad we weren't talking face-to-face, so the inspector couldn't see how my cheeks were burning.

"Yes, Inspector. Thank you for your time— Oh! One last thing? Is my dad still under suspicion?"

"He's a person of interest. No one's ruled out until we make our case. That goes for you as well, Ms. Turner."

Next I called Olivier Galopin, who agreed to come

over at six. Then I checked in with Dad, who was helping Caleb with homework and planning on grilling steaks for dinner.

Finally, I lost myself in my work for the rest of the afternoon, crawling under the eaves to assess some duct-work, and then measuring the new firebacks for the fire-places, which I hadn't managed to do yesterday. I was elated to find that they would fit without altering the brickwork. I brought the heavy iron pieces up to the second-floor bedroom we were using as a staging area for painting doors and faux-finishing specialty pieces, and discussed their refinishing with the painters.

I lost track of time, and was surprised when Olivier walked into Cheshire House, an athletic bag in each hand.

He smiled. "Working late?"

"How can you tell?" I wore my stained coveralls over today's skirt, leggings, and sweater. My hair had escaped from its ponytail and was full of dust and cobwebs from my excursions under the eaves. "Excuse me a second."

I called down to Katenka and asked her to join us. Then I stripped off the coveralls and washed up in the kitchen sink, trying not to feel self-conscious as Olivier trailed me through the house.

"What did you have for dinner tonight?"

"What? I . . . um." I wasn't used to being grilled on my food choices, except by my father, and even he had learned to tread carefully. I had eaten half a sandwich and a half a bag of chips leftover from lunch. "Had a little something. And you?"

"I haven't eaten yet." He looked at his wristwatch. "French hours. Difficult in a city like San Francisco, where so many places stop serving dinner at nine. Perhaps after, presuming we are still alive, I will take you to eat?"

"Let's play that one by ear, okay?"

He just smiled.

Katenka appeared at the top of the basement stairs, Quinn balanced on one hip. I introduced her to Olivier.

"You are Russian?" Olivier said. "Such a beautiful people. And look at you."

Katenka preened and smiled.

He's French, I thought. *He can't help it.* One lingering question answered: Olivier wasn't interested in me; he was like this with all women.

Besides, I wasn't interested in Olivier. He spoke American English too well. I needed a man with whom communication would be difficult. That way, I could remain blissfully ignorant of his thoughts, and he of mine. I pictured myself in my Left Bank garret, tapping away on an old typewriter—my hands kept warm in fingerless gloves, a tiny cup of espresso by my side—as I wrote a self-help guide for the romantically impaired: *What's That You Say? Miscommunication as the Key to Romance.*

"—don't you think, Mel?"

I came back to the unpleasant present. "Sorry. What's that you say?"

"I say I don't know where Jim has hidden the letters—I looked everywhere. Probably he has in his briefcase to read at work. I tell you, he is obsessed."

"Katenka, I am here," a woman's voice called from the doorway.

"Oh good. This my friend Ivana." Katenka gestured to the woman standing at the entrance. Ivana had honey-blond hair, and was taller and stronger-looking than Katenka, but the two had the same severe, serious look about them. "Ivana sit with Quinn for the evening, just in case. Ivana, this is Mel Turner."

Ivana took the baby, swung his diaper bag over her shoulder, and left the house without another word.

"Let's start downstairs," Olivier replied. "After you, ladies."

Olivier, Katenka, and I descended to the basement apartment. Olivier set his bags on the kitchen counter and extracted several items.

"This is an electromagnetic field, or EMF, reader."

"And what does that do?"

"It measures energy. Ghosts, spirits of all kinds, emit energy, or draw energy from their surroundings. That's why there's often a cold spot where an entity appears."

I struggled not to roll my eyes.

"It's all theoretical, of course. But think about it: Are you aware of all the radio waves transmitting at all times around you, the signals to satellites and broadcasting shows? They're there, and they're real, though there would be no way of knowing or detecting them without special equipment."

All good points.

The EMF reader in one hand, Olivier began walking slowly through the rooms of the apartment: the two bedrooms, the main living area, and the kitchen. In the bathroom I held my breath, half expecting the shower to turn on. Hot water had taken on sinister overtones in my mind.

At long last we returned to the kitchen counter.

"This whole apartment is a bit of a fear cage."

"Excuse me?"

He showed me the meter on the device. The needle was registering at seventeen and a half.

"Anything between seven and nineteen hertz has an effect on humans."

"Are you saying you're measuring ghost energy right now?"

Olivier smiled. "I believe what the device is registering here has an entirely natural cause. Pipes of a certain length and girth, combined with electrical wiring, emit vibrations that can affect us subconsciously." He turned to Katenka. "Have you had symptoms of nausea, dread, fatigue, paranoia?"

Katenka looked at me. "He doesn't believe me."

"On the contrary. I believe you are feeling these things, and with good reason."

"Is *ghost*, not fear cage."

"I do believe you," he said, his tone gentle. "You've both seen something. That's a big deal. Let's go check out the other floors."

"Just because I don't see ghosts, only hear them, don't mean they don't exist," said Katenka.

"But you did see them," I said. "The other day, when you fainted."

"I saw the door open."

"You didn't see any entities?"

She shook her head. "You?"

"I did, yes." At least Dog sensed them.

"What you see?" she whispered.

"It's hard to explain," I hedged. "Let's continue; we'll talk about it later."

We climbed the narrow stairs from the basement to the main floor. The needle on Olivier's machine immediately dropped. When we walked into the dining room, it jumped to seventeen.

"Let's keep going," Olivier said.

We walked slowly through the rest of the main level: the kitchen and pantry, the parlor, the sunroom, the small library.

"So to clarify," I said, leading the way up the stairs to the second floor, Katenka trailing behind like a reluctant child, "there's something called a fear cage?"

"It's essentially an EMF-saturated area, which is common in basements and attics because there are so many pipes and wires."

"Why would a particular frequency make us think we're experiencing something bad?"

"Humans seem to be hardwired that way. The frequencies that affect us are the same as those generated by dangers from our primordial past. Erupting volcanoes, the crash of large ocean waves, the roar of big cats like tigers. No doubt we learned to associate them with danger and fear. Those who heeded their instincts survived, and passed their sensitivity on to their offspring. Those who did not—did not."

"Evolution in action."

"Exactly."

The theory appealed to me. I wasn't a freak because I saw ghosts—I was simply more evolved.

We explored the five bedrooms and two baths on the second floor, then proceeded to the third floor and toured its six small rooms.

"All right, ladies," Olivier asked, a slight smile on his face, "ready to brave the attic?"

Chapter Twenty-two

*N*o. But I knew I had to face my fears. "Sure." I reached up for the cord and pulled the hatch open, then unfolded the ladder. Olivier went first. Katenka hesitated, then followed. I brought up the rear.

The attic was silent, still, and dark.

"This is the part that worries me," I said as I showed him the hidden closet.

"'*Memento mori,*'" Olivier read. "Remember we all die."

"What?" Katenka asked, sounding annoyed. "What this mean?"

"It's an old saying. Nothing to worry about." I hoped.

Olivier showed us the meter reading: eighteen hertz. It had crept higher as we approached the closet.

Katenka halted. "I go. Get baby from Ivana. She cannot keep him long, and I tell her I would not be late."

"We'll finish up here," I said.

She paused at the attic ladder. "Mel, I forget to tell you I hired cat-catcher to find the cat in walls."

"I haven't seen any signs of a cat, Katenka. I've looked all around, even under the eaves."

Katenka shrugged and hustled down the attic ladder.

"She's scared," I explained.

"Perhaps she is smarter than we," Olivier replied. He held my eyes, a smile playing on his lips. "It is a little frightening."

"But I thought you were the big brave ghost hunter."

His smile broadened into a grin. "Only a foolish man would have no fear of the unknown. I am only a man, Mel. And I hope not to be foolish."

"Could you at least *pretend* to be the big brave ghost hunter?"

He winked at me. I guessed that would have to be reassurance enough.

Olivier brought out a complicated-looking camera and took pictures of our surroundings from every angle. After scoping the place out with his electronic devices, he asked me, "Are you sensing anything?"

I shook my head. It figured. It was like the mysterious pain that subsides just as you arrive at the doctor's office, or the strange *ping* the engine stops making when you pull into the mechanic's garage.

"Do you want to try to call on them?" Olivier asked.

"On purpose?" I swallowed, hard. "Not really."

"It could be interesting. . . ."

"I don't even know how to go about it."

"If they're appearing to you spontaneously, they must sense a connection to you for some reason, or know that you are a medium between their spirit world and the natural world. Concentrate on being open to their energy, their needs."

Still I hesitated.

"Isn't this why you asked me here, Mel?"

I closed my eyes, took a few deep breaths, and tried to concentrate. I felt nothing, and opened my eyes: no weighty gaze, no shadowy figures, no flashes in my peripheral vision. No fierce whispers or sodden, gurgling ghost.

"Nothing," I said.

He nodded. "Then let's go."

We descended the ladder and the two flights of stairs to the main floor. I checked to see if Katenka was home to say good-bye, but all was quiet in the basement apartment.

"Let's go to my car for a moment and talk," Olivier suggested. We climbed in and he ran the heater to take the edge off the evening's chill. "What do you know about the history of this place?"

I told him what I knew about Dominga, her sons Charles and Andre, her daughter-in-law Luvitica, and her grandchild, Junior. And about Charles's gruesome return in a barrel of rum.

"Do you think Charles is one of the ghosts?"

"I think so. The footsteps I saw were surrounded by drops, like from some kind of liquid. I assumed it was water."

"Could be ectoplasm."

"Or rum?"

I couldn't see Olivier well in the dim light from the streetlamps. Cars drove by, their headlights illuminating our faces briefly. A couple passed by, arm in arm; a mom walked by with two boys dressed in karate uniforms. The homeless fellow had made a bed out of an old sleeping bag and blankets in the foyer to Emile Blunt's upholstery shop. I made a mental note to bring him a lunch tomorrow.

It was nice out here. Normal neighborhood activity. No ghosts.

"Listen," Olivier said, "this may be hard to believe, but when it comes to hauntings, I'm rather skeptical myself. It's rare for spirits to make contact. The likelier explanation is an overactive imagination or human mischief. But in this case . . ."

"What?"

"I believe you. And if what you say is true, I'd stay out of this house."

"That's not really an option."

Another Gallic shrug. "Then I don't know what to tell you."

"How about telling me how to get rid of them."

"I would have to take more time, set up a situation to make contact."

"You mean a séance?"

"If what you have told me is true, that you were able to speak with a ghost and help him to the other side, then you don't need a séance. You're already more powerful than most séance leaders, since you don't need the psychic boost that comes from a circle of believers."

"So where does that leave me?"

"The spirits are making contact with you. As frightening as that may be, you should let them. Get yourself in a safe place emotionally, and the next time they reach out to you, allow it to happen, without fear, if possible. Probably the attic would be the best place for contact."

My heart sank. "I was hoping you might suggest some sort of exorcism."

"You would need a priest for that. You can go in armed with holy water and crosses if that's a comfort to you, but it's more about your resolution than anything else. There's no magic elixir. The important thing is to remain resolute in their company. Remember, Mel, this is dangerous. You must protect yourself. Do not allow them to influence you."

"How do I do that?"

"Bring with you items that remind you of who you are — amulets, symbols. The item itself is not important; it's what it means to you that matters. If you can, do not go alone. But if you bring someone with you, make sure you can count on that person to remain resolute."

"How about you?"

"I do not think I am a good candidate. The ghosts did not appear to us just now, did they? Perhaps they do not like me. But they did appear when you were with Katenka."

I couldn't imagine Katenka would remain resolute. Then again, I hadn't shown much resolve, either, when I ran screaming from the basement apartment on the heels of a wet dog a couple of days ago.

"Have they appeared to you with anyone else?"

Graham. Should I ask? I imagined how I might approach him: *"Hey, Graham, how's it going? Look, I'd love it if you went back into the attic with me so we could allow angry spirits to manipulate us. Would tomorrow at ten work for you?"*

I blew out a long breath. "Assuming I make contact and remain resolute, what do I do then? How do I actually get *rid* of them?"

"Usually they will make this clear to you. Perhaps there are unresolved issues you can help them with. If they don't, you must demand they leave. Make it clear they no longer belong here. Repeat to yourself, and to them: 'I am alive and you are not. I belong to this world and you do not.' Something like that. It is crucial that you take control of the situation."

My phone rang. I glanced at it: Graham. Had I somehow conjured him by thinking about him? I took the call.

"Standing me up seems to be a habit with you," Graham said. "A less confident man would start to take it personally."

I had completely forgotten we were supposed to meet to go over the green designs for the Daleys.

"Oh, Graham, I'm so sorry. I got caught up with something here at Cheshire House." I glanced at my watch. Quarter after seven. "What's your schedule like? Can you hang out with my dad for a bit? I'll leave right now, be there in twenty minutes?"

"Sure. Get here when you can."

I turned back to Olivier.

"A date?" he asked.

"I forgot I had a meeting. I'm sorry."

"So no dinner for us?"

"I'm afraid not. Eat well."

"You, too. *Bon appétit, et bon soir.*"

By the time I got home, Graham was sitting with Dad, Stan, and Caleb, beer and soda cans in hand, watching a football game in front of the enormous high-definition television that was Dad's pride and joy.

"Where you been, babe?" Dad asked, his eyes glued to the television. "You hungry?"

"I'm afraid I lost track of time. Working late on that Union Street job. I'll grab something to eat in a little while."

"I thought you were gonna see that French guy tonight," said Caleb.

"French guy?" Dad finally looked up. "What French guy? No one tells me anything around here."

"Wait . . ." said Caleb. "Was I not supposed to mention it?"

Stan gave me a wink.

Graham followed me into the room down the hall that served as Turner Construction's office. Stan kept things tidy here: There were two desks, three filing cabinets, a drafting table, and a big box of blueprints in one corner.

"French guy?" Graham said. "Dare I ask?"

"I told you about him. The ghost tour guy."

"You're going out with the *ghost tour* guy?"

"I'm not going out with anybody, not that it's any of your business."

"Huh." He did not look pleased, which pleased me more than it should. "How's Raul doing?"

"Broken arm, one broken rib. But I called on my way home, and he was in good spirits."

"Good."

I sorted through the rolls of blueprints until I found the set for Cheshire House. I laid the heavy roll on the drafting table and spread it out. We flipped through the electrical, plumbing, and basic structural drawings.

"As you know, the only insulation in the attic is old newspapers," Graham said. "First order of business is to seal the air leaks and blow cellulose into the wall cavities and between the floor joists."

"Not a problem. We can remove siding if need be, but a lot of those spaces can be accessed through the eaves and crawl spaces."

"The old windows are awfully drafty. I don't suppose you'd consider replacing them with double-paned reproductions?"

One of my many pet peeves: replacing perfectly serviceable, gorgeous wood-and-antique-glass windows.

I gave him a look.

He smiled. "Didn't think so. All right, fifteen double-hung and twenty or so casement windows that leak so much they might as well be wide-open. We'll need to dismantle and refurbish the wooden parts, seal the leaks, repair the broken channels, retie the lead weights, and then order custom-fitted storm windows."

"I stumbled across a new resource for reproduction storm windows: Heartwood Lumber. Have you heard of it?"

"I haven't been over there for years. I'll check them out and have them give us a quote if it looks like a good product. How about gray-water reclamation?"

"I thought the city didn't permit that yet."

"Doesn't mean it can't be done."

"I'm not hearing any of this."

Gray water is the runoff from washing dishes and clothes, from showers and baths. As long as homeowners use environmentally friendly soap and don't pour anything toxic down the sink, this water can be filtered and used to irrigate ornamental plants. In drought-prone California, reclaiming water this way is an environmental boon. It also prevents flooding the sewer system with water that doesn't need to be treated. Though a brilliant idea, gray-water reclamation has few fans at city hall because building permit offices aren't set up to deal with the newfangled idea. More than a few environmentally conscious homeowners have their homes plumbed to code, and the minute the inspector signs off, they merrily dismantle the plumbing and install gray-water systems.

Everyone knew it happened, but a contractor could lose her license if she participated in this kind of code violation.

"Is this your idea, or Jim's?"

"Jim liked the idea. I think it's helping him let go of his dream of wind power. He floated the windmill idea by some of the neighbors and it didn't go over big."

"Hey, what was up with Jim, acting like you were making a move on Katenka?"

Graham shrugged.

"He totally lost his cool. It seemed . . . out of character."

"Katenka gives off something . . . It's probably just a guy thing. But she's a beautiful woman, and having her look at another man . . . That sort of thing can drive a husband crazy."

"Was she looking at you that way?"

"I think it's the only way she knows to look at a man. It's a kind of protective reflex, sending out signals that she needs to be taken care of until some schmuck comes along and does."

"I guess she found that in Jim. I'm curious, though. Doesn't it seem kind of odd that such a normal, attractive guy would have to go to Russia to get a wife?"

"What, you don't think it's true love?"

"He's educated, intelligent, well-off, and good-looking. You'd think a man like that would have no trouble meeting interested women in a place like San Francisco."

"You think he's good-looking?"

"Not really my type, but yeah. Sure. Don't you?"

"Can't ask a guy a question like that," he said with a shrug. "I guess he's okay."

I smiled. "He's not as handsome as some I could name."

He took a step toward me. "A man who might be more your type, you mean?"

Chapter Twenty-three

I nodded. "Matt's pretty good-looking, for instance."

Graham paused. The corners of his mouth tightened. "Matt."

"In a British bad boy sort of way."

He snorted. "'Bad' I'll grant you. But that 'boy' is fifty if he's a day."

"Late forties, maybe. And you know what they say: Age is only a number."

"He's far too old to party like he does."

"Why are we talking about Matt again?"

"You brought him up."

"Okay, let's get back to the subject. You don't find it strange that Jim went to Russia for a wife?"

"It's not like she was a mail-order bride, Mel. They met online and decided to get together. Like thousands of people do these days. She just happened to live in another country."

"I would think that in the Bay Area, an employed,

decent-looking, heterosexual man would have found a suitable woman easily enough. Unless something's wrong with him."

"Like what?"

"That's my point. Maybe he's . . . odd. Odd in ways that aren't immediately apparent."

"Odd in ways that would lead him to murder an old man in cold blood for . . . what? For wanting to buy his house? For yelling about the noise of construction?"

"I haven't figured out that part yet."

He started rolling up the blueprints. "You won't figure out that part, because there *is* no such part. I know you think finding true love is hard for women, but it's not all that easy for a guy to meet the woman of his dreams, either." He tapped me on the head, gently, with the roll of blueprints. "Even for those of us who are good-looking and employed."

"Didn't take *you* very long," I muttered as I rooted around in my satchel for the catalog on reproduction storm windows from Heartwood Lumber.

"Pardon me?"

"Nothing," I said, handing him the catalog. "Emile Blunt spoke Russian. Doesn't that seem strange to you?"

"More surprising than strange. Why?"

"Emile never struck me as a linguist."

"Maybe his mother was Russian. There are a lot of Russians in San Francisco. Have been ever since the gold rush days; and even before then, they traded furs up and down the west coast into Canada. Fort Bragg's an old Russian outpost. Go out to the Richmond district and you'll find fresh pierogi in every store. Good stuff."

"I suppose so. But the last time I spoke to him he acted as though he didn't know the difference between

Ukrainian and Russian, which would be really odd for a Russian speaker, wouldn't it?" I said. "How about this: Why would someone dig up the yard to disinter cats?"

"Excuse me?"

"The backyard of Cheshire House was dug up to remove the bodies of the cats that had been buried there over the years. But why? Hettie Banks wasn't charged with killing cats, and the folks at the animal shelter admitted her cats were healthy and well cared for. Hettie was released with a slap on the wrist, once the media flurry died down."

"You are just a bundle of questions tonight, aren't you?"

"I find myself in a very weird situation."

"I don't think it's good for your mental health."

"Thanks so much. Anyway, I have a mental health professional on call."

He grinned. "Great to see Luz the other night. But I have a few questions of my own. Are we going to keep avoiding talking about what happened up in the attic between you and me?"

"We already talked about it. I think the ghosts were influencing us."

"You think that was all?"

"That's not enough? Olivier says they sometimes pick up on latent emotions and exploit them."

"Olivier Galopin."

I nodded.

"What sorts of 'latent' emotions do you and this French guy have?"

"He didn't try to kiss me when we were in the attic, if that's what you mean."

Graham looked at me for a long time, then came to stand near me. Too near. "In the interest of science and ghost busting, maybe we should try it without ghosts around. See what happens."

My heartbeat sped up, and I tried to remain casual.

"I doubt Elena would approve."

Graham chuckled. "Probably not. All right, then. If I can't have a kiss, may I at least take home a copy of the blueprints?"

"Help yourself," I said.

As he left, I couldn't help but think: *He gave up awfully easily*.

The next morning I arranged for Steve Gilman, the foreman from Matt's Vallejo Street job, to spend some of his time at Cheshire House. Luckily, Matt's job was in its final stages so it wasn't too much of a stretch. I oriented him to the work in progress and familiarized him with the subcontractors he didn't already know. I also wanted to introduce him to Katenka, but no one was home in the basement apartment.

I was about to head out to meet Luz across town at the botanica when I looked up to see a large Heartwood Lumber delivery truck pulling into the driveway.

At the wheel was Dave Enrique.

"This is a surprise," I said as he swung down from the cab.

"I asked to make the delivery. I . . . I wanted to talk to you again."

"About what?"

He rubbed his arm, then took out a cigarette and lit it.

"You caught me off guard the other day, asking me about this place. I just wanted to say . . . Mrs. Banks would never hurt anyone. She may be eccentric, but she's good people."

"You came all the way over here just to tell me that?"

He hesitated, opening and then closing his mouth.

"I have a question for you," I said. "Any idea why someone would dig up the backyard?"

He looked alarmed. "You mean where the cats were buried? Someone dug it up?"

I nodded.

He cleared his throat and took a drag on his cigarette. "I think someone might have been looking for something they thought was buried with the cats. Something that should have stayed buried."

"Like what?"

Dave glanced up at the tiny attic window under the eaves and paled. He took a step toward the truck, then tossed his half-smoked cigarette onto the driveway and crushed it with his boot.

"I better offload this stuff and get back," he mumbled.

I looked at the attic window and saw a flash of movement, almost as if the darkness had become darker.

That did it. I didn't care what Olivier said; if I had to go up against ghosts, I wanted some kind of backup. If the botanica had gear for this sort of thing, I would get myself some.

I met Luz on the corner of Nineteenth and Guerrero, in the heart of the neighborhood called the Mission. The area is home to a lot of Latino newcomers, not only from Mexico but also Central America, Ecuador, and Puerto Rico. Some time ago outsiders discovered the vibrant nightlife here, so now the area was jammed with posh restaurants and music clubs right alongside humble taquerias and low-rent bars, and on weekend nights the streets were jammed with revelers from across the city.

The Mission also had two BART stations, making it easy to get around without a car.

The botanica called El Pajarito had a colorful storefront painted with birds and ivy. Inside, the shelves were jammed with herbs, candles, and figurines. Luz was distracted by a display of aerosol-can air fresheners whose labels promised everything from luck in the lottery to establishing domestic bliss.

No cans of Ghost-B-Gone, unfortunately.

"Here," Luz said, handing me a can with a bright yellow label. "You need some of this."

According to the fine print, Black Cat Spray would rid me of romantic rivals.

"Thanks, Luz. I really appreciate it."

"Anytime."

"I think *you* need *this*." I handed her a pyramid made of clear resin, in which was captured a little Buddha, a key, and gold sparkles. "Get in touch with your inner Zen Buddhist."

"Hey, if Zen Buddhism includes gold sparkles, I might just sign up."

Behind the register was a thin girl with long dark hair who couldn't have been more than twelve years old. Why was someone her age running a shop, I wondered, and why wasn't she in school?

Luz seemed unfazed. She lifted her chin slightly at the girl, and said, "*¿Está tu mama?*"

Without speaking, the girl disappeared through a bead curtain featuring the Virgin of Guadalupe.

"Shouldn't she be in school?" I whispered.

Luz nodded. "Seems like."

After a moment a woman ducked through the curtain,

still chewing, holding a coffee cup in one hand and a bag of roasted pumpkin seeds in the other. She looked to be in her late fifties, short and plump, her hair dyed a dark brown with a burgundy tinge and piled, lopsided, upon her head. She had a pleasant, round face.

She nodded to us.

"Gracias por hablar con nosotros." I thanked her for speaking with us in my less-than-fluent Spanish. "I'm sorry if we interrupted your lunch."

She waved off my concern. "I am Señora Moreno. Can I help you?"

"A friend of mine came in here a few days ago, asking for help with . . . spirits in her house. She's small, pretty, speaks with a Russian accent. She may have asked for a *limpia*?"

"Lots of people come in here," she said, sipping her coffee and looking down at a notepad on the counter. I wondered if botanica owners were like priests and therapists—did they have to maintain clients' confidentiality?

Luz leaned on the counter with one arm and raised her eyebrows in silent challenge.

"Well, whoever helped this lady screwed up," Luz said, her head waggling as she spoke. Her parents may have come from Mexico, but Luz was born and raised in East LA and had the urban head waggle down to an art. "'Cause these ghosts hurt somebody the other day. So either this person makes it right, or we start spreading the word that folks should go elsewhere for supplies and advice, *me entiendes*?"

Señora Moreno took another sip of coffee and picked at her teeth with her tongue, as though unimpressed.

She popped a couple of pumpkin seeds in her mouth and crunched. But after a moment, she nodded.

"I remember her. She was very scared. I offered her my services, but I was headed up to Reno on vacation and she did not want to wait. She wanted to try it herself. I sold her the necessary supplies, plus some holy water and talismans." She shrugged. "But then she didn't come back."

"The haunting seems to have gotten worse. Someone told me she might have chased off the 'good' ghosts but not the more serious ones."

I felt Luz's eyes on me, assessing, cynical. But Señora Moreno nodded.

"This is possible. This is why it's best for me to do it. The most important part of cleansing a house *es tener confianza, no*? To remain confident. This can be very hard for amateurs. They are frightened, and the spirits know this. I told your friend this, but she wanted to do it herself so I told her the standard procedure to rid spirits from a house."

"And that would be . . . ?"

"It is all outlined in this pamphlet, available for only ten dollars. Have some *pepitos*."

She held out the bag of pumpkin seeds. I declined, but Luz took a handful.

I flipped through the illustrated pamphlet. Hardly seemed worth ten dollars. But it didn't seem right to ask this woman to give her expertise away for free. Everybody's got to make a living.

"Tell you what," I said. "I'll buy my supplies here and I'll even buy the pamphlet. But give me a condensed version."

"The key to a *limpia* is to reclaim the space. I told her to send the little one away for the evening and to have her husband help her. Holding a lighted candle, start at the back of the house on each floor and move toward the front. Ring the bell, light the incense and a candle, sprinkle the holy water, and sweep, while declaring that the space no longer belongs to the ghosts, it belongs to her and her husband. Declaring ownership is very important. Do you understand?"

I nodded.

"After sweeping thoroughly, from the back to the front, you must take the broom outside and burn it." She sighed. "A lot of people don't burn the broom. I never understand this. Who wants such a broom?"

"I'll burn it," I said, though I felt more than a little foolish.

Luz nodded a shade too solemnly, and I nudged her with my elbow.

I ended up buying the pamphlet, some candles, a brass bell, a package of incense, and whole bunch of stocking stuffers for Christmas. For Caleb I bought the sparkly resin pyramid with a Buddha, as well as cans of Good Luck and Homework Help room spray. For Dad I chose a bag of antiaging peppermint tea, and for Stan a box of lucky charms in the shapes of animals.

"Would you be available to come to the house and do a *limpia*, if my client agrees?" I asked as I handed over cash.

Señora Moreno cast a disapproving look at Luz, who was roaming the aisles, snorting and laughing at the things she found. She picked up a small box and read the instructions aloud, chuckling. Moreno turned her attention back to me, reaching out and grabbing my wrist. Her hand was warm, strong.

"I'm worried about your Russian friend," she said in a low voice. "She had the sense of someone doomed. But you . . . you have the sight, no?"

I yanked my wrist away. "Why would you say that?"

She chuckled. "Why do you think I run a botanica and perform *limpias*, *mi muñeca*? I have had the sight since I was a child. I am not a . . . What's the word you use here?"

"A fake? A con artist? A charlatan?" suggested Luz, who had joined us at the counter.

Moreno nodded. "It is true that I sell many items that are not, in themselves, good luck or magic. And it is true that I sometimes encourage superstitious beliefs. But when people believe they will get well because they drink a certain tea, sometimes they do. And if they have faith that their bad luck will go away if they light a candle and recite the right words every night, then sometimes it does. I don't always help people, but I never hurt them."

Luz, rarely at a loss for words, looked chastened.

"So, *mi muñeca*, I will sell these items to you. If you have the sight, you won't need me there. I have two *limpias* scheduled in the next week, and I am no longer a young woman. Just remember to remain confident. This is the essential thing, much more important than saying the right words."

By the time we left the shop I was fifty bucks poorer, clutching a brown paper bag containing all the items I might need to rid a house of ferocious ghosts. I couldn't quite bring myself to believe it. I feared the resolution that Señora Moreno—and Olivier—emphasized might be lacking.

"Why did she call me *muñeca*? What's that mean?"

"Doll. It's a term of endearment. She liked you. Or at least she liked your fifty dollars. Anyway, I'm starving. You promised me lunch, remember?" Luz said. "Unless you don't have any money left after your occult supply run?"

"Tacos?"

"My favorite Pakistani restaurant is right down the street."

"We're in the Mission and you want Pakistani food?"

"It's really good. Besides, I'm Mexican, which makes Mexican food just plain old food. I feel like something exotic."

"Okay," I said, checking my phone for the time. "But I have to be out of here in under an hour. I'm down one foreman and I have to take Katenka to pick out her favorite knobs."

"I'm not even going to respond to that sentence. That dirty joke writes itself."

"You're a real pal, Luz."

Chapter Twenty-four

While we walked the three blocks to the Pakistani restaurant, I called to check on Raul. He had been released from the hospital, and was at home with his broken arm in a sling. When he said he would be back to work tomorrow, I could hear his wife yelling at him in the background.

"Don't you dare," I said. "Let your wife dote on you for a few days; get some rest so you heal faster. We pay scads into that workers' comp account—might as well use it. We'll get by."

At the restaurant Luz and I slid into a red vinyl booth. I suggested Luz order for us, and without even consulting the menu she rattled off *pappadums*, chicken *pakora*, *haleem*, chicken tikka kebab, lamb *rogan josh*, *aloo paratha*, and two mango lassis.

Once our feast was set before us, I confessed my worries about the ghosts and the murder of Emile Blunt.

She looked skeptical. "What could a murder across the street have to do with ghosts in Cheshire House?"

"I'm not sure. Nothing, maybe. It just seems too coincidental. Who would have a motive for killing the old guy? And it turns out Emile Blunt lived in Cheshire House for a while, and apparently he once saw ghosts in the attic."

"You think the ghosts crossed the street and went after him? Can they do that?"

"I don't think that's what happened," I said, surprising myself with my confidence. "I think . . . the ghosts influenced someone. The people who've lived in Cheshire House mentioned something. . . . Even I've felt their influence. It's as though they get to you."

"Are you talking about spirit possession?" Luz scooped up some *daal* with a small piece of *aloo paratha*.

"Not quite . . . It's more subtle than that. Okay, here's something else: It seems Hettie Banks, the woman who used to own the Cheshire Inn—"

"The crazy cat lady?"

"For lack of a better term, yes. Anyway, she inherited the upholstery shop from Emile Blunt. That's motive, right?"

Luz fixed me with a look and raised one eyebrow. "At what point did you start delving into a murder investigation? I thought you were just trying to get rid of ghosts."

"I told you—I think it might all be connected. And besides . . . my father's still under suspicion for Emile's death. I wouldn't mind coming up with a few other likely suspects."

"You don't think the SFPD might be better qualified for this sort of thing?"

"Of course. In fact I spoke with the investigator on

the case earlier today. It won't surprise you to know that she thinks I'm nuts."

"You told her about the ghosts trying to shut down your construction project?"

"Afraid so. Anyway, Hettie couldn't have killed Emile, could she? She's an old woman who's overly fond of cats. I can't imagine her shooting someone in cold blood."

"Don't underestimate little old ladies. Ever hear about that woman in Sacramento who ran a boarding-house and whose boarders mysteriously disappeared? The police found their bodies buried in her backyard."

"When was this?"

"In the late eighties, I think. Dorothea Puente bumped off at least nine of her tenants and planted them in the garden. Apparently she had quite the green thumb."

"Anyone ever tell you that you are a fount of really disturbing information?"

Luz laughed and helped herself to chicken *pakora*. "That's why I became a university professor. A mind like a steel trap, chock-full of useless trivia. This Hettie Banks must be rolling in it, if she sold that massive place on Union Street."

"She donated most of the money to the animal shelter."

"To make up for her hoarding sins?"

"So it seems."

"How was the neighbor killed?"

"Shot with his own gun, according to the paper."

"Not poisoned?"

"I don't think so. Why?"

"Poison's a woman's method."

"Surely women aren't the only ones who use poison."

"No. But it's more typical. Much safer than stabbing

someone. All in all though, when it comes to murder it is *much* more likely for the culprit to be a man. Any scary men lurking around?"

"There's one fellow, Dave Enrique, who used to live in the house. Something strange went on between him and Hettie's daughter, Janet. And he knew Emile. But that was years ago; I can't figure out how it would be related to what's going on now."

"Any other obvious suspects?"

"You know who I find suspicious, though I can't explain why? Jim Daley."

"Your client? What possible reason would he have to commit murder?"

"Emile Blunt was causing problems with the construction."

"You told me yourself that he had no cause to actually shut you down, so it sounds like it was just an annoyance factor." She served herself some lamb and topped it with a dollop of lime pickle. "Hard to imagine that would provoke someone like Daley to homicide. He's a wealthy professional, a loving father, with a wife he adores. Why would he risk all that over a minor dispute with a neighbor? Especially since the cause for complaint will end in a few months?"

"Good question. Why did Dorothea kill her tenants?"

"For their social security checks. Oh, she claimed she thought they were better off this way, since they were old and sick, but nobody bought it."

"So it was about the money."

"It usually is."

The botanica outing and lunch took longer than I'd anticipated, and I screeched to a stop in front of Cheshire

House a few minutes after four o'clock, the time Katenka and I had agreed to go look at knobs and tile.

The homeless guy was asleep across the street, so I put a bag of Pakistani food leftovers in his shopping cart, then went to find my client. But she wasn't there.

While I waited for Katenka to show up, I checked in with my crew, who were wrapping things up for the weekend. Everything was on schedule to begin the Daleys' wall prep next week, so I made sure we were number one on the painters' schedule. In this business there was always a risk: If you fell behind, even by a day, you risked losing your slot with the subcontractors, who had their own schedules to juggle. That would throw a monkey wrench into everything down the line.

I handed the crew their paychecks, and they took off to enjoy their Friday night.

Twenty minutes later, Katenka still hadn't arrived. I headed down the basement stairs and met Jim coming up. He held a happily gurgling Quinn in the baby sling, nestled against his chest.

"Oh, hi, Jim. I didn't know you were here. Is Katenka around?"

He shook his head. "That's why I'm here—I came home early to look after Quinn."

I held my forefinger out to the baby. He smiled, grabbed hold, and squeezed with remarkable strength. "Katenka and I had plans to pick out a few things at the Design Center. Any idea how to get in touch with her?"

"She took off for a bit. I could go with you, if there's a real time pressure."

"That's all right. I imagine she'll be here soon. She told me this would be a good time for her."

Jim hesitated, opening his mouth as if to say something, then closing it again. We were standing in the close quarters of the narrow stairway to the basement level. I moved two steps higher, which gave me the novel experience of being taller than Jim Daley.

"Is everything all right?" I asked.

"We had a fight."

"What about?" I sounded nosy to my own ears. But given my conversation with Graham last night, I was ready to jump to conclusions.

"Not that it's any of your business," Jim said, giving voice to my thoughts, "but we fought over staying here. In this house. She's completely illogical. One minute she's planning a party, the next she wants to leave."

"Jim, I know you're skeptical, but I think you need to at least consider that Katenka might be right. There's something odd going on in this house. Don't you think it would be better for all concerned, especially with a baby, to leave while we finish up?"

"You really think that by finishing the renovation you'll vanquish the spirits? If they've been here for more than a century, I hardly think a few new windows will chase them out."

"So . . . you mean you believe in them now?"

"I never said that."

I supposed that was technically true, though I was beginning to have my doubts.

"Jim, you know how I put together a scrapbook of all of Turner Construction's renovation projects? I wondered whether you might have any papers, something like that, anything at all that you've found in the house . . . ?"

He shook his head.

"No letters, maybe?"

"Nothing," he said, but he looked away. Short of call-

ing him a liar, that line of questioning wasn't going anywhere.

The baby gurgled and cooed, making us both smile.

"You know," Jim continued, "sometimes Katenka
gets angry and disappears for a while. In fact . . . at times
I think she might be seeing someone."

"I understand you two met online?" I said.

He nodded. "While she was in Russia. It seemed too
good to be true, and maybe it was. She's beautiful, and
wonderful, but . . . perhaps not the most reliable person
in the world."

Contractors are often in the position of learning more
than they want to about their clients' personal lives.
Homes are intimate spaces, and we spend so much time
with people that there's a natural blurring of boundaries.
But Jim had never treated me as a confidant. It was
Katenka who confided in me, in her guarded way.

"When was the last time you saw her?"

"About an hour ago. As I said, we had words, and she
took off."

"She's not answering her cell phone?"

"Didn't even take it with her. Flung it at my head, in
fact." Quinn began to whimper. "I need to take Quinn
out. Poor kid's been stuck inside all day, and we need
groceries."

"Of course," I said, retreating up the stairs. "I'll be
taking off, too, then, if Katenka's not here."

As we left, I noticed Inspector Crawford at Emile's
upholstery shop. Why was I so bothered by Katenka's
no-show? Maybe she really was angry at Jim and took
off. Or maybe last night's ghost hunt rattled her so much
that she couldn't stand to be here another minute. But
would she have left Quinn behind? I knew she found

him difficult, but it seemed hard to believe that she would simply turn and walk away.

Ever since the doubts about Jim had entered my mind, I couldn't shake them. I lingered at my car, returning a phone call and waiting for Jim to leave. I could have sworn I felt his gaze on my back.

Jim strapped the baby into the car seat, then took off. As soon as the car turned the corner, I crossed the street.

"Excuse me, Inspector Crawford?"

The inspector looked tired, frustrated. And not at all pleased to see me.

"Yes, Ms. Turner?"

"I wanted to ask you . . . to mention that . . ."

She gave me an "out with it" look.

"Katenka Daley seems to have gone missing."

"Missing? Since when?"

"Last night. I saw her earlier in the evening, but she left before we could say good-bye."

"She's 'missing' for less than a day, then? Isn't it a little early to be worried? Did she miss an important appointment?"

"Sort of. She was supposed to meet me."

"For something important?"

"We were going to pick out knobs at the Design Center."

The inspector lifted one eyebrow.

"When I say it like that, it doesn't sound all that important. But it surprises me that she would take off without her son, and without mentioning it to me."

"And her husband isn't worried?"

"If he had something to do with her disappearance, he wouldn't be worried, would he?"

"Do you have any reason to suspect her husband of foul play?"

"No, not really. Just a hunch."

The inspector looked at me for a long moment. Assessing.

"Chances are she's gone off for perfectly legitimate reasons. What do you know about her? Any local relatives, friends, anything like that?"

"There is one friend," I said. "Ivana . . . something. Russian, as well."

"Check with Ivana-something; maybe she's seen her. I'm a homicide cop, Ms. Turner. Even if Ms. Daley were missing for forty-eight hours and a search was begun, I'm not the one to talk to. That's a whole different department."

I nodded.

As she was about to enter the upholstery shop, she paused. "On the other hand, you happen upon any bloody knives, that sort of thing, you be sure to let me know."

Will do, Inspector.

Chapter Twenty-five

I let myself back into Cheshire House. Though the natural light was fading on this winter's afternoon, I didn't turn on any lights.

I checked the corkboard in the kitchen, but Ivana's information and the picture were gone. Katenka had mentioned Ivana lived two blocks away in a house with gold lions in front. How many gold lions could there be in this neighborhood? I slipped out the front door and headed down the street.

Sure enough, two blocks down I spotted a nice marina-style home with a pair of gold gilt lions guarding the front steps. The home wasn't ostentatious, but as anyone who's been house hunting in San Francisco could tell you, you can't touch anything in the lower Pacific Heights for under a million bucks.

The postage-stamp town garden had been pruned and trimmed with care but no imagination — the kind of gardening that expressed the desire to fit in with the neighbors rather than love for flowers and plants. The money was in the details: The home's paint was fresh and pressure-washed, the moss on the stone steps had been removed with surgical precision, and there wasn't a single cobweb or leaf in evidence.

Ivana answered the door, her eyes widening when she saw me.

"Hi, Ivana, remember me? From Katenka's house?"

"You are the builder—Mal?"

"Mel. Is Katenka here?"

She shook her head.

"Do you know where she might be?"

"She is not home?"

"No. She was supposed to meet me today but she didn't show up."

Ivana stood back and invited me in.

The formal, round foyer was floored in marble and ringed with doorways. One led to a dining room with a gleaming mahogany table and twelve chairs; another to a living room with formal furniture in muted tones; and a third, closed door I imagined led to the kitchen. A grand stairwell with a beautiful marble balustrade led to the second story.

Ivana waved me into the living room, where I took a seat on an oyster-colored linen sofa that was so stylish and so uncomfortable I imagined it must have been chosen by an interior designer more focused on appearances than livability. There was a touch of gold gilt on the feet of the couch, and the coffee table legs were carved to look like heads of lions.

"You would like something?" Ivana offered. "Tea or coffee? Vodka, maybe? Or my husband keeps scotch, if you prefer."

"No, thank you. I'm fine."

"But you are worried for Katenka," Ivana said as she sank into a leather club chair. "You are here because you are worried."

"We had an appointment to look at some items at the San Francisco Design Center. It's not like her to miss a meeting."

Ivana nodded.

"How did she seem last night?" I asked. "Did she say anything about being upset?"

"I did not see her, not after I pick up baby. When I saw you."

"Didn't she come for Quinn last night?"

"Jim came for him."

"What time was that?"

"About eight o'clock."

"Jim still has the baby with him. Would Katenka have gone off without him?"

"Quinn is with Jim?" She looked alarmed, and shook her head. "Jim was very jealous. Getting more so."

"How do you and Katenka know each other?"

"We danced together."

"I didn't know that. Was this in Russia?"

"Oh no, here. In San Francisco." Ivana inspected her manicure. "They called us dancers, anyway. I was never much talented. But then I met Larry and he gave me good home. All is good now."

She had certainly landed in the lap of luxury, I thought. But based on the silver-framed wedding photo atop the credenza, I doubted the jowly, balding man twice her size had been her romantic ideal. Then again, what did I know?

"Did Katenka meet Jim in one of these clubs?"

"Not exactly . . ." She was quiet for so long I didn't know whether she would finish the thought. "She met Jim after."

"I thought they met online while she was in Russia."

"I have said too much. I . . . She and Jim met first, maybe. Before I knew her." She consulted a thin gold watch on her left wrist, and stood. "I must go. I have Pilates."

"At this hour on a Friday night? Sounds ambitious."

Ivana led the way to the front door.

"Could you tell me the name of the club you and Katenka danced in?"

Her pretty lipsticked mouth was pressed into an ugly line. "I have said too much. I am sorry. Please ignore me. I don't speak English very well."

"I think you do."

"I get confused."

Ivana was hard to read. What could she be thinking right now, with that flat affect? At the moment I would have traded my knack for seeing ghosts for the ability to read minds.

"Do you have a photo of Katenka I could borrow?"

Without a word, she returned to the living room, rooted around in a drawer at the roll-top desk, and showed me a snapshot of her and Katenka, looking younger, both smiling. "It is when we first arrived." She took a pair of scissors and cut herself out of the picture. "Okay?"

I nodded. "Okay. Thank you, Ivana."

"If you . . . if you talk to anyone, other than Katenka, I mean . . . please to don't tell them about me. Don't mention my name."

I nodded. "I promise. It won't come up."

As I walked down the street toward my car, my mind was a whirl. For all I knew, Katenka had gone off, without her son, for reasons of her own. But what if those reasons were related to Emile's murder and her haunted house? How, I had no idea. I had gotten close to the Daleys during the renovation and I needed to reassure myself that Jim hadn't harmed his wife. Her sudden disappearance was worth looking into, especially since I knew someone who knew something about girlie shows. Someone who owed me. Big time.

Zach Malinski.

It was a Friday night, so he might not be home. But it was still early, and I imagined Zach's evening didn't start until later. Maybe he was taking what Luz used to call a "disco nap," a late catnap that allows you to stay up all night at the club. On the other hand . . . we hadn't exactly kept in touch after our last run-in, when he locked me up in a salvage yard. For all I knew, he was in prison.

I drove to the corner of Golden Gate and Divisadero, then circled the block three times until a parking spot opened up. Zach lived in a forties-era building that featured five-foot-high arts-and-crafts-style wood paneling and marble thresholds. Z. Malinski was still listed in Apartment 112. I tried the buzzer. No response.

A woman with a stroller started to maneuver her way into the building, so I held the door and followed her in.

I scooped up a *People* magazine from the demilune table that held the tenants' overflow mail and went past number 112 to the end of the hall, where a door opened onto a set of back stairs and an emergency exit. I left the door open a crack and took a seat on the next-to-bottom stair, where I could see who came and went.

I enjoyed the novel sensation of being hidden and

unknown, observing but not being observed. I put my phone on vibrate and flipped through the magazine, intending to catch up on celebrity gossip. The only problem was I didn't recognize most of the people in *People,* and the few I did recognize were in an article entitled "Where Are They Now?" Was I really that old? Maybe I just didn't watch enough TV. The last television program I remembered seeing was a house-flipping show that Luz and some other friends had insisted I join them in watching. It was kind of fun ridiculing the host's shoddy workmanship and throwing popcorn at the screen, but I hadn't been invited back. I had the sneaking suspicion my antics had gotten me blackballed.

I heard noises in the hall, and peeked out to see a trio of young women in four-inch heels teetering down the main stairs, all dolled up for a big night on the town.

I glanced at my steel-toed boots. Bet they'd make a big splash at the downtown club scene. I had no plans for this Friday night. When I'd checked in earlier, Caleb was heading out to the movies with a group of friends, and Stan and Dad were planning on eating leftovers and settling in to watch *Top Gun* on DVD.

Speaking of leftovers . . . It had been a long time since the Pakistani food. I wondered, just for a moment, what Olivier was having for dinner. What would it be like to have someone like Olivier trying to seduce me with food?

And speaking of seduction . . . My mind drifted to Graham. When he was younger he had been so dashing, handsome and brash, roaring up to job sites on his motorcycle. He had mellowed. A lot. Now he was . . . I closed my eyes and shook my head, exasperated with myself. He was taken. Period.

The front door opened again. Zach. His head was bent as he sorted through the mail in his hands while he walked down the hall. He paused outside his apartment door, reading a postcard, as he fished for his keys in his pocket.

Quietly I slipped out of the stairwell and came to stand next to him.

He glanced up. His eyes widened in surprise, then wariness.

He took an involuntary step back, then smiled. "Mel! Great to see you! You're not armed, are you?"

"Does the Glock in my purse count?"

He held his hands up, grinning now, though there was a flicker of worry in his sherry-colored eyes. "You know what I always say, no need for firearms among friends."

"Oh, I don't know, Zach. I think I'd best keep the upper hand this time."

He ducked his head. "Well, I'm man enough to enjoy a woman being in charge. Once in a while."

An elderly woman came out of her apartment across the hall, leading a small white dog on a leash.

"Good evening, Zachary," she said.

"Mrs. Eldridge, don't you look lovely this evening in that red hat. Heading out for a hot date?"

"Oh, you." She smiled and swatted the air. "How you do go on. Is this your lady friend?"

"This is my good friend Mel Turner. Mel, meet the lovely Mrs. Eldridge."

We exchanged pleasantries, and she tottered down the hallway.

"Come on in," Zach said as he unlocked the door. The apartment was tiny but charming: Off the small foyer was the bath, a single room just big enough for a queen bed and a desk, a closet, and a cramped galley kitchen. Large windows looking out over the street kept the snug apartment from feeling claustrophobic. The walls were lined with five-foot-high cherry-stained wainscoting topped by a little shelf, which Zach had filled with photographs and various mementos from his travels.

"'Good friend'?"

He smiled.

"Don't you think that's stretching it a bit?" I continued. "We didn't exactly part as friends."

"That's not entirely true." He took a seat in the desk chair, interlaced his fingers over his flat stomach, and leaned back. "I bear you no ill will."

"Shame I can't say the same."

Another flicker of doubt in his eyes.

"Why aren't you in jail?"

"I didn't do anything wrong. I was just caught up in a series of events . . ."

"Give me a break."

"Also, I struck a deal with the DA. Turned state's evidence."

"Ah."

Our eyes held for a moment. He smiled that crooked, charming smile. Last time I saw Zach had not been pleasant. But to be fair, we had spent time together before that, and despite all that happened I felt a certain . . . comfort with him. I couldn't quite explain why. He was younger than I, by several years, and extremely handsome in an earnest, sleepy-eyed way. But despite his ever-present smile, his expression was sad.

Tall and muscular, he looked older than I remembered. His clothes weren't expensive, but they suited him: classic jeans, white T-shirt, black leather jacket. Today he had on a blue-and-green scarf against the cold.

"Nice scarf," I said.

He grinned. "My mom knitted it. You don't think it's lame?"

"I like it. How come you're home on a Friday night?"

"It's not night yet. It's late afternoon in my world."

We were silent for a few minutes, Zach waiting for me to make the first move.

"I need help."

"Excellent," he said, sitting up and rubbing his hands. "I happen to be looking for work."

"I don't mean your photography skills."

"You and the rest of the world, unfortunately. The state of journalism today is a crime. I'm looking for anything at the moment."

"How about McDonald's?"

"Except fast food."

"I'd like you to talk with your friends at the Vixen's Lair about a Russian woman who might have worked as a dancer in one of the clubs downtown."

I handed him the photo of Katenka.

"Do you recognize the club she's in, by any chance?"

He looked at it a beat too long before shaking his head.

"You're sure?" I pushed.

"I may need money, Mel, but I'm not stupid. I don't tangle with this sort of thing."

Chapter Twenty-six

"What sort of thing?"

"The people who bring these girls in, they're . . . not very nice people."

"The women come here legally, though, right?"

"Sometimes, sometimes not. And even if they're legal at first, they might overstay their visas. Anyway, if she worked in one of the clubs, chances are good she doesn't want them to be reminded of her, either. If she got out, then it's all good. Why stir up trouble?"

"It's the only thing I can think of. She's gone missing. I'm worried."

"And the cops?"

"Her husband hasn't listed her as missing yet."

Our eyes held for a beat. "And you think her husband had something to do with her disappearance?"

"I don't know," I said. "I have no real reason to think so. I just . . . I can't imagine why she would disappear. They have a little boy, a baby." I supposed it was possible

Katenka had simply gotten fed up and run, or was so scared of the ghosts that she bolted. But she was arranging that birthday party for Quinn, and no matter how awkward she seemed with him . . . she was also fiercely protective. I couldn't shake the feeling that she'd have to have a reason to run.

"What the hell," Zach said with a shrug. "I need the cash."

"You're going to charge me?"

"I just told you I was looking for work. I have a very reasonable hourly rate."

"Yes, but you owe me. Big time. Do this for me and I'll call it even." I handed him a twenty-dollar bill. "For expenses."

"Gee, thanks."

"Let me know what you find out." I rose to leave.

"Aren't you coming with me?" he asked.

"I've got buildings to build." And ghosts to banish.

"It's Friday night. Why don't you let me take you out?"

"I thought you didn't have any money."

He grinned. "I've got a twenty in my pocket; let me at least spring for a cup of coffee. Or how about McDonald's? I could pick up an application."

I couldn't help but smile.

"Thanks anyway, Slick, but the last time we met you essentially kidnapped me."

"I was trying to keep you safe."

"Calling the cops would have been preferable to trapping me in a salvage yard."

"Leave it to you to fixate on the details."

"I'm leaving now. Let me know what you find out." I headed for the door.

"Are you sure?" he asked, reaching around to open the door for me. "You, me, a twenty-dollar bill and a Russian girlie club—what's not fun about that?"

Mrs. Eldridge was coming back down the hall, her little white dog yapping in excitement.

Zach let out a loud sigh. "Guess I'll ask Mrs. Eldridge instead. Last time we went out she drank too much and started dancing naked on the bar, though, didn't you, Mrs. Eldridge?"

"Oh, you dickens," she said with a smile, waving him off.

"At least let me walk you to your car, Mel," Zach said.

"I'm fine." I hurried down the hallway, dropped the borrowed magazine on the credenza, and headed out of the building before I could change my mind. What was wrong with me? I had been whining about not having a date, and not only was Zach good-looking and interesting, he made me laugh. But he was young. Also, he was a criminal who had sort-of kidnapped me. Important to keep that in mind.

Absorbed in my thoughts, I neglected to pay attention to my surroundings. It was never a good idea to let down one's guard at night. This was a big city, after all. Things happened. Like now.

Someone grabbed me from behind. Before I could think, there was an arm clasped around my throat.

"*Stay out of it, or else,*" a man's voice hissed in my ear.

What a cliché, I thought as a strong hand shoved me against my car, slamming my face into the metal doorframe. Pain shot through my cheekbone and engulfed my skull, muddling my thoughts.

Instinctively, I fought back, pushing away my assailant's arm and stomping on his foot with my heavy work boots, then kicking his shins, hard. He grunted and doubled over, and I spun and drove the tip of my steel-toed boot at his kneecap hard enough to cause serious damage. Screaming, I ran back to the apartment building. Since I knew the front door was locked, I headed for Zach's window, which was a good five feet above the sidewalk, yelling his name.

Zach flung the window open and leaned out, bare-chested.

"*Mel?* Are you all right?"

I scanned the area. No sign of my attacker.

"Are you okay? What the hell happened?"

Before I could find the words to explain, he leapt nimbly out the window, landing on the narrow strip of lawn, ready for action in bare feet and jeans.

"*Where'd he go?*"

"I don't know. I think he's long gone."

"Who was it?"

I shook my head. My assailant had been a tallish guy, and I thought he had been wearing a ski mask and gloves. That description could fit a good portion of the city's population, including Zach. But it couldn't have been him; he had the perfect alibi.

Zach pulled me to him and cradled me to his chest, murmuring soothing sounds.

Not that this was the best time to notice, but Zach must have been working out. His lean swimmer's physique had beefed up considerably since the last time I'd seen him.

"You okay?" He touched my face gingerly.

My cheek throbbed and I could feel my eye swelling. But I cleared my throat and stepped away, nodding. "I'm fine. Thanks."

"You want to call the cops?"

I chewed on my lip, then shook my head. Inspector Crawford already thought I was nuts, and even if she believed me, without more to go on there was no way they'd find the guy.

"Let's go inside," Zach said, then paused. "Hold on. No key. Well, no problem. I'll hoist you up; you go through the window and open the door for me."

"You most certainly will not hoist me anywhere," I said, uncomfortable with the thought of him trying to lift a, uh, healthy woman like me. What if he couldn't do it? And even if he could, I was wearing a short skirt and lacked grace. No, such a scenario could only end in disaster. "I'll hoist *you*. I'm at least as strong as you are."

He chuckled.

"Or you can ask Mrs. Eldridge to open the door," I suggested.

"I could, but my apartment door would still be locked."

"Didn't give a thought to grabbing your keys before jumping out the window?"

"I was focused on rescuing you. I was being gallant, thank you very much."

"Yes, you were. Thank you. Too bad the guy had already run off."

"Not my fault."

"I should get home, anyway. Want me to boost you?"

"Nah." Zach cocked his head, assessing the height of the window. He stepped back to get a running start, leapt in the air, grabbed the window ledge, then gracefully swung his body up and over the windowsill.

I was impressed. "What are you, a gymnast?"

"Misspent youth."

"I'll bet. Anyway, thanks."

"Anytime. I'll just wait here and watch until you leave."

I turned, then hesitated. "Zach, this guy isn't, in any way, working with you, is he?"

"You did *not* just ask me that. When are we going to get past that one little incident, so long ago?"

"Just wanted to cover my bases. Let me know what you find out about the Russian."

I hurried to my car, climbed inside, and locked the doors. I waved good-bye to Zach, who was watching from the window, and drove off.

I didn't really think Zach had had anything to do with what just happened—after all, he was in no way connected to any of this business. But this meant someone had been following me. I watched my rearview mirror anxiously all the way home.

I *hate* being followed.

I limped home to find all the boys—Caleb and a friend, Dad, Stan, even Dog—in the living room watching TV. They were sharing a huge bowl of popcorn, which was the one food—besides tofu—that Dog didn't like. Unless, of course, a popcorn kernel was loaded with butter and salt, in which case he was all over it. Dog's velvety snout was in constant motion, sniffing and waiting to make a move.

"Hey, what happened to you?" Dad asked, noticing my swelling, bruised cheekbone.

"Got in the way of my own hammer."

"That's not like you, babe." Dad frowned. "You got too much on your plate?"

"I'll be more careful. I promise."

I took a bag of peas from the freezer and held it to my face, then slumped onto the sofa next to Caleb. He no longer enjoyed snuggling, but that didn't keep me from stealing a little physical contact from him when I was feeling particularly needy . . . and tonight qualified. Caleb was gracious, allowing me to lean into him for all of five minutes before easing away. It was amazing to see him grow up, though I missed the cuddly five-year-old pirate.

I watched about twenty minutes of an animated sit-com the guys found hilarious before my eyelids began to droop. I pushed myself off the couch, hugged Caleb, said good-night to his friend, kissed Stan, and leaned over to give Dad a hug.

As I smelled the lingering scent of tobacco on Dad it dawned on me: The guy who attacked me had smelled of cigarettes.

Chapter Twenty-seven

Usually I work on Saturdays, catching up on the million-and-one little things that I can't see to during the week as I rush from job site to job site. But today, I vowed, I would check in with my foremen, then take the rest of the day off.

Well, not "off" in the sense of sipping piña coladas on a beach. But today I would trade my hard hat for a ghost-chasing hat, whatever that might look like.

First I stopped by Cheshire House to see if Katenka had returned.

No one was home in the Daleys' basement apartment, but I found Raul in the main house, his arm in a sling, going over some paperwork.

"Raul, what are you doing here? Go home and recuperate. The General commands it."

"I will, boss lady. I just wanted to make sure we're ready for everything on Monday," Raul said, then looked up from the paperwork and did a double take. "What happened to your face? Are you hurt?"

The swelling on my cheekbone had gone down, but a quick glimpse in the mirror this morning revealed a bloom of color on my cheek: cherry red, greenish gray, blue. It wasn't becoming.

"Little accident. Nothing serious. And I already took care of everything for next week. Now please, go home and let your wife pamper you."

He smiled but looked troubled.

"I want to show you something."

"What is it?"

"I've been trying to figure out how I fell. The ladder was positioned well; Bertie did his job. And I know I didn't lose my balance. So I got to thinking maybe something was wrong with the ladder."

"Wrong how?" This was worrisome. My dad was a stickler for properly maintaining equipment, and I had followed his example to the letter. At least, I thought I had.

"I wondered if maybe the ladder had been tampered with. So I checked it out."

"And had it?"

He shook his head. "No, not that I could tell. But look what I *did* find."

He led the way up the stairs, to the section of balustrade that collapsed when I fell against it the other day. "See this?"

The railing had been sawed most of the way through, leaving a clean cut, not the jagged edges an accidental break would leave.

"And here . . ." Raul showed me another spot on the third-floor catwalk.

"Those cuts have been there awhile," I said. A fresh wood cut is a bright, whitish yellow. Older cuts appear darker because wood oxidizes over time. Both of the cuts Raul showed me were a dark brown.

Raul nodded. "I checked the entire railing carefully and didn't find any other cuts. How did they get there? Who would do such a thing?"

I had no answer for him.

Raul's phone rang. "My wife's outside," he said, looking sheepish. "She gave me a half-hour furlough while she ran to the store. Mel, I know you're careful, but . . . This is serious. Be more cautious than ever."

"Thanks, Raul. I will."

I walked him out to the car and exchanged pleasantries with his wife, then retrieved my supplies from yesterday's trip to the botanica and went back inside the house. It was time to stop the supernatural nonsense once and for all. Mounting the stairs, I wondered if it was wise to go into the attic by myself. I thought about waiting and trying to get Graham to go up with me, but I hesitated to subject him to possible danger. Besides, I wasn't sure I wanted to allow these ghosts to reopen a romantic can of worms with Graham.

Olivier had explained it was vital to be resolute before contacting the spirits. Last night's attack had served to strengthen my conviction. I had been physically threatened by a human as well as by ghosts, my foreman had been injured, and my complicated relationship with Graham had been rendered still more complex.

I'd had it with these spirits.

With each step I climbed, I focused on banishing my fear, replacing it with determination and a sense of calm. I started chanting to myself, *I am alive, a part of this world. You are not.* The winged angels of death carved in the woodwork seemed to follow me with their eyes, as if mocking me. *I am alive, a part of this world. You are not.*

On the top floor, I took a deep breath and released it slowly, caressing the warm gold of my grandmother's wedding ring that I wore around my neck. I pulled open the hatch, brought down the stairs, and ascended into the darkness of the attic.

Daylight streamed through the small vents, but otherwise the space was shadowy and forbidding. I switched on the overhead lightbulb and, using my flashlight, inspected the old dead bolt on the hidden door. I tried each key from the antique key ring. None worked.

I turned away to grab my tools, but this time when I crouched down in front of the lock, the door was ajar.

As I reached out toward it, it snapped shut.

Something scurried past in my peripheral vision.

A shadow hovered over my shoulder, dark and angry.

My heart leapt to my throat, and I squeezed my eyes shut for a moment, pondering fear cages. Could I be experiencing a biological response to electromagnetic stimuli? Or was I, in fact, communicating with the former inhabitants of Cheshire House? Inhabitants who had to be convinced to move along to the light, or the other side, or wherever it is that ghosts are supposed to go? Maybe I should have thought this through a little more thoroughly. . . .

But for now, I had to try to speak to it . . . to them.

"Is this Charles Carter?" Nothing. "Andre? Dominga? Luvitica?" I intoned one name after the other, concentrating on calling them, communicating with them. I clasped the band of gold, centering myself. *I am alive, a part of*

this world. You are not. I am alive, a part of this world.
You are not.

Still nothing.

Okay, plan B.

Kneeling on the dusty floor, I laid out the items from
the botanica: a bell, bundles of herbs, holy water, candles. I felt a little foolish, and wondered if I had become
the sort of person I used to make fun of, the "Berkeley
woo-woo type." But if I had, did it matter?

I lit the candles, then held the smudge bundle over
the flame. As smoke arose from the herbs, I repeated
aloud: "I am alive, a part of this world. You are not."

I heard something, a sound so low I wondered if I'd
actually heard it, or if I'd imagined it. It reminded me of
being awakened from a sound sleep by Caleb calling to
me when he was younger. I couldn't tell if it was real or
a dream, so I would tiptoe into his room to find him fast
asleep, chubby boy cheeks flushed with warmth, holding
his plush rabbit close to his chest.

After my marriage ended, I would still awaken, certain Caleb was calling me, only to realize that I was in
my dad's home, far from the little boy I loved so much,
wondering if he was all right.

This was that kind of sound. There, but not there.

"What is it you want?"

Silence.

But now I could feel them, sense them along my skin,
an engulfing sensation, like entering an air-conditioned
store on a hot, humid afternoon.

I felt anger, and desire. Longing. Lust. *Need.*

I picked up the bell, then went to the far corner of the
attic and rang it, intoning, "I am alive and you are not. I
am part of this world; you are not. Leave this place."

A woman's laughter rang out, as it had when I was in the basement. Malicious, immature. Once I got over the sinister shock of it all, I was reminded of girls snickering behind their lockers in high school.

As I walked the perimeter of the attic, I noticed a neat stack of ancient newspapers, as though someone had pulled them from the walls and floor. Could someone have been up here, cleaning up?

They were yellowed and brittle with age. The one on top contained a nuptial announcement, with a formal wedding sketch of Charles and Luvitica. She was beautiful and very young-looking; he was rather gaunt-looking, though not nearly so haggard as when I saw him in the bathroom mirror downstairs the other day. So the wet footprints did, indeed, belong to Charles.

I lifted the paper, which fell apart in my hands. Below it was another, reporting Charles Carter's demise from kidney failure while on a sea voyage to Chile. He was survived by his wife, Luvitica, his mother, Dominga, and his younger brother, Andre.

I felt I was being watched. The next thing I knew, wet footprints appeared before me.

"Charles? Can you tell me what happened?"

I turned back to the papers. The next in the stack was dated two days later, and had been folded to display a small article about Andre Carter going missing. Maybe Charles *was* communicating. He couldn't speak to me, so was he trying to tell the story through the old papers?

It dawned on me that Charles spit up liquid when he tried to talk. But the dead don't breathe. How had liquid gotten into his lungs? Perhaps he hadn't died of kidney failure, after all.

Then I felt a blackness over my shoulder—it appeared

to chase Charles away. The newspapers began to scatter, whirling through the attic, as though flung by invisible hands.

I heard the woman's laughter again, and I saw something in the shadows, shifting and growing.

A newspaper landed on the burning candle and burst into flames.

I ran to extinguish it, stomping on it with my booted foot. Papers were flying through the air now, the neat stack dispersed. I blew out the remainder of the candles, but turned on my flashlight. Daylight sifted in through the ventilation screens, but the place was still dim.

I looked all around me, but Charles had disappeared.

But the shadow loomed on one side of the attic, and a ghostly woman laughed on the other. Two different entities, then. And Charles. All in this house. I was hoping their unhappy trio was the extent of it.

I stroked my grandmother's wedding ring, and tried to regroup.

"Luvitica?" I called.

More laughter. And a faint, "Hmmmmm."

"Show yourself," I said. Nothing. "This is no longer your house. Leave this place."

The candles began to fall over, one after the other. The bell rang of its own accord. I tried not to respond in fear to the eerie parlor tricks. I told myself to hold on to my resolution to rid this house of these ghosts, once and for all.

"What do you want?" I demanded.

Urgent whispers, unintelligible, from behind the hidden door.

"Do you know what happened to Katenka?" I asked, taking another tack.

More laughing.

And then . . . an image of the horsehair settee popped into my mind—as if the ghosts had guided it there.

"I am alive, a part of this world. You are not," I said. I had to get control over them before they were able to manipulate me to do their will.

I heard a high-pitched giggle, mocking, as if daring me. I felt rage building inside me, but pushed it away.

"I am alive, a part of this world. You are not," I repeated.

There was sudden silence. I waited, opening my senses to further communication with them. I sensed nothing, heard nothing.

Had it worked? Had I banished them? As much as I wanted to, I couldn't quite believe it. That had been too easy. I held still, listening, feeling, but as minute followed minute and I still sensed nothing, I dared to hope.

I descended the attic ladder to the third-floor hallway. The air seemed to shimmer, shadows hidden within shadows—it all seemed sinister. They were still here.

An image flashed in my mind: the settee.

I walked slowly down the stairs, pressing my back against the wall for safety, taking care to stay away from the railing. Each step seemed to squeak, and the wind rattling the windowpanes sounded like far-off laughter.

In the dining room was the settee. The settee I had laid Katenka's still form on after she fainted the other day. The settee Katenka intended to bring to Emile's shop the day he was murdered. I had wondered at the time why she was focused on it when there were so many other things to worry about. As I approached, I fully expected to see indentations in the dusty horsehair cushions, as though the ghosts were sitting there, watching me. But I saw nothing. I took a seat.

It was supremely uncomfortable. One area bulged out, the edging pulled up on one side. I looked closer. The upholstery was held down not with upholstery tacks but with staples, the kind used in a desk stapler. I snagged my fingernail under the staples and pulled them out, one by one, until I could fit a hand under the upholstery. I reached in. My fingertips felt something hard yet yielding, grasped it, and pulled it out.

An envelope. Filled with cash.

I counted it. One hundred twenty-dollar bills. Two thousand dollars.

It was an odd way to pay for an upholstery job. Unless that wasn't what the money was for.

Had Katenka been paying Emile for something else? Had the Russian-speaking Emile known about her past and blackmailed her? Had Katenka killed Emile to put an end to the blackmail, and then fled, afraid she would be discovered?

And if so, why had she waited so long?

My phone rang. I glanced at the screen.

Zach.

"I got that information you wanted," he said without preamble.

The voices started up again around me, bickering now. Sniping at one another. It wasn't as frightening as the nasty laughter in the attic, but it was much more annoying. It was like speaking over a phone with a bad connection, when you hear the echo of your voice and try to ignore it. They were giving me a headache, as well as a sincere appreciation for those poor souls afflicted with schizophrenia.

"Did you find her?" I asked loudly, trying to drown out the voices.

"No. But I found something else. Meet me at Caffe Trieste in twenty minutes. Why are you shouting?"

"I'm sort of in the middle of something," I said, lowering my voice. I tried plugging my free ear with my finger. "Just tell me what you found."

"No."

"Why not?" I thought of all those movies where someone refuses to divulge a secret on the phone, saying instead: *"I have critical information to solve the mystery; meet me in an abandoned warehouse down by the docks at midnight."* That never turned out well.

"Because I want to buy you coffee. I've been trying to buy you coffee since we met."

"This isn't a *date*, Zach, for heaven's sake." The whispering grew louder, snider. The ghosts were making fun of me. "Just tell me."

"You need caffeine. I can tell. If you can't meet me right now, then how about this evening?"

"No," I said, rubbing my temples. I needed Olivier to do his miraculous headache cure. Or bigger hands to do it to myself. "Fine. I'll meet you there in twenty. But if you wind up dead, don't come whining to me."

"If I *what*?" Zach said. "Why would someone kill me for this information?"

"Why not? That's what always happens in the movies."

He laughed. "I'll take my chances. Caffe Trieste is pretty mellow this time of day."

I snapped the cell phone shut and gathered my things.

"I'll be back," I said to the ghosts, channeling my inner Terminator. As I slammed the door behind me I could have sworn I heard a ghostly Bronx cheer.

*   *   *

A small part of me felt like a chicken for not finishing what I'd started with the ghosts, but the biggest part of me felt a palpable sense of relief as I stepped outside into the fresh air.

Besides, my resolve had been seriously eroded. I needed time to recuperate, to decide where to go from here. And my now nagging headache should be helped by the caffeine.

I noticed the homeless man sitting on the corner, singing "Jingle Bells." He had attached a holiday wreath with a bedraggled red bow to the front of his shopping cart. It was nice to see somebody embracing the holiday spirit.

As I passed by him, he stopped singing and shouted, "No, I *don't* have any heroin, as a matter of fact. Why would you ask me that?"

After my bizarre experience at Cheshire House, this made me wonder: Maybe he and the other talkative street folk weren't mentally ill. Maybe they were conversing with invisible spirits. I stopped in front him and searched my peripheral vision. Nothing.

"You okay, lady?" the man asked.

"Sorry," I said. "Hey, are you hungry? I almost forgot—I brought some lunch. My dad's a good cook."

"Sure," he said. I fetched a brown paper bag from my car and handed it to him. He peeked in.

"Chicken and rice with broccoli," I said.

"I like Thai better," he replied.

Only in San Francisco.

"Sorry. It's potluck at my house. I eat what my dad cooks."

"Okay, thanks," he said. "I'm honored. Got a spoon?"

"It's in the bag."

I was about to turn back to my car when I noticed a

couple of long, thin, brown cigarettes peeking out of his shirt pocket. Pricey, European cigarettes.

Expensive habit already, and I get hooked on the imports.

"Hey, you hang out here a lot, right?" I said. "You talked to the police about the fellow who was killed the other night?"

"Didn't mean to snitch on you," he said, clutching the leftovers closer.

"No, of course not," I hastened to say. "I just wondered if anyone else went in, maybe someone you forgot to mention to the police?"

He shrugged. "Sometimes my memory's not so good. Especially if it's not jogged by a charitable donation."

What an operator, I thought, though I kind of admired him for it. I reached into my pocket and pulled out a ten. "How's this?"

He nodded and took the bill. His fingernails had that crusted, ground-in dirt that came from going too long without a shower.

"Fellow came by, said he used to live here a long time ago, in the house across the street, back when it was a boardinghouse."

"What did he look like?"

"Latino guy, mustache. Gave me a twenty, some cigs. Good guy. But I guess he served time and he didn't wanna talk to police."

"What do you mean?"

"Dude had prison tats. You can tell 'cause they're done with ink from ballpoint pens, not like regular tattoos." He tapped his head. "I figured that's why he asked me to keep the info on the down-low, if you know what I'm sayin'."

"Did you hear anything after he went into the upholstery shop? Did you hear a gunshot?"

He shook his head. "Didn't hear anything but them arguing. Then I left to go see a friend. I mind my own business, mostly."

"Could you hear what they were arguing about?"

"Crazy talk, somethin' about ghosts in an attic. And people say *I'm* nuts."

"Anything else?"

The man tilted his head. "Yeah. Asked about a key."

"A key to what?"

"A door, I think he said."

"What about it?"

He closed his eyes and didn't answer. I waited.

His eyes popped open. "He asked if the key to the door was safe."

Chapter Twenty-eight

As I drove to meet Zach, I thought again of the letters Katenka told me Jim had found, the letters that seemed to be influencing him. I felt sure the key to it all was in the house's past. If I could get ahold of those letters, perhaps they could shed more light on the house and the family who had once owned it. The ghosts hadn't wanted their history known, had "told" Hettie Banks to destroy the files at the historical society. They must have had a reason.

Just as I was pulling up to a parking spot, my phone rang. I didn't recognize the number.

"This is Mel," I answered.

"*Mel*. Thank goodness. I don't know where to turn. I haven't been able to get in touch with Katenka for *days*."

"Elena?"

"Yes, of course. Have you spoken with her? There are so many things to go over for the party . . ."

I let her vent for a moment, only half listening,

wondering what to say. If Katenka had stepped out for a couple of days to cool off, I imagined she still wanted the party to take place. It was her son's first birthday, after all. But if something unspeakable had happened to Katenka, an elaborate Russian-themed birthday party would be in poor taste, to say the least.

I hoped Graham hadn't confided to Elena my fears about Katenka and Jim. That would be awkward.

"I think you should make the decisions for the moment, Elena. Katenka has been out of touch, I know. But this is why you're the professional, right? You make all the right sort of party choices."

"But the event's only two days away!"

"I realize that, but since you only started planning it a few days ago, percentage-wise, two days is huge. Think of it that way."

"What? I don't understand."

"I have to go now, but I promise I'll let you know when I hear from Katenka. For now go make some party favors so everything will be just glorious, okay?"

"I . . . all right. Thank you, Mel. I appreciate it."

I made a gagging noise upon hanging up, then felt bad. What was I, twelve? There was nothing wrong with Elena. She was perfectly nice. And it wasn't out of line for her to be worried about the party that was supposed to take place in two days.

I parallel-parked in a residential area a couple of blocks from Caffe Trieste, an unassuming little coffee shop that has occupied a quiet North Beach corner for about as long as anyone can remember. It's a local favorite and serves the best coffee in the world, hands down.

Zach was waiting for me at a small table by the window. He gestured to the barista as I sat down.

"I ordered you a double latte."

"Nonfat, please," I called to the barista.

"Fat lattes taste better," said Zach with a smile. "How about a chocolate croissant or something? A sweet for the sweet?"

"Tell me what you learned." I was *not* in the mood.

"You're a tough nut to crack, Mel. Know that?"

"Maybe I'm just a nut."

He gazed at me intently. "Somehow I doubt that."

"Zach, please. What did you find out?"

He sighed. "Katenka said she met her husband online, when she was living in Russia, yes?"

I nodded.

"That was stretching the truth. She worked in the city long before she met Jim, online or otherwise. Paid a pretty penny to be brought in and 'allowed' to work at an underground club called Jelly's."

"Hard to picture Katenka as a dancer."

"That's because she wasn't, not in the strictest sense. The women at Jelly's do a certain kind of dancing, if you catch my drift. It may not be what she thought she was signing up for in Russia, but once they're brought here, they're stuck. If the women run away and file a complaint with the police, all they'll get out of it is deported back to Russia. Either way, they lose."

"That's outrageous."

"Things are tough in the former Soviet Union. There's a line a mile long of women trying to get out, and there aren't many legal ways to do it. Anyway, Katenka was one of the lucky ones. The bartender said she didn't work there for long. Turns out she met up with an old man—would that be her husband?"

I shook my head.

"I got the sense this guy was something of a barfly. The bartender didn't know his name but said he was an American who spoke Russian. Learned it from his grandparents, who were immigrants, according to the bartender."

Emile Blunt, I thought. "What happened then?"

"Far as the bartender knew, that was the whole story. Katenka didn't show up for work one day, slipped away somewhere. Must have laid low for a while with her sugar daddy. Within a month she sent money to pay off her debt with her employers, so they let it go. Probably used her as a 'success story' to lure other women. Come to America, marry a rich man."

"The man was rich?" I asked. Maybe it wasn't Emile.

"All men in America are rich, haven't you heard?"

"Guess I missed the memo."

Zach handed me the photo of Katenka that Ivana had given me. I searched her pretty face, the trace of a smile I had rarely seen on her.

"By the way, you're in my debt."

"How do you figure that?"

"I had to slip the bartender a Benjamin to get him in a chatty mood."

"A Benjamin? Oh, that's . . . a hundred?"

Zach gave me a crooked grin.

"I thought you said you were broke," I pointed out.

"I am. It's my mad money."

"A hundred bucks is your mad money?"

"I don't often get mad."

"And that's it? This doesn't tell me where to find Katenka."

"No one's seen her for years now. But it does tell you something about her background."

"Did the bartender say anything more about the old man? Does he still come in?"

"He apparently disappeared around the same time as Katenka."

"Anything else?"

"One thing that stuck in his mind—the guy was into taxidermy, stuffing dead animals."

It was Emile, then, for sure. How many old Russian-speaking taxidermists could there possibly be in San Francisco?

So Katenka had a deep, dark secret and a history with Emile Blunt. As his mistress? Or had Emile suggested Katenka find his lonely, wealthy neighbor Jim online so that the two could meet and Emile could then . . . what, milk her for money? Was the money I found in the settee one of her payments to him?

I sipped my latte and turned possible scenarios over in my mind. Could Katenka have killed Emile, tired of the blackmail? Or had Jim Daley discovered what was happening and killed Emile to keep him quiet about Katenka's past? Maybe to punish Emile for his relationship with Katenka and for stealing Jim's money through blackmail? Or was Jim Daley a jealous husband who, upon learning the truth about Emile and Katenka, had killed them both?

Maybe.

Then again . . . Dave Enrique argued with Emile the night he died. Could he and Emile have been enemies since their days at the Cheshire Inn? Could there have been some kind of romantic triangle involving one or both of the men and Janet, Hettie's daughter? I rejected that idea. Emile was old enough to be Janet's grandfather, and Dave was a good ten or twenty years Janet's senior. A romantic triangle involving those three seemed far-fetched.

Plus, it was icky.

Besides, Hettie Banks and Emile Blunt were former flames. And white cat hair had been left on the sofa in Emile's shop the night of the murder. Cat hair meant cats, which suggested Hettie. She might be getting up there in years, but it didn't take much strength to pull a trigger.

I thought about calling Inspector Crawford again, but decided against it. I had nothing even remotely resembling evidence to implicate anybody in Emile's death, and for all I knew Katenka came home last night, and was even now enjoying a champagne brunch with Jim and the baby at the Palace Hotel.

Zach interrupted my reverie. "Penny for your thoughts?"

"Beg your pardon?"

"Penny. For your thoughts."

"My mother used to say that."

"So did mine. What's up?"

"Nothing. Listen, Zach, I have to run. I don't have a Benjamin on me. Can I send it to you?"

"Why don't I give you a call? We'll get together when you have more time, and arrange for repayment."

"Okay, whatever works. And thanks."

"Anytime."

I pondered possible suspects and scenarios as I walked to my car. Before I started up the engine, Hettie called.

"Need a favor."

"Okay. . . ."

"Will you feed my cats?"

"I . . . uh . . . why? What's going on?"

"I can't get to 'em for a while. Key's under the mat. There's food in the cupboard. They share a can morning and night. Oh, and change their water."

"Where are you?"

"I'm down to the police station."

"Are you in trouble?"

"It's not looking good, tell you the truth. They say I had motive, opportunity, left some of Pudding's hair on Emile's couch, and even took a souvenir from the crime scene like they say some disturbed people do."

"Souvenir?"

"They found a rhinestone cat collar on Pudding. I didn't put it on 'im."

"Have you called a lawyer?"

"I'm not worried about me. Heck, I hear in prison they got free medical care and cable TV and everything. But promise me you'll take care of my cats."

"What about Janet? Have you called her? Could she help?"

"Janet hates cats almost as much as she hates me. She oughta be happy now, though. Guess she'll get a building on Union Street after all. Seems least I could do is leave her that upholstery shop if I'm going to San Quentin." I heard a commotion in the background. "Listen, I gotta go. Are you gonna do this for me, or not?"

I took a deep breath and let it out slowly. "I'll take care of them."

An hour later I walked into my dad's house with a struggling cat under each arm and a bag of cat kibble slung over my shoulder. I was scratched up and down my arms, covered in fur, and in a truly foul mood. I also had a newfound respect for Janet Banks and the feral feline rescue squad.

Dog went nuts upon sensing felines. The cats hissed and broke free, leaping from my arms and running to hide.

Dad dropped his chopping knife and after much human yelling and canine barking, Dad grabbed Dog by the collar, dragged him outside, and shut the kitchen door.

"You're adopting cats now?" Dad demanded. "What the hell's gotten into you?"

"You okay, Mel?" asked Stan.

I dropped the bag of food on the floor and went to the sink to wash my hands. Between my mottled cheekbone and the red furrows on my arms, I was starting to look like an extra in a zombie apocalypse movie.

"Learned something new today: Cats don't like to ride in cars," I said.

Corralling the cats at Hettie's condo had been hard enough, but I finally managed to get them out to the car. The moment I started the engine, both cats lost their minds. At one point Pudding was literally standing atop the steering wheel while Horatio paced back and forth across the backseat, howling. It was a long ride home.

"Some cats don't mind cars." Stan chuckled and coaxed Horatio out from behind a cupboard and into his lap. Pudding was nowhere to be found.

I leaned against the counter as I dried my hands.

Dad returned to chopping onion and celery. "Gonna be a damned menagerie in here by the time you're through."

"We're doing a good deed," I said. "And it's only temporary." I hoped.

"That's what you said about Dog. And Caleb . . ."

"Hey, Caleb's nonnegotiable. He and I are a package deal, so if you don't want him here, just say the word and I'll move out."

"Me, too," said Stan.

Dad shrugged. "Nah, Caleb's a good kid. I put him and his buddy to work out in the yard today, cutting back those shrubs by the garage."

"Is he here?"

"Out with a couple of friends, jogging around Lake Merritt. Said he'd be back for dinner, asked if he could invite them along. I said sure."

"Thanks, Dad."

"Not sure about those cats, though. You remember the time you brought home that flea-bitten Siamese?"

"That was one of your other daughters. Charlotte always liked cats."

"You sure? I could have sworn it was you."

"I'm sure. I was there."

He shrugged and transferred the onions and celery into a pan of heated olive oil, where they sizzled, sending out an enticing aroma. My stomach growled.

"Mel, why don't you go take a shower while Bill finishes supper and I introduce Dog to the cats?" suggested Stan. "They'll get along fine once they know one another—you'll see. This one here's a real sweetie."

"Thanks, guys. You're lifesavers. What would I do without you?"

Chapter Twenty-nine

The next day the phone rang while I was still in bed, pretending to sleep. I wasn't sleeping, of course, because now that I awoke at five every morning for work I had become the sort of person who can no longer sleep past dawn. Plus, there were two cats and a dog sleeping in the room, and at least two of the creatures snored. Pathetic.

I reached for the phone, covers still drawn over my head.

"Hello?" I croaked.

"Morning, sunshine."

I sat up. "Graham?"

"Sorry to say this isn't a social call. Matt's about to lose it over the tile in his kitchen."

I sighed. "What's up?"

"Apparently they're the wrong height, so the kitchen floor will be higher than the existing wood floors in the hall and dining room."

"Significantly higher?"

"About three-eighths of an inch."

I heard Matt's voice in the background, slightly hysterical, exclaiming, *"Whoever heard of height? Width and length, but height? Is that Mel? Tell her to come save me!"*

"I'll be right there."

So much for a day, much less a weekend, off work.

"Why are you meeting with Matt at this hour?" I asked when Graham opened Matt's door.

"Green consultation with the architect over breakfast. Apparently I'm now on call twenty-four hours a day. OSHA's looking better all the time."

"Mel, thank heavens you're here," said Matt as he rushed up to us. "I'm beside myself."

I checked out the kitchen floor, and the new shipment of tile. Three-eighths of an inch was too much of an elevation shift to bridge with a simple wooden threshold. It would never look right.

"The tile guy should have alerted you, Matt. I apologize on his behalf. I'll follow up with him, but for now you have a decision to make. You either have to take out the subfloor—which is a pretty big deal—or simply choose a different tile."

"But I had my heart set on those," Matt said.

"I'll go tile shopping with you, if you want. It'll be fun." That was an exaggeration. What it would be was a huge time-suck, like all shopping trips with clients. But if Matt's project fell behind, so would Cheshire House. Since we shared the same workers and subcontractors, one problem led inexorably to another, like toppling dominos.

"Okay, if you'll come and hold my hand. It's hard to decide these things."

"Sure I will." I checked my BlackBerry. "We can do lunch on Tuesday or Wednesday, if you want."

"One more thing. I think the ceiling in the library is too low."

I froze. This wasn't a three-day tile job fix we were talking about. This was serious.

"You want to redo the roof."

"I want it done right."

Was it the effect of the cameras? Was he becoming a prima donna?

"I have to level with you, Matt. It'll be exorbitantly expensive. Raising the roof means new permits, and requires getting the neighbors' consent because a raised roof may impact the view of the houses behind you. There's something called discretionary review here in San Francisco, which means that if the neighbors consider your project 'exceptional and extraordinary' they can request a review by the city planning commission, even if the project has already been given approval."

Matt gave me a blank look.

"Bottom line: If you get approved—and you probably won't—it means a delay of at least several months, possibly more. Not to mention the additional construction costs, which will be substantial. If you really want to do this, the first people to convince are your neighbors. You'll also have to talk to the architect to commission new drawings. In the meantime, I suggest we leave the roof as it is."

"One good thing: If we change the roof we could put solar panels up there. Graham was just explaining their advantages."

I glared at Graham. He smiled.

"That's a special permit process, as well," I said. "But

then as my mother always used to say, in for a penny, in for a pound."

"How many pounds?" asked the Brit.

"Many, many pounds."

Graham walked me to my car.

"Have you heard from Katenka?" he asked.

"No sign of her."

"Elena's been trying to get in touch with her about the party, which is coming up."

"Yes, she called me yesterday."

"Don't suppose you know anything new?"

"Actually, I asked someone to look into the club where Katenka used to dance, when she first arrived from Russia. Remember Zach Malinski?"

"Zach, as in that kid from the fiasco at Matt's house last summer? The photographer?"

"The photographer, yes. But he's hardly a kid."

"The man who *kidnapped* you?"

"It wasn't a kidnapping, exactly. There were extenuating circumstances."

"Are you insane?"

"I think we're getting a little off track here; my point is that Katenka didn't meet Jim the way she claimed. She was here, in San Francisco, working at a club."

"What kind of club?"

"The sleazy kind."

"So maybe they were embarrassed about it, and made up the online story to sound more respectable."

"No one remembers meeting him at the club."

"All that means is he isn't that memorable. I could have told you that."

"But what if she led him to believe she really was in

Russia, teaching Sunday school or something, and he found out the truth, and did something to her?"

"Look, I find it hard to believe Jim would do such a thing, but assuming you're right, why aren't you talking to the police?"

"I mentioned it, but the inspector didn't seem to think there was much to it. And Jim's my client, after all. If I had some sort of proof, anything at all, I wouldn't hesitate. But how awful would it be to accuse the man if he's innocent?"

Graham nodded. "It's a tough one. But listen, as soon as she's listed as officially 'missing,' the police will be looking at Jim long and hard anyway. As sad as it is, it's often a loved one who does the unspeakable."

"Somehow that fails to make me feel better."

"Hey, this is really getting to you, isn't it?"

"These women just seem so . . . vulnerable. Remember that Russian in Piedmont a few years ago, who was killed by her engineer husband? Her situation was a lot like Katenka's."

"Mel, you can't go around impugning every nerdy guy who marries a Russian. Katenka is probably with a friend, cooling down. I don't think you can jump to conclusions with something like this."

"Why wouldn't Jim file a missing persons report?"

"It hasn't been that long. And these days . . ." He shrugged. "With homeland security and everything else, you might not want to get someone with a questionable visa involved in the system."

My phone rang. Caleb.

"I'm in the middle of something, Goose," I said. "Can I call you back?"

"Bill asked me to call," he said, and I heard a woman's high-pitched voice in the background. "We've got company."

"Who is it?"

"The lady from the house you're working on. The Russian."

Chapter Thirty

"*Katenka*? She's at the house?"

"Yeah. And she's got the kid with her."

"Is she okay?"

"Seems okay. Kinda upset, though. Can't get the baby to stop crying. Bill's not that happy."

"Put her on the phone."

There was a crashing sound, and the crying grew louder. I heard male and female voices raised. The dog barked and a cat yowled.

"It might not be, like, the best time?" Caleb said. "How 'bout you just get home as soon as you can?"

"I'm on my way."

I hung up to find Graham looking down at me, a self-satisfied smile on his face. I couldn't help but smile back.

"All right, all right. You were right. She's fine. Sounds like she's already driving my dad crazy, though. I'd better get back."

He reached out and tucked a curl behind my ear.

"You might want to develop a little more faith in humanity, Mel. In men, in particular."

I rolled my eyes, but nodded. "Maybe you're right."

I arrived home to find things had settled down considerably. Stan was regaling Katenka with a long story from his childhood back in Bull Hill, Oklahoma, and Katenka listened with that breathless, big-eyed expression she reserved for the male of the species. Caleb had taken the baby up to his room to find a children's book in his old bookcase we had never emptied out. And Dad had decided to cook a traditional Sunday "lupper," a lunch/supper combo to be served early in the day. He was chopping and grousing in his cheerful, gruff way.

"Katenka, I was so worried about you," I said.

"Really?" she seemed surprised, then pleased.

"Does Jim know you're here? How did you get Quinn?"

"I picked baby up from Ivana. She was watching him this afternoon."

"Does Jim know where you are?"

She shook her head.

"Let's go in the other room," I said, heading toward the living room where we could have a little privacy. "Excuse us, guys. Girl talk."

We both took seats, and Katenka resumed her typical flat affect. "Katenka, when you disappeared . . . I really thought something might have happened to you."

"I was in hotel on Fisherman's Wharf. They had a special; it was cheap. I watch cable, eat crab. Be by myself for a day or two. Get away from ghosts. This is too much to ask?"

Now she reminded me of me. Luz was right: It *did* sound whiny.

"Everyone needs a break sometimes. But you should

tell your husband and your friends." Presuming your husband wasn't a murderer.

She shrugged, but looked chastened.

"I was . . ." I hesitated, wondering how to phrase it. "I was so worried that something had happened to you, that I looked into your past. I learned how you came into this country."

"You can't tell anyone, Mel," she said, alarmed.

"Were you paying Emile for his silence?"

She swallowed hard. "Emile met me at the club, helped me leave, let me stay with him. I was grateful to him for this. Then he told me about his neighbor, Jim; helped me to meet him online. I didn't think . . . I didn't want to hurt anyone. Just wanted to stay here, have a nice home."

"Did Jim find out about this? Did he know about the blackmail?"

"No." She sounded very sure.

"So that night, when Jim went to talk to Emile, it was just about the construction issues?"

She shrugged and played with her key ring, which was in the shape of Mickey Mouse.

"Katenka?"

"I was upset. I told Jim Emile said mean things to me in our language. I shouldn't have told him that. Jim became very angry, went to defend my honor. I could not stop him."

"But Jim didn't know about the blackmail, or your relationship to Emile?"

"No! Of course not."

"Do you think Emile told him that night?"

She looked frightened. "No. I am sure of this."

I didn't see how she could possibly be sure of that. "Were you there?"

"No, I stay with baby in the house."

"Katenka, I don't think you should keep this a secret from Jim," I said. "He's your husband. He has a right to know."

"I did nothing wrong. I did what was necessary."

"I understand, but—"

"*No*, Mel. You do not understand. You have happy family, good life. Look at all of this." She gestured around the room.

At first all I could see was broken windowpanes, unfinished trim, cracked and unpainted plaster. But in the window stood a Christmas tree covered in funky decorations from my own happy childhood, and newer ones from Caleb's. On the mantel were framed pictures of my mother, my sisters with their young families, a Turner family camping trip. At the bottom of the stairs were several pairs of athletic shoes and boots, belonging to a small group of loyal, loving guys who cared for me. And at my feet lay a big, brown dog that had once saved my life.

"You are so lucky," she continued. "How do you possibly understand what I must do?"

I didn't know what to say, because of course she was right. We both remained silent for a long time.

Pudding, the white cat, strode along the coffee table, stepping daintily over Katenka's crowded key ring. I found myself checking for an odd old key of some sort, one that would fit the hidden room in the attic. Hettie said Pudding had been wearing the rhinestone collar from Emile's place, but she hadn't mentioned a charm hanging from it . . . The homeless guy said Dave Enrique and Emile Blunt were arguing about a key . . . Could that charm I first noticed on the stuffed cat in Emile Blunt's upholstery shop have been some sort of key? Was it possible?

When Katenka finally spoke, her voice faltered with

emotion. "I love him now, you know. Jim is a very good man. At first I wanted green card, security—this is true. But he is always there for me, always good. How will he believe I love him if he knows about this?"

"Don't you think that if Jim loves you, if he's a truly good man, he would understand?"

"Maybe." She shrugged and brought out a stack of yellowed papers. "I bring you the letters from the attic. I took them from Jim's briefcase. They are not good for him. You keep them, please. You keep all the old things you find in that house. I don't want any of them."

"Thank you, Katenka. I think these letters will be useful."

"You must help me to go home," Katenka said. "Tomorrow is party."

"Speaking of the party . . . have you checked in with Elena? Last time I talked to her she was hyperventilating."

"What is hyper—what you said? I don't know this word."

"Sorry. Elena is very concerned. I told her to keep on with the party planning, but she would love to hear from you."

"Dinner's on!" yelled my Dad from the kitchen.

"Right now, you need to call Jim and let him know where you and Quinn are. I'm sure he's very worried."

She bit her lip.

"Let the poor thing eat first," said Dad, standing in the doorway to the living room.

"Oh yes, thank you," said Katenka, springing off the couch. "I call after. Smells good, Bill."

"Babe, grab the silverware, would you?" Dad told me as Katenka took a seat at the dining room table.

"Oh, let me get you a napkin," Stan said, rolling into the kitchen.

Caleb arrived with a happy Quinn on his hip, and started pouring water with his free hand.

Fluttery and helpless, Katenka knew how to work her crowd. Dad and Stan were falling all over themselves to make sure she was happy. Even Caleb was being helpful and gallant in a rather clumsy, teenage way.

"Call him now, or I will," I said, handing Katenka the portable phone. Now that I was sure Jim hadn't killed his wife, and I was very nearly certain he hadn't killed Emile, I was very much on his side.

She made a face, but then made the call.

We sat around the dining room table since the farm table in the kitchen couldn't accommodate us all. Dad had dug up an old high chair from the basement and set it up for Quinn. Dog and the cats joined us, hoping for tidbits.

Within half an hour Jim Daley arrived on our doorstep, tears in his eyes. After a private meeting, he and Katenka joined us again at the dinner table.

Dad presided over the table, which he had set with a poinsettia-and-lace tablecloth, pouring cheap wine from a gallon jug and passing the dishes from left to right. I thought how, if my mother were here, she would have turned this gathering into an impromptu party, full of warmth and laughter, as she always had. Thanksgiving without her had been hard, and I expected Christmas to be even tougher.

But we were doing all right. Crazy menagerie that we were, we made the lupper a celebration of homecoming.

Jim wound up drinking too much wine, so Katenka and I made up the extra room for their little family.

Dad fell asleep in front of the television, Stan finished up some work on the computer, Caleb cleared the table and excused himself to go text his friends, and I washed the dishes and then retired to my room.

I read very old letters until my tired eyes could no longer decipher the faded, old-fashioned writing in the wee hours of the morning.

When I finally fell asleep, they haunted my dreams.

I woke up on Quinn's first birthday pondering my new insights into the world of Cheshire House's ghosts.

Assuming Elena hadn't had a coronary, there would be a party tonight on my haunted job site. Oh boy.

My dad believes in big breakfasts. I'm more a coffee-on-the-go girl. So he was pleased to have a grateful audience as he served up plates full of omelets, bacon, and hash browns. Katenka and Jim oohed and aahed over the food, and were acting like a honeymooning couple at a bed-and-breakfast.

As I was leaving, Jim opened the door for me, then followed me out.

"Katenka told me she gave you the letters I found at the house," he said. "I'm glad she did. I don't know why I lied to you about them."

"That's okay," I said. "I was pretty caught up in them last night, myself. They're absorbing."

"That's one way to look at them. I think they were . . . I don't know. If I weren't a rational man, I would say, well, they just creeped me out. Let's leave it at that. Listen, if you still want us to move out while you finish the project, I think I'm ready to talk about it."

"That would be wonderful, Jim. It might even help us to speed up construction a little if we don't have to worry about you and your family."

"Thanks for everything, Mel. You folks at Turner Construction really do go above and beyond."

"Well, we do like to keep our clients happy," I said with a smile. "See you later at the house."

I went straight to Matt's to read the riot act to Rodrigo, the tile layer. He should have known to check the tile height long before it had been ordered, and there was nothing worse than subcontractors screwing up and making the general look bad.

Then I called and asked Luz to meet me so I could think through what I had learned from the letters.

"Lunch?" she asked.

"I can't today —no time. Besides, if you and I keep eating these huge lunches, I'll be as big as the houses I work on. I was not blessed with your miracle metabolism."

We settled on coffee at a diner on Hayes. I had a nonfat latte, and Luz ordered a mocha and an almond croissant, explaining that pastries counted as "part of coffee."

I launched into the story I had been putting together with the information from Brittany Humm, my own interactions with the spirits, and the love letters between Andre and Luvitica.

"So Luvitica and Andre were having an affair. I think Andre must have had a fight with his brother over Luvitica. The violence escalated, and in the heat of the moment, Andre killed his brother. To hide what he'd done, he put Charles's body in a barrel of rum and arranged for the ship's captain to take it with him on the trip to Chile."

"Why would he do such a thing?" Luz asked.

"There were always lots of barrels loaded onto a ship before a trip, and Andre had a connection to the sugar plantation—he may have known the captain personally."

"No one noticed Charles was dead?"

"How would they know? Andre makes all the arrangements, pays for a ticket in Charles's name and bribes the captain or a steward to swear Charles came on board. All the captain had to do was to send the rum barrel back to San Francisco once they arrived in Chile and say he died en route."

"That's awful."

"That's not the worst of it. Given how Charles's apparition appeared, I don't think Charles died from the fight with his brother. I think he drowned in the barrel of rum."

"Poor guy. What happened to Andre? He went missing, right?"

"So it seems. I'm assuming that when the barrel was delivered, Dominga insisted on laying out the body before burial. It must have been plain to see Charles had been mortally injured. Andre ran, fearing discovery."

"And Luvitica stayed behind with Dominga?"

I nodded. "The last two letters from Luvitica were never sent to Andre—I doubt she knew where to send them. In them, she claimed the baby she was carrying was his, not Charles's."

"Boy, talk about a dysfunctional family," said Luz as she popped the last of her almond croissant into her mouth. "Listen, I've got to run soon—class in an hour. What was it you wanted me to weigh in on?"

"I just wanted to make sure I'm making sense: If I'm interpreting the letters correctly, one of the ghosts is Charles, trying to reveal the truth about his death. I think telling his story will take care of his spirit, help him move on. But the shadow ghost . . . Oliver told me sometimes ghosts are overwhelmed by shame and anger, quite literally staying in the shadows. I can feel the rage and despair every time this one comes near me. I think Andre must be manifesting as the black shadow. Andre must have been eaten up with shame over sleeping with his brother's wife, and then killing Charles."

Luz and I both sat silent for a moment, subdued by the tale. It was just plain sad. Even an almond croissant couldn't fend off depressing thoughts over the Cheshire House's tragic history.

"But if Andre's the shadow ghost, then he must have returned to Cheshire House at some point, right?" Luz said. "And probably died there?"

"How do you suppose he died?"

"Maybe Andre came back to make amends, but was so haunted by the ghost of his brother that he killed himself out of guilt and remorse. That would fit with the shadow thing, as well, right?"

I nodded. "So I have to force Andre out of the shadows, and then convince him and Luvitica to leave the house. I just have no idea how, exactly."

"And what about the mother, Dominga? Where does she fit into this?"

"I'm not sure."

"Have you seen her ghost?"

"Not really, though the voices bicker quite a bit, and I think I heard two different female voices at one point. But . . . I don't know how to explain it, but her personality doesn't come across as strongly as the others, and I don't feel threatened by her. I'm going to assume that she, like Charles, just needs to have the truth told."

"Wow. Four ghosts. Reminds me of that Sartre play *No Exit*. Imagine being trapped in eternity with people you despise. What a drag."

"You can say that again. But if I make this work, maybe they'll all find their way to their respective exits."

Chapter Thirty-one

"Mel, thank goodness you're here," said Elena the minute I walked into Cheshire House. Graham stood behind her, his arms full of child-sized costumes. "We have to stop all that work upstairs. The dust is getting everywhere."

Elena hadn't wasted any time—I had to give her that. In the front parlor of Cheshire House stood a beautiful eight-foot Christmas tree covered with bright paper decorations and multicolored lights. Giant Russian nesting dolls sat in the corners of the parlor, surrounded by presents wrapped in layers of colored tissue. Dozens of sparkling snowflakes hung from the ceilings, and the usual construction-site smells of wood and plaster had given way to the aromas of scented candles, roast meat, and honey.

The baby monitor crackled, and I could have sworn I heard whispers. "Are Katenka and Jim downstairs with the baby?"

Elena nodded. "Katenka says they won't come out of

the basement until they're fully dressed. Not like I couldn't use another pair of hands around here . . ."

"I thought the party wasn't until six," I said.

"It's not, but there's so much to do. Everything has to be perfect. Graham, you can arrange those things right there in that chest."

He dumped the costumes into the brightly painted "dress-up" chest decorated in Russian-style toile, then gestured to me with what I'm sure he thought was a subtle nod. Elena zeroed in on it immediately and glared first at him, then at me.

"Um, Graham, could I show you that weather-stripping thing? Upstairs?" My improvisational skills could use a little work.

"Sure. Elena, why don't you run and pick up the adult costumes you rented? Once we check out the weather stripping we'll come give you a hand."

She checked her watch. "Oh, good heavens, you're right. I'm late. I'll be back as soon as I can. Oh, and can you be sure that cat woman leaves before the party? Last thing we need is cats running around."

"What cat woman?"

"Katenka hired someone to catch a cat stuck in the walls."

"Oh. Will do." Graham and I mounted the stairs to the second floor. "What costumes is Elena renting?"

"The newly reunited Daleys will be playing the roles of the Snow Maiden and Father Frost. Apparently it's a Russian tradition. According to what Elena tells me, though, the Snow Maiden is supposed to be Father Frost's granddaughter, which makes it kind of creepy that they can't keep their hands off each other. Good job with the couples counseling, Mel."

"Thanks. It's my strong suit."

I had hoped to rid the attic of ghosts before the party, so I was carrying my so-called ghost-busting equipment in a canvas bag. But I wondered: If I tried to banish them now, would they mess up the parlor, throw things around as they had with the newspapers in the attic?

That seemed like exactly the sort of peevish thing Luvitica would do.

On the other hand, could I risk waiting until after the party? What if they sensed that I had learned the truth about them? Would they make an appearance? Turn over the punch bowl? Crumble the gingerbread? Reanimate the roast goose? Or something much worse . . . something truly sinister? I believed Andre and Luvitica had tried mightily to keep their history hidden. Knowing who they were was key to ridding the house of them. Why, I wasn't sure, but I would use the information.

Once out of earshot, Graham turned to me. "Do me a favor and cut Elena a little slack, will you? She hasn't actually put together many events since she's gone out on her own. She used to work for a big party planner who called all the shots. And Katenka's disappearing act hasn't made things easy."

"What did I say? I'm the one who made Katenka call her last night. How about a little credit?"

He smiled. "Thanks."

"Anytime. Now, want to return the favor?"

He looked doubtful. "Depends."

"Are you feeling resolute?"

"I'm sorry?"

"I was planning to go up to the attic and rid this place of ghosts," I said. No use beating around the bush. "I tried it before by myself, but I think I need you with me."

"Graham?" Elena's voice drifted up the stairs. "Would you come help me move these boxes into the car before I go?"

"Be right there," Graham called to her, then turned back to me. "I thought your French guy told you the ghosts were influencing us the last time we were up there, picking up on 'latent emotions.'"

"That's why I need you to come. Two of the ghosts were in love, or at least strongly attracted to one another. When you and I are up there . . ." I trailed off when I realized what this sounded like.

"They pick up on our attraction to each other?"

"Something like that," I mumbled, embarrassed.

"You're attracted to me?"

I rolled my eyes.

"So they're sort of ghostly lie detectors?"

"Look, Graham, I am not having this conversation. Are you going up with me . . . or are you chicken?"

"What, are you going to double-dog dare me next?"

I laughed despite myself. "Are you coming or not?"

I decided I didn't want to wait. If the ghosts made a mess, there was still time to clean up before the guests arrived. I couldn't guarantee Elena would survive the shock, but that was a chance I was willing to take.

"Whatever you say, boss. Just let me go help Elena, and I'll be right there."

"Great," I said, feeling relieved at the prospect of getting these spirits taken care of, once and for all. "I'll go tell the workers to knock off early, keep down the dust. Meet you at the attic door in ten minutes?"

He nodded and left.

I checked in with Steve Gilman, the temporary foreman, and asked him to shut things down for the day. I answered a couple of questions regarding the built-in cabinets in what was to be Quinn's room, and crossed a few "done" items off the punch list. Finally, I asked if anyone had seen the "cat woman," and was waved upstairs to the third floor.

As I walked up the final flight of stairs, I could see the attic hatch door was open. The ladder had been pulled down.

Was someone up there . . . or was I being invited?

I heard the clomping of heavy boots and a jingle of keys overhead. It sounded more like a construction worker than a ghost. I was happy to note I heard no whispering, no voices at all.

"Hello?" I called, stepping up a couple of rungs and sticking my head into the attic.

The boots belonged to none other than Janet Banks. The large key ring I had noticed hanging from the ignition on the bus now hung from a chain around her waist, and she wore a pair of heavy leather gloves that reached nearly to her elbows.

"Janet? What are you doing here?"

"Whoa . . . Mel." She reared back, as though I startled her. "That Russian lady hired me to come back and search for cats. She thinks we might o' left one here. Says she hears it in the walls sometimes." Janet crouched down and looked under the eaves with a flashlight. "Thing about felines is, they're tricky. Real smart. Gotta hand it to 'em."

Her pale eyes flickered over me. "You shouldn't be up here."

"You're right; neither of us should. This isn't a good time to search the place. They're getting ready for a party downstairs."

"Yeah, I noticed. The Russian lady and her husband told me they're gonna be the Snow Maiden and Father Frost, whatever that means. But that diced potato-carrot dish looked great. Nice and gloppy. Gotta love a culture that puts mayo in their salads, am I right?"

"Right," I said. I wanted Janet out of here, *now*. I was finally putting a few things together, and they added up to keeping Janet out of the attic. "Actually, I'm hungry. Aren't you? Let's go check out the salads, shall we? The favorite traditional one is called 'salad Olivier,' just like the ghost buster. Funny, huh?"

"Ghost buster?" Janet demanded. "What ghost buster?"

"Olivier Galopin. He helped us to rid the house of ghosts."

"I . . . You're saying they're gone?" Her eyes started to dart around the attic. "No way."

"I thought you didn't believe in ghosts."

"Right. I don't. I believe in what's real." And just like that, she pulled out a gun. "You might as well come the rest of the way up. You've meddled your way in this far."

My heart leapt to my throat. I wondered whether I could just drop down off the ladder before she had a chance to shoot, but she held the gun with confidence, like someone who knew her way around firearms. I recognized the signs, thanks to plenty of shooting-range bonding with my dad.

"Janet, listen to me. The ghosts are able to influence people, that's what hap—"

"Shut up." She gestured toward the closet door with her head. "And go open that closet for me."

"I can't. I've tried. And when I tried to take the hinges off, the tools broke."

"Get up here *now*."

I climbed the last few steps of the ladder, wondering when Graham would arrive.

"Try this." She handed me a metal piece stamped with a design: semicircles of acanthus leaves cupping a winged skull.

"Where did you get this?"

"It's mine. Emile had it. He stole it from me, way back when he lived here. I looked everywhere for it, even dug up the cats in the yard thinking maybe Mom buried it."

"I think he was trying to keep you safe by hiding it."

"All this time it was on that stupid collar on the stupid stuffed cat in Emile's shop. I went to speak to him that night, talk to him about why my mother would have given away this house. . . . It was *his* fault she gave it all to those damned cats."

I calculated my chances of wrestling Janet to the ground. She was no waif, but Graham should be here soon. If I could keep her talking . . .

"You shot Emile?"

She nodded. "I didn't really mean to, but I'm not all that sorry, gotta tell ya. He refused to admit it was all his fault, kept going on about how the ghosts weren't good for anybody. They were more friends to me than anyone else in this house. And then I saw the key that I'd been looking for, for so long . . . and I just went nuts. Anyway"—she caught her breath, eyes shining with excitement—"open the door."

The strange key felt almost as though it was guiding itself into the dead bolt. It slid in, and I heard the tumblers fall. The rusty hinges scraped and squeaked as the door swung open. I peered inside the dim space. Janet's flashlight beam shone in from behind me.

There was no rum barrel. But it looked more like the

inside of a crypt than a closet. Three cobweb-strewn coffins were stacked on shelves along the interior wall.

The small bronze plaques adorning them read: CHARLES CARTER, LUVITICA CARTER, ANDRE CARTER.

Behind me, Janet started laughing, an eerie kind of laughter that reminded me of Luvitica's. Organ music began to play, far-off and ghostly.

"Janet, listen to me. Don't let the ghosts influence you. Think about what you're doing."

"You think I *haven't* given it a lot of thought? Driving that Shellmound loop over and over, round and round, I've had a *lot* of time to think. That old man Emile took my happiness from me, and then the cats and this whole house took the rest. Round and round I go, all day, every day. . . . But it doesn't matter anymore. None of that matters."

She started to sway, her arms up in front of her as though embracing a ghostly dance partner. Then I saw it. Barely there, a shadow figure hovering near her. Janet seemed like someone else, outside of herself, pleasure written all over her face. But she still had the gun in her hand.

I felt waves of desperate yearning, desire, anger, and jealousy. The energy of the spirits reached out to me and tried to overwhelm my resistance. I stroked my grandmother's ring around my neck, concentrating on it, keeping myself grounded in the here and now. Reminding myself who I was, pushing away the rage and desire.

"Andre, Luvitica, you don't belong here," I said loudly, focusing on not giving in to the fear. "This house belongs to the living. We are alive, and you are not. Leave this place."

Janet laughed again, her tone malicious. Luvitica-like.

"Mel?" I heard Graham yell to me from below.

"Stay away, Graham!" I cried out, no longer wanting him here, at risk. The situation felt out of control, unpredictable.

Ignoring me, Graham hurried up the ladder. He took in the scene, his stance cautious but ready to fight. His gaze held mine: searching, questioning. If only I knew what to tell him.

As he stepped forward into the attic, the black cloud shifted, faded into the shadows. Janet faltered, falling to the floor.

The black cloud surged forward once more, and a new look came over Graham's face. Remote, angry . . . cold.

"It's *me*, Graham. We are alive, you and me; this is not Andre's world. Do you understand me? Graham, stay with me."

The shadow hovered just over his shoulder.

Desperate to make him connect with me, I flung myself into his arms and kissed him. Hard. I didn't let go, willing myself—and Graham—to remain in the present, centered, bound to the here and now.

After what seemed like forever, I could feel Graham coming back to me. He deepened the kiss.

I saw flickering lights in my peripheral vision, sensed a black shadow over my shoulder, along with feelings of rage and jealousy and shame washing over me. But I wouldn't let them in. They would not influence us. I forgot about them, losing myself in the kiss.

Unfortunately, in that moment I had the ghosts under control . . . but I hadn't considered the living.

"No!" Janet shouted. "He's *mine*!"

Graham shoved me to the floor just as the gun went

off. He followed me down, then turned and tackled Janet's legs, bringing her to the floor before she had a chance to aim again.

I scrambled up and jumped on her. She was vicious, large, and angry. But I'm no waif. She pulled my hair and shoved me, reaching for the gun, but I kicked it away. Together, Graham and I finally managed to wrestle her to the floor.

We flipped her over and I used a bundle of old twine to truss her up tighter than Katenka's roast goose.

"Let me *go*!" she yelled, squirming. Then she started to cry while she raged. "You don't understand! This is *real*!"

Now instead of organ music I could hear a commotion downstairs, raised voices, loud footsteps on the stairs. They had heard the gunshot.

Tying the last knot in our twine, I met Graham's eyes.

"You okay?" he said, his voice low with concern.

I nodded. "You?"

"A little off my game. But I'll live. Let's get the hell out of this attic."

Chapter Thirty-two

An hour later Graham and I were sitting at the top of the stairs as the flurry of police activity died down. Inspector Crawford had taken our statements, put Janet under arrest, and told us she'd be in touch.

"Help me understand what happened," Graham said.

I gave him the abbreviated version of what I'd figured out with Luz earlier.

"And the part where you kissed me?"

"It's sort of hard to explain. . . . I think it focused our minds on the present reality, denied Andre his influence over you."

"Interesting ghost-busting technique."

"I'm still a novice." I shrugged. "I sort of fly by the seat of my pants."

He gave me a half smile, then reached out and touched my cheek, stroking the still-livid bruise softly. "Did you figure out who gave you this shiner?"

"Janet had an admirer on the bus she drove—a sweet

fellow, but he probably would have done whatever she asked. I bet it was him," I said. My nervousness made me talkative. "As for these ghosts . . . I think Dominga, feeling the family had been disgraced enough, covered up Andre's death and entombed him in the attic. And Charles was already there as well. Maybe she planned to move their bodies somewhere more permanent later . . . Who knows?"

"And Janet got the idea of cutting the banister, hoping to kill her own mother, Hettie Banks?"

"It's important to remember that Janet wasn't entirely in her own head. She was a miserable child, an adolescent when she first started associating with the ghosts. That's a very volatile time, often correlated with paranormal activity. I think she was influenced by them so strongly that she wasn't completely in control of her actions."

"That will be a tough sell when she's talking to the judge. So who's in the third casket?"

"Luvitica. She probably wanted to be with Andre. I'm guessing Junior didn't adhere to the full disclosure rules when he sold the house. He told Hettie to stay out of the attic, and she did."

"But Janet didn't."

I shook my head. "Janet must have found the key to that closet and stirred up the ghosts. Emile took the key from her, and maybe he or Hettie tried to seal up the closet, make it hard to find. Hettie sent Janet away to live with her father, but she returned to help chase down all the cats after her mother was arrested."

"Why did she kill Emile? Just for that key?"

"I think she was angry at him for many things, including hiding the key from her. She was also angry at her mother for leaving the money from the sale of Cheshire House to the animal shelter, so she set up her own mother to take the fall for Emile's death. Janet probably thought she would inherit the place from her mother if Hettie went off to prison."

"I think I need a drink. Suppose there's any good vodka to be had at a Russian Tree party?"

The Snow Maiden, Snegurochka, hurried over to us as we descended the stairs. Her hazel eyes were huge with worry—and with hope.

"You are all right?" Katenka asked.

I nodded.

"Good. The police talk to us, but I could not help with much. Please to join the party. Try the salads. Very traditional for Tree celebration."

I'm not exactly a mayonnaise fan. But I helped myself to some goose and caviar, and had to admit that the *sbiten* wasn't bad. Especially when spiked with vodka. I noticed a sign in front of the punch bowl alerting parents to the dangers of young children ingesting honey.

The parlor soon filled with neighbors and friends, some of whom spilled out into the entryway and dining room. The presence of the police had caused quite a ruckus, but Elena had managed to distract the children by suggesting they open the presents. Torn tissue paper littered the floor like multicolored confetti.

"It is our tradition to wrap the presents several times," Katenka explained. "Each layer is marked with the name of a child. First child takes off first layer, and passes it to next child named. Until finally the name on the last layer is the one to receive gift."

"That's a lovely custom. This party turned out great,

Elena," I said as the party planner joined us. "You sure came through in a crunch."

"Really?" She sounded breathless.

"Really. I'm impressed. A lot of my clients give big parties and events—if you give me a stack of your cards I'll hand them out."

"That's so thoughtful, Mel. Thank you."

"No problem."

"Oh! I have to check in with the caterer, get the birthday cake ready," said Elena. She hurried off toward the kitchen.

"What happened upstairs, Mel? Can you tell me?" asked Katenka.

"It's sort of complicated."

"I cannot believe that Janet, the cat-catcher . . ." She shrugged. "And the . . . entities?"

"I think they're gone. I can't promise—maybe we should get Olivier back out here with his machines to test things, just in case. But it feels different to me. It's hard to describe, but the place feels benign now. Like a great old house full of metaphorical rather than real ghosts."

"I don't know this word, 'metapharcal.'"

"Sorry. I just mean that the ghosts are gone, I think. Now it's just a beautiful historic structure."

"It is a home," Katenka said. "Our beautiful home."

"Yes it is."

Chapter Thirty-three

There were no further signs of ghostly activity in Cheshire House. Katenka and Jim had the caskets pulled out of the attic and buried. They asked us to seal off the entire attic, though, just in case. It was an easy fix—some sheetrock, a little mud on the edges, a little paint, and it was a done deal.

I kept the strange key to the secret closet and hung it on my own key chain as a reminder of death, and of life. *Memento mori.*

Raul was driving his wife so crazy at home that she sent him back to work. The Daleys, true to Jim's word, moved into an extended-stay hotel, so the Cheshire House renovation was progressing at a nice clip.

I was back on the job, and today was overseeing Jeremy, the talented carpenter, while he was creating ornate on-the-job scrollwork with a jigsaw. Meanwhile I was using a nail gun to build up a lush, multilayered gingerbread trim around the front door. The exertion of using the heavy nail gun, the smell of the fresh sawdust, and even the intermittent, deafening *rat-a-tat-tat* of the compressor calmed my nerves, letting me know I was back to my real work.

There was only one problem. Lately, in addition to being sensitive to ghosts, I seemed to be hypersensitive to at least one living, breathing man: Graham Donovan, green builder extraordinaire.

For instance, I didn't have to turn around to know he had come to stand behind me while I nailed up the last wooden curlicue. I waved at Jeremy, and Graham and I descended the steps to escape the noise of the compressor.

"What's up?" I asked, real casual-like, as we went to stand in the narrow alley at the side of the house.

"Stan tells me you're in the ghost-busting business for real now."

"I wouldn't go that far. But I do have a lead on a fascinating new renovation in the Castro. The owners are actually hoping their ghosts will stick around."

Stan was still fielding calls from folks looking for help with their ghosts, and though I wasn't about to start doing this sort of thing full-time, I had noticed one particularly intriguing job: an old colonial revival whose owners wanted to convert it into a bed-and-breakfast . . . a *haunted* bed-and-breakfast. Apparently the building came ready-made with ghosts, and the owners wanted me to take on the renovation while squaring it with the spectral residents.

"Uh-huh," Graham said, his dark eyes searching my face. "If you're going into this sort of thing for real, you and I might need to work on your new ghost-busting technique."

"What technique would that be?"

"That mouth-to-mouth technique."

"Ah. What about Elena?"

"Elena and I have decided we're better friends than lovers."

"Oh, I'm sorry . . ."

He grinned. "Liar."

"Anyway, I already told you that new ghost-busting technique . . . that was sort of by the seat of my pants. An experimental type deal."

"It might need some fine-tuning. If you're going to go around chasing ghosts, we'll definitely need to practice. Hone our skills."

"I do love skilled labor."

"I know you do, boss lady."

Author's Note

The entirely fictional events in *Dead Bolt* were inspired by a true strange tale from San Francisco's past. The Atherton Mansion, at 1990 California Street, was built by a rather dysfunctional family in the late 1800s. George Atherton lived there with his wife and mother, and, according to legend, tried to "escape" the women by boarding a ship bound for Chile. While at sea George died of kidney failure. His body was preserved in a keg of rum and sent back to San Francisco, where it was delivered to his family's doorstep. The poor butler opened the mysterious keg to discover his former master pickled in rum. The women of the house came to believe George's lingering spirit was haunting them. They sold the grand mansion, which changed hands several times before becoming a boardinghouse in the 1920s. Former tenants have complained of cold spots, mysterious knocking, and other strange events; some even claim to have seen actual apparitions.

'm not a necromancer, so I can't see ghosts. Normally.
But tonight felt like a different story. The brightly
lit streets of downtown Oakland were host to women
seemingly from another era, in beaded flapper dresses,
glamorous 1930s-era gowns, and vibrant swing costumes.
Accompanying the feathered-and-spangled partygoers
were men clad in tuxedos with tails, white bow ties, and
shiny black shoes.

A black Model T Ford, polished and gleaming, glided
to a stop in front of the magnificent Paramount Theatre,
and the couple that emerged could have stepped out of
the pages of *The Great Gatsby*.

Among these apparent spirits-from-another-time was
a sprinkling of witches.

"The top hat is wrong," murmured Aidan Rhodes,
one such witch. His blue-eyed gaze flickered over the
formally attired man who opened the theater door and
welcomed us to the Art Deco Ball.

"Top hats are elegant," I replied. "They're *never* not
right."

"But it's not authentic. Top hats were already out of style by the twenties. And, my dear Lily, you of all people should know: the devil's in the details."

"I hope you don't mean that litera—"

I was shoved from behind. Aidan's strong arms caught me before I toppled off my unfamiliar high heels and plunged down a short flight of stone steps.

"Oh! I'm so sorry!" exclaimed a young woman as she steadied herself. "It's these dang shoes!"

"Miriam, you okay?" asked her gray-haired escort as he wrapped a beefy arm around her shoulders.

"Fine. Just clumsy. I'm more of a barefoot gal."

The woman named Miriam had hazel eyes that echoed the sea foam shade of her dress, and her honey-colored hair was covered by a glittery beaded cap. Unlike many of tonight's guests, who had clearly modified or sewn their dresses, this young woman's gauzy number was authentic. It was a diaphanous flapper dress; beaded and fishtailed, it hung loose on her creamy shoulders. My vintage-clothes-dealer sensibilities kicked into high gear, leaving me wondering where she had found such an incredible gown in mint condition.

"I know the feeling," I commiserated. "No harm done. I have to say, your dress is beautiful."

"Thank you. Yours, too." She smiled. Her expression was warm, but strangely . . . vacant. Off-kilter. Though undeniably pretty, her face appeared flushed but pinched, as though she were feverish.

And from her vibrations I could sense . . . something was wrong.

Wrong, and yet familiar. Had we met before? I hadn't sold her the dress she was wearing—I would have remembered such an exquisite antique gown.

Unfortunately, when the young woman stumbled into me, I had been distracted by the touch of Aidan's warm hands; they had, as usual, sent an annoying yet intriguing *zing* of electricity through me. So whether the disturbing vibrations I noticed emanated from Miriam's garment or from the woman herself, I couldn't know unless I touched her again.

As she turned to continue up the steps, I reached toward her bare shoulder.

"Leave it," Aidan whispered, resting a white-gloved hand on my arm. "It's not that kind of night."

I hesitated, and lost my chance. The young woman and her escort disappeared into the crowd.

"I suppose *you* wouldn't offer to help her until you'd run a credit check on her," I said, miffed at his interference.

Aidan sold his magical services. Many talented witches did. We're human—we need to eat and pay rent just like everyone else. Still, it galled me. It seemed so crass to cash in on our special abilities. I prefer to keep my talents separate from money, which is one of the many reasons I opened Aunt Cora's Closet, my vintage clothes store, where I earn a legitimate living the old-fashioned way, just like every nonwitchy merchant on Haight Street.

Usually. I might utilize my witchy wiles from time to time to gain an edge in the cutthroat vintage clothing business ... but I tried to keep it to a minimum. It seemed only sporting.

Aidan, unfazed, smiled as he led me into the grand lobby of Oakland's Paramount Theatre. The 1920s Art Deco extravaganza was the ideal locale for the annual Art Deco Preservation Ball.

I paused, taking it all in. The massive carved glass

"Fountain of Light," over thirty feet tall, dominated the entrance, casting a rich amber glow throughout. Overhead a vitreous green panel was bordered by labyrinthine fretwork and diamond-shaped gold patterns. Flanking these were vermilion piers, bas-relief sculptures, white-veined black marble trimmed in silver gilt, a plush red carpet, and accents of burnished gold throughout.

They sure didn't make movie theaters like this anymore.

In one corner a man with slicked-back hair stood near a grand piano, singing a lilting tune from the twenties. And the crowd was, to a person, dressed to the nines in outfits from the heyday of the Art Deco movement.

It didn't take a wild imagination to feel as though we had just stepped into a ghostly reenactment of a high-society soiree from days gone by.

"Do me a favor?" Aidan asked.

"Hmm. That depends. . . ." With a powerful witch like Aidan, an offhand promise could lead to something one didn't intend: a life of servitude, for example. It paid to be a little paranoid.

"Relax and enjoy yourself tonight? As a woman, not as a witch."

I laughed. "I'll try. The woman part I've got down. It's the dancing bit that's making me jittery."

"Surely you've been to a formal dance before. What about senior prom?"

"Closest I came was a hootenanny, when I was eight." That was before the good people in my hometown decided to shun me.

"Well then, this *is* a special occasion. Chin up, my dear. You're making a grand entrance."

"I'm as nervous as a long-tailed cat in a roomful of rockers."

"You shouldn't be. You look stunning," he whispered. "Just look."

I scoffed but followed his gaze, glancing at my reflection in the mirrored wall.

Land sakes. I *did* look nice. I don't know why I was so surprised. I often tell my customers that when their clothes change, *they* change. No reason this transformation wouldn't apply equally to me.

I had chosen the dress carefully . . . or perhaps it had chosen me. I had been planning to wear a peacock blue cocktail gown from the 1930s, but when I received a call from an elderly woman in Bernal Heights with two generations' worth of fine formal garments hidden away in her crammed walk-in closet, my options increased exponentially. The moment I picked up the tea-stained silk chiffon, I knew I had found my dress. The fabric was embossed with beads and flat gold-leaf sequins in a twisting-vine pattern. Simple spaghetti straps led to a deep V-neck, and the bottom was trimmed in a sassy beaded ruffle. Two handmade silk roses sat on the drop waist, along with a velvet sash.

Perhaps most important, something about the vibrations of the garment gave me courage, the fine fabrics brushing against my legs as I moved, making me aware of my skin. The dress had been altered so that it fit perfectly: it was loose, as any flapper dress should be, but made the most of my figure.

My friends Bronwyn and Maya had tortured my straight hair into a wavy Marcel style, then gathered it into a chignon at the nape of my neck and decorated it with a glittery beaded hairnet. My lipstick was a brilliant red, and I wore matte makeup and eyeliner.

My only complaint was my shoes. Bronwyn and Maya had nixed my usual comfy footwear, insisting the shoes be appropriate to the event. Thus I wore reproduction heels that made me miss my Keds with each uncomfortable step.

Still, the reflection showed that all the effort had been worth it. I fit in here, with these other would-be spirits from the roaring twenties, and elegant thirties, and swinging forties. . . .

Until I saw something in the mirror, something besides me and the crowd.

A frisson of . . . *something* passed over me. I'm not a sensitive, and have no special gift of sight. Even my premonitions are vague and generally useless, arriving as they do only seconds before something happens.

But this time, I could have sworn I saw the image of a woman sleeping amidst vines and briars and roses. As I watched she reached out to me. . . . I raised my hand to the mirror. . . .

"Lily?" For the second time that evening, Aidan laid his hand upon my arm to stop me. His voice was low, but adamant. "What are you doing? You should know better than to place your palm against a mirror. Especially in a theater."

As soon as we returned to our table, Susan grabbed my hand, saying, "We have to go powder our noses—girl talk!" to the men, and pulled me along with her.

"I adore the belowstairs ladies' lounge. Let's go to that one. Isn't this place incredible? It was built back when people really knew how to design things." Susan often spoke without requiring a response. But instead of being annoyed, I found her enthusiasm charming. "Back then, a restroom was a place one could actually *rest* in, to escape the menfolk, and to gossip, I suppose. Speaking of which . . . are you and Aidan an *item* now?"

"Of course not," I said, noting the breathlessness in my voice. I held the rail as I descended the great sweep of stairs, worried about my heels and distracted by the gowns surrounding me.

Attending the Art Deco Ball was not an easy gig for someone in my line of business. I was beginning to feel like I had Vintage Clothes–Related Attention Deficit Disorder.

"Check *this* out," said Susan when we reached the bottom of the stairs and entered the ladies' lounge. The outer chamber was encircled by gilt-framed mirrors, each with a narrow glass shelf and delicate iron chairs in which to sit and apply makeup. In each corner was a pair of upholstered armchairs, and there was a brocade chaise longue set in the back. The interior chamber was the actual lavatory, with stalls made of marble, hung with mahogany doors.

There was a line for the toilets, so I sat down before a mirror to fuss with my hair. I brought my comb out of my vintage Whiting-Davis mesh purse before realizing that the complicated chignon made combing my hair impossible.

"Excuse me. Hello, again. Would it be too much to ask if I could borrow that?"

It was the young woman I had met on the front steps, Miriam. Her honey-colored tresses had escaped their pins and had half tumbled to her shoulders.

"Oh, of course. Here, let me help you."

I caught her hair up in the comb as best I could, but I was clumsy—I wasn't the kind of child who grew up practicing "day at the hairdresser" with friends. I did what I could with the heavy mass, twisting and gathering. As I fussed with the long silken locks, I took the opportunity to concentrate on Miriam's vibrations. They felt chaotic, as if they were detached from their source. Decidedly odd. She seemed displaced, her expression still vacant. And again, I had a strong sensation of familiarity.

"Are you feeling all right?" I asked.

She met my eyes in the mirror. "Of course." But her words rang hollow, and her eyes were too shiny.

"You're Miriam, right?" I asked.

She hesitated, then nodded.

"I'm Lily Ivory. You seem so familiar—have we met before?"

"I don't think so. . . . Oh wait! On the stairs earlier?"

"Yes. I meant another time, maybe?"

She shook her head. "Thanks for the help."

"You're welcome." As I slipped the comb into my bag, I noticed a few strands of her hair were entangled in the teeth. Just then a stall opened up, so I grabbed it.

A few minutes later, as I washed my hands, I overheard women speaking in the outer lounge.

"Now that's what I call using the restroom."

"She's lounging, all right. Too much champagne, maybe?"

"Hey, are you okay?"

I rushed out to the lounge.

Miriam lay upon the chaise longue, eyes closed, sea foam silk fanned out around her. She had the odd stillness of one who wasn't merely sleeping.

"Wake up, sweetheart." An elderly woman gently

shook Miriam's shoulder. "Are you okay? Want us to find your escort?"

They all stood back when I approached, as though I were a physician who would know what to do.

I knelt beside her. "Miriam?"

My heart caught in my throat. Bright red flags of color on her cheeks stood out against an unnatural ashen pallor. I placed a hand on her brow, and felt her neck for a pulse. It was weak, thready. But it was there.

"Call nine-one-one," I said over my shoulder.

The orchid corsage pinned to Miriam's collar caught my eye. Lovely pale pink flowers tinged in violet formed a perfect contrast to the sea green of her dress. A few trumpet-shaped flowers formed a pale background. But as I looked closer, I spied beneath the foliage a bit of black ribbon, the glint of needles, and an ugly tangle of black thread. And I smelled . . . cigarettes?

This was no normal corsage.

ALSO AVAILABLE

FROM

Juliet Blackwell

If Walls Could Talk
A Haunted Home Renovation Mystery

Melanie Turner has made quite a name for herself
remodeling historic houses in the San Francisco Bay
Area. But now her reputation may be on the line.

At her newest project, a run-down Pacific Heights
mansion, Mel is visited by the ghost of a colleague who
recently met a bad end with power tools. Mel hopes that
by nailing the killer, she can rid herself of the ghostly
presence of the murdered man—and not end up a
construction casualty herself...

**Available wherever books are sold or at
penguin.com**

OM0055